AQUA CRYSTA

To
Bill, Ben and Barney
for all our early morning walks
through the "Harvestlands"

AQUA CRYSTA

Part 1

Next to No Time

AQUA CRYSTA

Part One

Next to No Time

by James David

Illustrated by Rex Aldred and James David

First Published in the United Kingdom in 2004
by Moonbeam Publishing

ISBN No. 0-9547704-0-4
EAN No. 978-0954 770402

Bibliographical Data Services
British Library Cataloguing-in-Publication Data
A catalogue record for this book is available
from the British Library

Printed and bound by:
The Max Design & Print Co
Kettlestring Lane, Clifton Moor,
York YO30 4XF

'A single candle flame
flickers and dances.
As it squats, swells and
stabs the air,
the magic it weaves
falls not only upon
the glistening crystal walls
of the Cavern, but across
the blackness of the night
that cloaks the Northern Moors
and our Harvestland.'

from 'Lepho's Journal'
(written during the 453rd
Harvest Expedition)

Chapter 1

'Not in a million years!' thought Jessica, as she gazed at the low, milky, crescent moon sailing through the silver-tinged clouds that billowed above the tree-tops.

"It could *never* have happened!" she whispered, tracing with her finger the bright stars of the great roller-coaster Plough, which lead her eyes to Polaris - the North Star, and then across the blackness to Queen Cassiopeia and her doomed daughter, Princess Andromeda.

As the moon glided in and out of cotton-woolly canyons and across deep, dark, starry seas, her mind was racing between the towering trees of the forest that afternoon.

“It just *cannot* have happened!” she muttered to herself, reflected in her bedroom window.
A moment later, pictures of the forest faded and she was suddenly the poor Princess Andromeda, chained to rocks facing the ocean’s threatening, crashing waves - her long copper hair draped over the harsh rocks, already being fingered by the swirling, grasping waters of the hungry tide.
She felt breathless as she tasted the first salt water on her lips.
She gasped the dying air and her heartbeat thundered in her chest.
She squinted through the spray and sensed the seawater filling her nose and ears.
Soon the waters would have her. She would be dead.
Jessica closed her eyes and tried to calm herself. Her breathing slowed together with her heart and she ran her fingers through her own long, coppery hair. Thankfully, it was perfectly dry.
She opened her eyes.
There was no engulfing tide.
Gone had the rocks and chains.
She licked her lips and found not a trace of salt.

She breathed a sigh of relief and wished at times she wasn’t at the mercy of her own imagination. The forest that afternoon had been bad enough, playing games with her. The last thing she needed were the ghosts of Greek myths playing more tricks, especially in the night sky and especially just before she got into bed!
She risked a glance up into the night sky, not to tempt the ghosts, but to assure herself that it was *just* a night sky, however starry and beautiful.
She knew that in the ancient story, Princess Andromeda was rescued by the gallant hero Perseus on his flying horse, Pegasus...and there, as bold as ever, was the Pegasus constellation...with its great empty square of

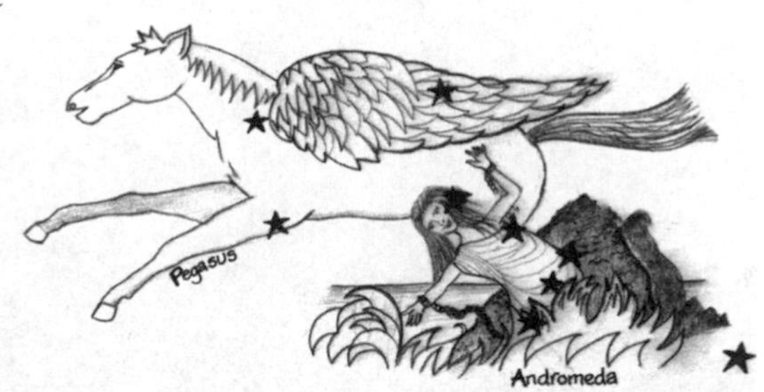

four brilliant stars, like the corners of a vast picture frame. Jessica gazed into its deep, intense blackness...and once again, images began to appear in her mind...or were they drawn on the sky's twinkling canvas itself? They were so clear! Clearer than she had ever seen before. Surely this couldn't be her imagination...inside her head...it all seemed so real!
A pure, dazzling white creature rushed between the trees of the forest - the same forest as the afternoon - crashing through the undergrowth, jumping low, mossy stone walls one after another.
It wasn't a winged horse...but a deer...an albino deer! That was the creature! And as soon as she recognised it for what it was, the images faded to be replaced by a single candle flame - a giant one, a vast one, taking the whole of the Pegasus picture frame - a single candle flame...flickering and dancing. Then that, too, faded and vanished, leaving just the magnificent empty blackness of Pegasus and a strange emptiness in Jessica...although she knew she had been touched by something mysterious and magical!

She stared at the empty square hardly believing what she had seen. The only thing of which she was certain was that the pictures she had seen in Pegasus were not hers...not of her own imagination...but somehow she knew that they were meant *for her*...and *for her alone!* Of that, she was absolutely crystal clear!

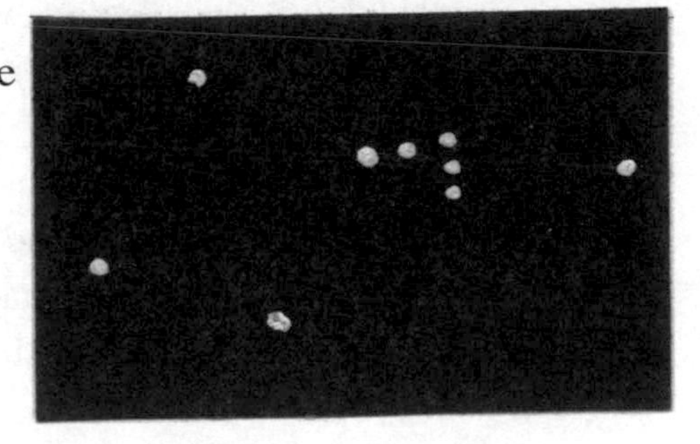

The crescent moon disappeared behind a thick drift of cloud that had crept from nowhere but now filled nearly half the sky. Jessica closed her bedroom curtains and wished, but only in a half-hearted sort of way, that she could pull a pair of curtains across her imagination and stop the never-ending stream of images that always seemed to flood through her head. She shook off her slippers and tiptoed across the bedroom carpet. Perhaps sleep would do the trick. After all she never seemed to have dreams...or at least she could never remember them if she did. She didn't have nightdreams and nightmares like everyone else...just daydreams and daymares!

She switched off the bedside lamp and slid under her cosy duvet. She curled up snugly and nestled her head deep into her soft pillow. Soon she would be asleep and in forgotten dreamland, far from the conjurings of her vivid imagination.

She closed her eyes and hoped for the best. Shutting her eyes would shut out the forest.

She could escape from her thoughts...but as soon as another empty canvas appeared behind her closed eyelids, instantly it was full of images. There was just *no* escape!

There they were again...trees, trees and more trees! Would they ever go away?

At least she felt comfortable and safe in bed, unlike the fear she had felt that afternoon in the forest! In the next room she could hear the familiar bleeps from her brother Jamie's computer. He was supposed to be asleep, but he always managed a quick last game before he settled down. Dad would never notice. The rat-a-tat of his ancient typewriter and the faint thudding rhythms of his 'Sixties' music came from his new den downstairs.

Jessica snuggled further down into her cosy bed and pulled the edge of her duvet up around her chin. She opened her eyes and gradually was able to make out the shadowy shapes of the furniture in her new bedroom. Back in the Scottish Highlands she'd shared a tiny bedroom with her brother, but here in Yorkshire she had a bedroom of her own for the first time. It was great, although it was strange not having anyone to talk to just before going to sleep. But then again, it was nice to have a bit of peace and quiet...a place of her own! Jamie, who was a couple of years younger, could be a real pain in the neck at times...a real nuisance...but it certainly was strange not to hear the creak of his bed when he turned in his sleep, or his breathing, or even his non-sensical mutterings as he talked in his dreams. In some ways she missed him being close. For a nine year old he was pretty good company!

As she looked around her bedroom, her 'night-eyes' soon became accustomed to the dark. The only light was a thin strip beneath her bedroom door coming from the landing, together with a milky glow from the night sky that crept through a chink in the curtains where they didn't quite meet at the top. She could just make out her wardrobe and dressing table as the shadows of branches outside danced on her curtains.

Instantly, they brought back the fears of the afternoon.

The two of them had decided to explore the part of the forest that lay closest to their new home. They'd walked down the grassy track from the cottage's front porch. Not heading the quarter of a mile or so towards the narrow moorland lane, but the other way...into the forest. Edged with tall evergreen spruce trees on both sides, the track became narrower and narrower...until it sort of just petered out in a miniature jungle of golden ferns. They couldn't have been more than five or ten minutes from the cottage, but the trees were so much taller here...their trunks as thick as dustbins...just right for felling!

That was what their father was here to do.

The plantation he'd managed in Scotland was now telegraph poles, garden fences, paper and all the other things trees are turned in to. With any luck, the chain saws wouldn't start buzzing here for years. That would give Jessica and Jamie plenty of time to explore and to get to know this forest as well as they'd known the last.

They'd both had mixed feelings about leaving the Highlands. Their dad's last job had come with a beautiful wooden chalet on the edge of a village surrounded by mountains and waterfalls.

The countryside had been terrific... magnificent...with its autumn colours and winter snows, not to mention the white-water rivers full of leaping salmon, the red deer, red squirrels, cunning foxes and the sleek, cheeky pine-martens like out-sized weasels. It had been a wonderful place to live. Even school had been brilliant with its one and only teacher, Miss McDougal, having taught both of them from the age of four.

Leaving it all hadn't been easy, but once their beloved forest had been felled, sawn up and loaded onto lorries, life there hadn't quite been the same. The trees had become part of their lives, friends almost. Over the years they'd discovered all the nooks and crannies, all the secret paths and hidden dells, and all the camping spots. Now they had another forest to get to know...and that's what they'd started doing that afternoon.

They'd reached the end of the grassy track with no sign of a path to follow between the trees as thick as dustbins. Jamie had set off through the ranks of towering spruce, running over the drifts of fallen, brown pine-needles, and Jessica had followed.
Back in Scotland she would have let Jamie go by himself as he knew the forest like the back of his hand, but here, in the unknown, she knew that they must keep together.

Jessica watched the shadows of the branches dancing on the curtains. She pictured herself running through the trees following her brother. He was *so fast*! Darting like a young deer between the trees, leaping from one needle drift to the next, he'd vanished in moments.
She'd stopped to listen.
It was so quiet.
No bird song. No running water. No wind.
Nothing.
Where *was* he?
Why couldn't he have waited for her?
"Jamie!!" she'd shouted. *"Jamie! Where are you? Are you hiding?"*
She'd listened again, her heart thumping in her ears.
But there was no reply.
She'd looked all around but there was no sign of him.
Not one single cracking twig could be heard.
Nothing.

Jessica rolled over in her bed. The computer bleeps from Jamie's bedroom had stopped. Her dad's typewriter was silent. His ancient music had stopped. The landing light had been switched off. The cottage was as quiet as the forest had been that afternoon.
The silence and the shadows on the curtains reminded her of the feelings she'd felt then.

During all the years of exploring the forest in Scotland she'd never once felt afraid, but this afternoon had been different...*very different!*
"Jamie!!" she'd called again, her voice beginning to tremble. *"Jamie! Where are you?"*
She'd started to run, weaving in and out of the silent spruce trees. On and on she'd plunged into the darkening depths, stopping now and again, listening and calling in the hope that Jamie's freckled face and ginger mop of hair would suddenly appear from behind a tree.
Once, maybe twice, her long hair had got caught in the rough, grasping, lower twigs.
Breathlessly, she'd untangled herself...hurriedly, as though, somehow, time itself was running out.
Her heart was now pounding in her ears and she was beginning to realise that she was panicking and not acting sensibly. Why hadn't she stayed back on the grassy track where Jamie had vanished in the first place? After all, he had a far better sense of direction than she had! In fact, he had probably made his way back to the track by now...and was wondering what on earth had happened to *her!!*
Still panting, she'd wiped the back of her hand across her sweating forehead after freeing her hair from the twig.
She'd glanced back the way she'd come. Then she'd swung her head round and peered into the dark depths of the forest that lay before her.
She'd suddenly began to feel light-headed and dizzy...
...and it was exactly at that moment that she'd seen it!
The wall.
There, straight ahead, in the gloom beneath the towering trees, with pine-needle drifts lapping its side like frozen waves, and made from all shapes and sizes of stone, all green and mossy. Not even and cemented like a garden wall, but more like a wall around a farm field with gaps between the stones and not a single trace of cement. Ferns sprouted from some of the gaps and gently swayed above the rocky barrier like flags from a castle battlement.
Not that the wall *was* a barrier, for the stones were piled no higher than Jessica's waist and much of it had collapsed. But it was quite wide.

Certainly wide enough to walk along the top of, in both directions, as it wound away through the forest like a great stony serpent.

Jessica tossed and turned in her bed and then suddenly sat up and stared at the curtains. She shuffled back and sat on her pillow, resting her head on the bedroom wall behind.

Somehow...strangely...seeing the wall had made her feel less panicky. She'd swept her hair back, her heartbeat had slowed and she'd gazed at it calmly...and with a certain amount of curiosity! It seemed so out of place, half buried beneath the trees, and seemingly with no purpose. She'd stepped towards it, gently touched the soft mosses and ferns and then sat on a lapping drift of pine-needles, leaning against the stones with a top one as a mossy, cushiony headrest.

She'd looked up into the uppermost branches of the spruce trees and into the cloudy sky beyond.

From her bed Jessica glanced up at the bedroom ceiling. She could see the white, fluffy clouds of the afternoon. She could hear the silence. She could smell the damp moss on the wall and the familiar scents of woodland.

But then, just as a patch of blue sky appeared in the blanket of white and sunlight lit the uppermost tips of the trees...she'd heard a sound, silhouetted against the silence...the sound of a faint, distant horn...coming from behind her!

Then another note had sounded!

Then another!

They'd come from the wall!

She'd jumped up from the pine-needle drift as though she'd been stung, and stared at the mossy stones, one by one.

"*Jamie? Are you there?*" she'd called.

She'd waited for an answer but none had come.

Then she'd knelt and peered into the dark, damp gaps between the stones, and even put her ear to one. She'd listened intently, expecting to hear more from the invisible horn...and, as though not to let her down, another note, then another, sounded from beyond the wall. All at once she'd been gripped by fear again! Fear of not knowing what was making the sound nor where it was coming from, and of course, the fear of still being lost in the middle of nowhere.

Jessica covered her ears as she watched more clouds drift across her ceiling and dust away the patch of blue. She slid back under her duvet and pulled it up again tightly around her chin and ears to smother the sound of horns. She gazed at the dancing shadows on the curtains and the clouds above her.
"JAMIE! WHERE...ARE...YOU??" she called out at the top of her voice.
Within seconds there was a clatter of knocks on her bedroom wall.
Jessica blinked and looked at the wall near the dark shape of her dressing table.
It was Jamie.
"What's the matter with you?" came a faint voice from the dressing table.
"What are you shouting about? I'm trying to get some sleep!"
"NOTHING!" Jessica shouted back at the dressing table,
"I'M ALRIGHT! I MUST HAVE BEEN DREAMING!"
"But you *don't* dream!" argued the annoyed dressing table. "Now count some sheep and get to sleep!"

Jessica covered her head with her duvet and snuggled her head, once again, into her soft pillow.
She felt as confused as ever!
Had she heard the sound of a horn coming from the wall beneath the towering spruce trees?
Had there been a wall at all?
Had she even been in the forest that afternoon?
Then, of course, there were the pictures in the night sky - the ones in Pegasus, the ones she was sure were meant for her.
She just *had* to discover the truth, but for now, sleep crept up and took her away from candle flames, albino deer and musical walls. The dull world of dreams had captured her, but the magical truth was not far away...

'The flame we call 'Lumina'
has danced her dance for as long
as anyone can remember...
and beyond even that!
Indeed, her candle has stood
on the table by the
Larder Steps for over
four and a half Harvestland
centuries.....and yet its smooth
whiteness is unblemished by any
trace of molten wax.
Its eternal wick never diminished
by the passage of time.
And its ancient, Abbey crafted
beeswax never consumed by the
frail flame it holds aloft.'

from 'Lepho's Journal'
(written during the 453rd
Harvest Expedition)

Chapter 2

A shaft of sunlight slanted across Jessica's bedroom, falling on her face. She opened her eyes, squinted and turned over to avoid the glare. She looked at the delicate pattern of flowers and leaves on the wallpaper just inches from her nose and, with a finger, traced a long twisting stem of ivy. The design was old-fashioned but she liked it. It was like waking up underneath a hedge in summer. She imagined a damselfly or a ladybird appearing from behind a leaf, or a tortoise-shell butterfly fluttering from flower to flower.

But just as she was beginning to hear crickets chirping and bees buzzing, the brambles and wild roses suddenly started clicking and bleeping! It could only mean one thing - her brother was awake!

And then, just as the fragrance of meadowsweet was tickling her memory, the aroma of toasted tea-cakes told her that her dad was up and about too!

In almost one bound she threw back her duvet, sprung out of bed, pulled on her dressing-gown and swept back the curtains.

The sun was shining brightly and the trees looked beautiful, each branch tipped with brilliant green candles - this year's new growth.

But as soon as she saw them her energy seemed to vanish as she remembered the vast candle in the sky the night before, Jamie disappearing, herself running panic-stricken through the forest, the tumbledown wall and the sound of horns. Surely none of it could have happened! Could it?

At that moment, Jamie flew into the room like a whirlwind and dived straight on to Jessica's bed as though he was diving into a swimming pool.

"What was the matter with *you* last night?" he gasped, as he started bouncing up and down and attempting a somersault.

Jessica turned from the window and looked at her brother.

"What do you mean? What was the matter with *me* last night?" she asked, a touch uncertainly, pretending to unknot a tangle in her cascade of copper hair.

"Last night! Don't you remember? I heard you as clearly as anything through the bedroom wall!" he laughed, glancing towards Jessica's dressing-table.

"Heard what, Jamie? What *are* you going on about?" snapped Jessica, a little irritably.

Her brother stopped bouncing and gazed intently at the dressing-table.

"Sorry, sis, I've got it wrong!" he replied, with a hint of mischief in his voice. "It must have been your dressing-table shouting in its sleep. That's it! Problem solved! Sorry I mentioned it! Let's go and tuck into dad's burnt offerings...!"

With that, he sprung off his sister's bed and galloped towards her door.

"Jamie! Be serious for a second!" shouted Jessica, even more annoyed, and grabbing the back of Jamie's T-shirt, yanking him back into her bedroom.

"Tell me again what you heard, you little horror!"

Jamie struggled to free himself, and slowly turned to face his sister, who still had hold of him by the scruff of his T-shirt, although with increasing difficulty. Then he looked up at her with his usual, innocent, butter-wouldn't-melt eyes.

"Well? What did you hear?" hissed Jessica, almost nose-to-nose with her brother. "Tell me or I'll have you fried and on toast for breakfast!"

"That's not...a very...balanced meal... at all!" gasped Jamie as his sister's grip began to tighten.
"Too much gristle and carroty hair, you mean?"
Jamie looked daggers at Jessica and then he contorted his face into an expression his sister knew only too well! His head fell to one side, his eyelids started blinking like demented butterfly wings and he put on the soppiest smile you can imagine. Jessica knew exactly what was coming and twisted her brother's T-shirt even tighter around her wrist.
Jamie's impression of her drove her wild!
"You dare, little brother! You just dare!"
"JAMIE? WHERE ARE YOU?" squealed Jamie in his very best big-sister voice.
Instantly, Jessica released her grip and stared at her brother blankly.
Then she turned and gazed out of the window again.
She was puzzled. Very puzzled.
"We *were* out in the forest yesterday, weren't we?" she asked quietly, her eyes fixed on the uppermost branches of the trees beyond the back-garden fence.
"What...did...you...say?" panted Jamie from the bed he was now using as a trampoline.
"The forest...yesterday? We did...Jamie, stop it for goodness sake! You'll land up going through the floor into dad's den if you carry on like that!"
Jamie's gymnastics stopped and Jessica sheepishly looked at him, her fingers fiddling with the cord tassel of her purple dressing gown.
"The forest...yesterday? We did go there, didn't we?" she mumbled.
"Of course we did, Jess!" exclaimed Jamie with surprise. "Surely you haven't forgotten our first exploring trip? It was great! I even lost you for a while! But I found you sitting by a w...!"
He was interrupted by a loud call from downstairs.
"Come on you two! Breakfast's ready and it's on the table!"

Jamie leapt off Jessica's bed, bounded along the landing and stopped at the top of the stairs.
"Race you to those burnt offerings in the kitchen!" he laughed, beaming at his sister.

But Jessica was in no mood for races. As her brother darted downstairs, she followed slowly and thoughtfully, the images and sounds of the day before once again streaming through her mind.

After breakfast, while they were doing their best with the washing up, their father cleared a space on the kitchen table and unrolled what looked like a large map. To stop it rolling up he roughly put salt and pepper pots and jars of marmalade and jam on the corners. Then he nipped into his den and turned off the *Jimi Hendrix* album that had been blasting out all through breakfast - one of the advantages of not having neighbours as he was always saying. Fortunately his children had come to enjoy most of his Sixties music. Although it had to be admitted *Jimi Hendrix* was a touch heavy first thing in the morning!

"Right," he said, "can you two leave that washing-up for a minute and have a look at this?"

Glad of any excuse, Jessica and Jamie dried their hands, knelt on a couple of ricketty kitchen chairs and gazed at the detail on the map. Their father's blue eyes twinkled as he pored over the dozens of square miles of his new kingdom. He smoothed the map with his right hand, which was easily as big as a small frying -pan, and then stroked his bushy black beard with the other...a sign to Jessica and Jamie that something important was coming.

Mr Dawson looked at his children, slipped on his glasses and spoke quietly in his native Yorkshire accent - one that felt at home again. (His children incidentally spoke with a similar accent tinged with light Scots, as they had spent almost the whole of their lives north of the border)

"Now I know we've only been here three days," he began, *still* stroking his beard, which meant that something *doubly* important was coming, "and I know for most of that time you've been unpacking and sorting out your rooms...but I think it's about time I introduced you to our new forest, so that you can gradually get to know it as well as you knew the *Queen Mary* back in Scotland..."

"Oh, we've started already!" burst Jamie. "We had a stroll up the track yesterday afternoon!"

“And *you* got yourself lost!” said Jessica.
“What d’you mean? *I* got lost? It was *you* who got lost!” laughed Jamie.
“Now hang on, you two!” said their father, keeping his children apart with his small frying pans on their shoulders as though they were a couple of boxers. “No arguing! Just listen. Getting lost is exactly what I’m talking about!”
He looked at them both with blue eyes that had turned to steel without a twinkle to be seen.
“The first rule is this...” he said firmly. “During the rest of the summer holidays, I want you two *always* to stick together. *Always!* Understand?”
He slid his glasses down his nose and peered over them at his children.
“Yes, dad! We promise!” burst Jamie for both of them.
“You can see the size of the plantation,” he went on. “It stretches nearly five miles in every direction from the middle. We’re here, almost on the edge, Look, there’s the cottage!”
He pointed with a fork.
“What are all those lines?” asked Jessica, following their jagged network all over the map with her finger.
“They’re the ancient stone walls around the old fields,” replied Mr Dawson.
Jessica looked up at her father in astonishment, pictures of the mossy pile of stones flooding before her as clear as crystal.
“But why are there walls criss-crossing a forest?” she asked.
“The *Mary* in Scotland was planted on rough grassland and mountain sides,” explained her father, “but here the trees were planted on land that used to be sheep farms. There are old stone farmhouses and barns scattered all over the place, some of them built three, four or even five hundred years ago! Look...here...and ...here.” He pointed again with his fork.

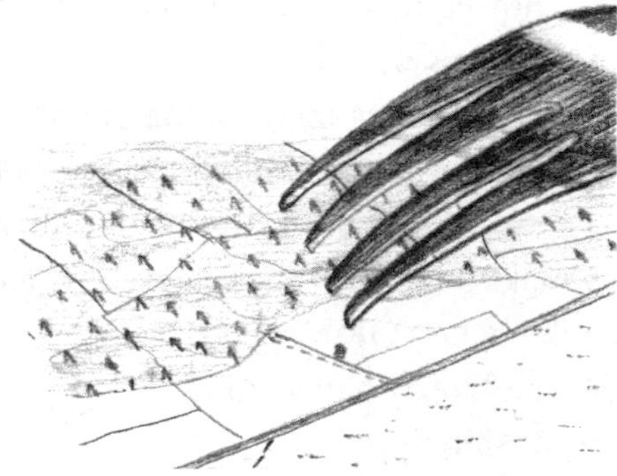

"What about all the farm tracks?" wondered Jamie. "Are they still there?"
"No, son, they're all overgrown now and lost, but you can still find the odd farm pond and sheep shelter. There aren't even any footpaths. It's going to be a tough job opening up the forest when the time comes for the big chop. There are only a couple of decent forest roads!"
"When will the felling start, dad?" asked Jessica dreamily, the sound of the horn from the day before softly playing in her mind.
"I really don't know. It could be weeks...months...or even years! I've got no idea. But when I get the go-ahead, it's going to be one heck of a job!"
"Well, let's hope it's years and years away, so we can really get to know the forest!" said Jamie, enthusiastically.
"And that brings us back to what I was saying. First rule, remember?"
"Stick together!" burst Jamie.
Jessica was miles away, lost in thoughts of ancient, ruined farmhouses and lost roads winding across the bleak moors. She loved the past and she could be whisked back into the mists of time at the drop of a hat!
Her father clicked his fingers and jolted her out of her daydreams.
"First rule, Miss Dawson?"
"Oh, sorry about that, dad!" Jessica muttered, as though she'd just woken up. "Er...*stick together!* That's it, isn't it?"
Mr Dawson smiled and reached over to the kitchen dresser.
"And the second rule is this. Make sure you've always got one of these with you!"
He showed them a much smaller version of the large map, about the size of a tea-towel.
The cottage was marked, the grassy track down to the moorland lane and all the old farmhouses, barns and walls.
"There's a whole pile of them in m'study next to the record-player so make sure you *always* have one each, folded up in your back pocket. OK?"
The children nodded and soon they were back at the sink finishing the washing up.

"Not much in the way of *Mary's* waterfalls and caves, but all those old buildings look interesting!" remarked Jamie, as he juggled a couple of handfuls of soapsuds.
"I can't wait to explore again!" said Jessica dreamily, as she absent-mindedly dried a mug and gazed through the little kitchen window into the forest just beyond the back garden fence. She was bursting to get back to yesterday's wall, the strange calm and the sounds of the horn.
"How about exploring again today, Jess?" suggested Jamie, as he pulled the plug and swished the suds away.
Jessica was lost in her thoughts.
"Hey! Wakey, wakey! I'm not going to have a mug left if you don't stop drying it!" joked Jamie.
"Sorry, I was miles away! What did you say?"
"I said have we to go exploring again today?"
But his sister didn't get a chance to answer, as just at that moment their father popped his head round from the hallway.
"How do you two fancy a trip to the coast today? It's a great day! The sun's shining! We can have a super time!"

Jessica was thrown into turmoil. On the one hand she was dying to get back to the wall...but on the other, she couldn't resist a chance to see the sea for the first time in ages. But, as she firmly told herself, the wall had been there for hundreds of years! It was hardly likely to vanish before they got back!

So, in a flurry of excited activity, the three of them prepared a picnic. In next to no time, they were in the Land Rover heading down the bumpy, grassy track, the *Beatles' 'Penny Lane'* playing loudly in their ears and in their eyes, as the barber shaved yet another customer and the fireman rushed in from the pouring rain!
"Bye, cottage! Bye, forest! See you later!" called Jamie, peering through the rear window.
"We can't keep calling the cottage *'Cottage'* and the forest *'Forest'!"* laughed Jessica, breaking off from singing along with her father.
"In Scotland we had *'Ben More'* and *'Queen Mary'!"*
"Well, we'll have to name them then, won't we?" said their father.

"We'll think of a name for the cottage and make a sign to go over the front door!"
"Isn't the name of the forest on that big map you showed us?" wondered Jamie.
"No, I haven't seen one. We'll just have to make one up. Any ideas?"
"What about *'Deep...Dark...Gloomy...Spooky Forest'?"* suggested Jamie.
"Don't be daft, Jamie!" tutted Jessica. "You can't keep saying *Goodbye, 'Deep, Dark, Gloomy Forest'* every time we leave!"
"You missed out '*Spoo..oo..ooky*'!" joked Jamie in his best ghostly voice.
"OK, OK, you two!" butted in their father, turning down the stereo.
"Let's have a sensible suggestion. How about *'Queen Elizabeth'* to remind us of the *Mary*?"
"It's not bad," said Jessica half-heartedly, "but *Elizabeth's* a bit long. What's short for *Elizabeth*?"
"*Lizzie...Betty...Bessie...Beth*...take your pick!" replied Mr Dawson.
"I don't like any of those," insisted Jamie, "and anyway, what about having a King's name this time, like *William*...or *Henry*...or *Edward*?"
"Well we can't have *'Edward'* to start with! That's dad's name!" Jessica pointed out.
"But what about *'George'*?"
"Yep, I'll go along with that!" agreed Mr Dawson, fingering the stereo's volume button, anxious to get back to his *Beatles'* tape.
"All in favour say *'Aye'*!"
"Aye!!" they chorused as they came to the end of the grassy track, and so it was decided.
A moment later, as the green, battered Land Rover turned onto the narrow moorland lane, Jamie called,
"Bye, *'George'!* See you soon!"
"Bye, *'George'!* See you soon!" echoed Jessica...but in almost a whisper.
With a wistful backwards glance towards the edge of the forest, she secretly could hardly wait to get back to its dark, magical depths. She had been well and truly captured by the forest's enchantment. Its spell was working and it, too, could hardly wait!!

"Yet, however small and slender
the solitary flame,
she means everything to us all.
Lumina is truly cherished....
if she dies...we die...
the magic will be no more...

But now, the Guardians of Lumina
frown as they sit at their table,
worry etched across their faces.
Lumina seems agitated, less strong,
her dance interrupted...
as though a breeze is blowing
through the Cavern...
a final breeze...
a breeze of death and
extinction!"

from 'Lepho's Journal'
(written during the 453rd
Harvest Expedition)

Chapter 3

The narrow lane was tree lined for a while, but soon the great expanses of the North Yorkshire Moors stretched as far as their eyes could see. It was almost the end of August, so there was just a hint of light purple over the the gently rolling landscape. By early September the heather would be fully in flower and the moors would be a sea of deep purple.

The odd, squawking grouse flapped over the lane as they drove along, and curlews, with their long curved beaks, warbled above them. Mr Dawson pointed out the distinct remains of a wide Roman road crossing the moorland, with a group of hikers marching along it like Roman soldiers, but with brightly coloured backpacks and plastic map-cases, instead of shields and swords!

A little further on they stopped by a tiny church on the edge of a village called Goathland. As Jessica and Jamie clambered down from the Land Rover onto the short, sheep-nibbled grass, their father called out,

"Anyone fancy going on a mouse-hunt?"

"A *mouse-hunt*?" Jessica asked curiously. "Dad, what *are* you talking about?"

"Follow me and you'll see!" beamed her father, as he crunched up the church's gravel path past inscribed gravestones and dark green yew trees. In the small church porch he whispered,

"I've spotted one already! Can you see it?"

After some rather puzzled searching, Jamie at last noticed a tiny mouse climbing the church door just below its brass handle.

"There's one!" he shouted. "It's a wooden one carved in the door!"

Jessica and Jamie crouched and stroked the smooth, humped back of the mouse. Their father explained that the carpenter's trademark was a wooden mouse and after more searching inside the church, they found another half-dozen, especially around the wooden altar.

"But how did you know about them?" asked Jamie, as they drove on through the village. "Have you been here before?"

"I certainly have, son! Back in the *Nineteen-Fifties*! We used to spend our week's summer holiday at a place on the coast near

Whitby. Every year we used to come. Me and your Gran and Grandad. We lived in Leeds then, so it was wonderful to escape the noise and grime once a year, even though it was only for one week! We used to come by train..."

"Didn't you have a car then?" chirped in Jamie.

"No, not many families did in those days. But we didn't mind! It was great fun coming on the railway, changing trains at different stations and making sure you didn't lose your luggage! I used to have m' own snitchy, brown suitcase with rope wrapped around it to stop it from falling open as I pelted along a platform trying to catch the next train! I always used to have it so jam packed that it was nearly bursting...and then there were m' bucket and spade and m' fishing net in m' other hand, and a great big straw hat plonked on m'head. I must have looked a right old sight, especially having baggy khaki shorts waving round m'knees, long grey school socks and tatty sandals on m'feet!"

Jessica and Jamie smiled at the thought of their father as a child compared to them today in a Land Rover and wearing bright multi-coloured shorts and T-shirts, dazzling fluorescent socks and red and blue trainers.

"But how did you get up here to the moors if you didn't have a car?" asked Jessica, as they drove past hordes of tourists and hikers mingling with the half tame sheep in the middle of Goathland.

"You'll see! Just ahead!" pointed Mr Dawson.

A moment later, a large stone building with tall chimneys came into view at the end of the village. Clouds of white smoke billowed above its grey roof, but it wasn't coming from the chimneys! Then came a shrill, ear-piercing whistle!

"There's your answer! Right on cue!" laughed Mr Dawson. "We used to come here by train, too!"

As they rounded a bend and squeezed over a narrow bridge, Jessica and Jamie looked down at the quaint, old-fashioned railway station. The two platforms were bustling with even more tourists scrambling in and out of open carriage doors, as the black, gleaming engine patiently waited, belching smoke from its chimney and steam from its pistons.

"We'll definitely have a ride on the *North Yorkshire Moors Railway* soon!" enthused Mr Dawson, hardly able to wait himself!

They drove along a winding moorland lane which climbed out of the village, occasionally slowing down to give sheep a chance to cross. Soon they came to the main road over the moors leading to Whitby and just as they came to the crest of a hill, Jessica shouted out excitedly and pointed into the distance.
"There's the sea!!"
Before them was the vast steel-grey sweep of the North Sea stretching away to the horizon. Mr Dawson pulled into a small car-park and they all gazed at the magnificent view.
"Norway's about four hundred miles over the water," he said, fiddling with his *Beatles*' cassette, "and that's Whitby nestled down there. You can see the ancient ruins of Whitby Abbey on the cliff top. It all seems exactly the same as it was when I was a lad. Come on, let's get down there!"

As '*The Long and Winding Road*' suitably came to an end, they were in the centre of the hustle and bustle of the little seaside town. Cars were everywhere and Mr Dawson certainly noticed the difference from the last time he was there! They drove along the main street passing the smart, old railway station, the swing bridge over the river and lots of colourful fishing boats moored by the quayside. Then they climbed a steep road cut into an orange cliff and stopped at the top near a large white hotel.

They looked over the harbour with its twin stone piers jutting out to sea, and staring back at them from the other side were hundreds of tiny windows belonging to scores of tiny, red-roofed houses clinging to the hillside. Above the patchwork of houses was the huge ruin of Whitby Abbey and its squat St Mary's Church perched on the very edge of the cliff, surrounded by gravestones.
"The graveyard over there is where the spooky tale of *Count Dracula* began," pointed out Mr Dawson, "and Captain James Cook, the great explorer, lived here before he joined the navy!"
"Is that him?" asked Jamie, nodding towards a statue of a man with a grey and white herring gull perched on his head.
"That's right, and look at that archway next to him with tourists strolling through!" pointed Mr Dawson. "It's the jaw-bone of a whale!"
"Cor! It's gigantic!" gasped Jamie, imagining the size of the whale it had come from.
"But surely there aren't any whales off the Yorkshire coast?" asked Jessica.
"No," laughed her father, "it's just a sort of reminder of years gone by when Whitby was a whaling port, sending sailing ships far north into the Arctic Ocean to catch whales for their oil and bones!"

They carried on and turned the corner by the large *Royal Hotel*. Once again they could see the vast sea stretching away to the clear horizon and more cliffs along the coast.
"That's where we used to stay every year!" Mr Dawson suddenly exclaimed, as though he'd met a long lost friend. The children looked along a couple of miles of golden sand to a small village tucked beneath the cliffs.

"That's Sandsend! Come on, let's go, then we can have a paddle and explore the beach! We'll come back to Whitby on another visit when it's quieter!"

Soon they were driving along the coast road hugging a long, sandy beach, the hustle and bustle of Whitby left far behind.

"There used to be a railway running along here as well as a road!" noticed Mr Dawson, slightly puzzled. "They must have taken it up as well as the railway viaduct that spanned the valley at Sandsend. Things have definitely changed around *here*!"

They drove into the village and parked on a large car-park.

"This car-park wasn't here either! It was just rough land and a couple of cottages," mumbled Mr Dawson, sounding a touch disappointed. "But look, there's the old railway station up there!" he beamed at last. "At least they haven't knocked that down! That's where we used to stay!"

"You used to stay in a *railway station*?" laughed Jessica.

"You're pulling our legs, dad!" burst Jamie.

"Well we didn't actually stay *in* the station," admitted their father, grinning from ear to ear, "but we stayed in a railway carriage next door!"

Jamie stared at him in total disbelief.

"You *have* to be joking this time!" he gasped. "People don't have holidays in *railway carriages*! Do they?"

His father, still grinning, quietly nodded as they all scrambled out of the Land Rover grabbing the picnic things. Then, without saying a word, he darted through a gate in the corner of the car-park and galloped up a steep flight of steps set in a grassy bank.
"See you at the top!" he called. "And all will be explained!"

Jessica and Jamie raced after him and at the top of the steps they found themselves on a narrow cinder track almost overgrown with dog-rose bushes. As they tried to catch their breaths, their father explained that they were standing on the old single-line railway track and even pointed out the remains of the old station platform.
"The railway used to run along the very edge of the cliff!" he recalled. "I can see now the little fires caused by sparks from the steam engines falling in the long grass. We used to stamp them out after breakfast, after the 7:19 from Whitby had just rattled away from the station. We used to play in the stream under the viaduct. That was best when a train passed over us with all the smoke and the sparks. And then there were the ponies on the beach...and the tunnel further along the track! We used to go in there after the last train each day...and come out black as coal from all the soot on the walls!"

Mr Dawson, lost in his childhood memories, sat on the edge of the platform and gazed out to sea. It was a beautiful spot, with the wide, warm sands stretching all the way to Whitby and its Abbey ruins sitting on the cliff-top. People were scattered all along the beach, with hundreds of children paddling in the gentle waves and building sandcastles. Yachts bobbed on the grey sea and kittiwakes and fulmars wheeled in the air above the cliffs. Bees buzzed in rose bushes and crickets chirruped in long, swaying grass. Jessica pictured her father as a boy sitting in the same position with his sandalled feet dangling from the platform.

"You didn't *really* stay in a railway carriage, did you, dad?" she asked, as she poured ice cold orange juice from a flask into three paper cups.
"We certainly did!" insisted her father. "They were just behind the platform, on a siding over there. There were two carriages coupled

together and painted green and cream. We used to call them *'camping coaches'*. I can remember, as if it was only yesterday, climbing the metal steps to get in them...and then inside, all the seats had been taken out to make three or four rooms out of the old compartments. There was a kitchen at one end with a paraffin stove, a table, chairs and a cupboard. Then there was a sitting room...I think. Yes, that's right...and then two bedrooms with bunk beds and storage chests. There was no electricity, of course, just gently spluttering oil lamps!"

He stared at the place the carriages had once stood, now long since overgrown with straggily rosebay willow-herb. But he could see them alright, standing there in their smart colours, welcoming families of holiday-makers from all over the country.

"I can see Mr Simpson now, the station-master, walking along the platform in his crisply pressed uniform and his polished buttons. He had a pocket-watch on a chain and a shiny, silver whistle. He used to keep the station as prim as a new pin with the help of Mrs Simpson. There were great big tubs of flowers all along the platform and large signs saying *'SANDSEND'* with polished brass oil-lamps above them. They were very proud of their station were Mr and Mrs Simpson!"

"How did you pass the time all week?" asked Jamie, tucking into a salad sandwich and fending off hover flies.

"Well, there was the beach, of course...and the ponies...and fishing...and exploring...and I used to go on country walks and camp in the hills with the local lads. I got to know some of them pretty well, coming back summer after summer. We became good friends. There was Jack...and Douglas...and Simon...oh, and William...and then there was Jonny and his sister Jane, who always had the carriage next door during the same week every year. I often wonder what happened to those two. They were great friends, but then they suddenly stopped coming and I never saw them again. I wonder where they are now...and their miserable, old uncle who used to bring them every summer. Now he *was* a strange old so and so..."

For the next few hours, Jessica, Jamie and their dad had a wonderful time down on the beach. Mr Dawson wandered around Sandsend village for a while re-living his memories, and even met a man called Joe, one of his special summertime mates. When the tide did eventually drive them off the beach at about tea-time, they enjoyed a snack in one of the village cafes and then piled into the baking Land Rover, all three of them well and truly shattered.

Soon they were back on the moorland road leading away from Whitby and the sea. The ruins of the Abbey disappeared as the great expanses of hazy, purplish moorland swelled before them. Over the steam railway and past the mouse church they travelled until they had their first glimpses of *George* in the distance.
Since leaving the forest in the morning, Jessica had hardly given a thought to its mysterious walls and strange sounds...but as they trundled along the narrow lane, closer and closer to the thousands of trees, she imagined herself lying by the low wall, her head resting on its mossy stones. She was once again falling into the forest's mystical grasp. She closed her eyes, just as her father swung off the lane and onto the grassy track which lead to their cottage.

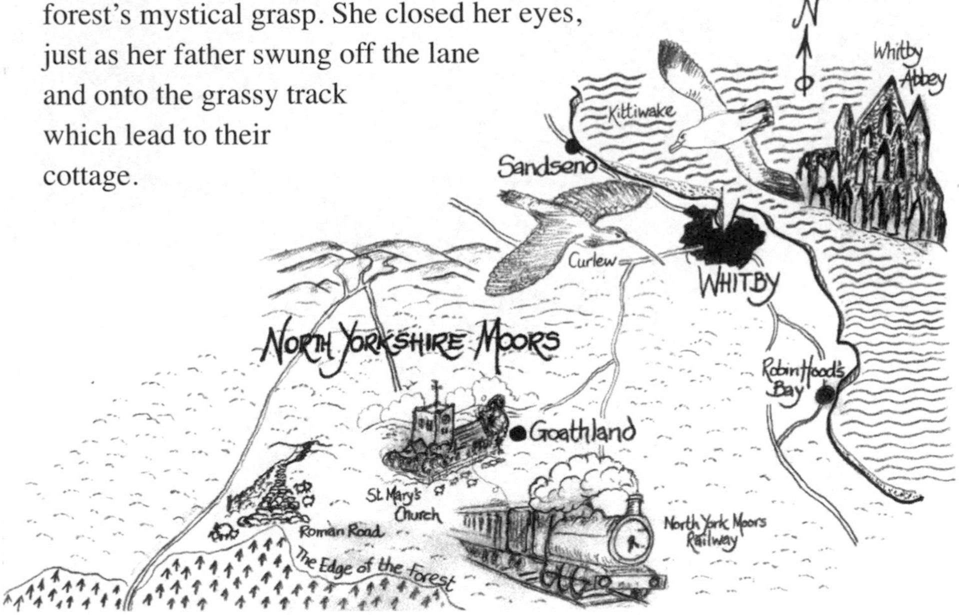

Suddenly, Mr Dawson braked hard, Jessica jolted forward and her eyes sprung wide open. What she saw ahead of them on the track made her gasp in amazement!
It was an astonishing sight!
A sight that sent shivers up and down her spine!
This just *had* to be magic!

Chapter 4

Scattered along the track and standing absolutely motionless, as though made of stone, were a dozen or more slender deer, each one of them staring back at their onlookers with great, brown eyes set beneath pairs of sharp, erect ears. But it was not these beautiful, dark brown, gentle statues that held the gaze of Jessica, her father and her brother...it was the spectacular, smaller, young animal that stood in the midst of the silent herd, as though guarded and protected by the rest. Its fur was of the purest white, with dark pink, almost red eyes set like rubies in fresh snow.

The albino fawn seemed to glow with a magical radiance all of its own, and strangely, around its neck was a slim band of iridescent, dancing colours like a miniature rainbow.

Jessica recognised the fawn instantly, but uttered not a word. She had watched it gambol within the bounds of Pegasus the night before. That had been a warning, but here was the messenger itself, in flesh and blood, standing before her!

But what was the message? What had she to do?

All at once, the young albino leapt from the track followed by its keepers and in a moment they had all vanished into the forest, as though an artist with a single brush stroke had washed them from a delicate watercolour. They were gone, but their magic had touched their three observers, leaving them strangely muted.

Mr Dawson, after what seemed an eternity, gently drove forward, everyone staring into the trees hoping to catch another glimpse of the deer.

But they had well and truly dissolved into the greenery and were now safe in the depths of the forest. Jessica alone knew that, somehow, the herd had done its duty. Her eyes had met the albino's.

She had felt the tingle of a special, mysterious one-to-one recognition. Something would follow, but what...she had no idea.

"Roe Deer," whispered Mr Dawson, "not the Red Deer we had in Scotland. Did you see the white patches on their rumps?"

Jessica and Jamie quietly nodded.

"And what about that young albino? That was amazing!" enthused their father. "I've never seen one before!"

"But what about the colours around its neck?" asked Jessica dreamily, still stunned by what she'd seen.

"What colours? I didn't see any colours!" smiled her father. "It must be that imagination of yours playing tricks again! Did you see any son?"

Jamie looked at his sister then up at his father's face...and then shook his head.

"No, I didn't, but did you see the way they all leapt off the track at once as though someone had pressed a button?" burst Jamie. "That's it! A perfect name for the *cottage...Deer Leap!!* And it will always remind us of our first trip...!"

"...And our return!" whispered Jessica, still wrapped in her daydream.

"Yep! I vote for that!" said Mr Dawson. "It's all agreed then? What about you, Jess?

Are you happy with *Deer Leap?"*
Jessica nodded slowly, almost hypnotised by the trees drifting by.
"She's called *Chandar,*" she said softly.
"No, *Dear Leap,* Jess!" insisted Jamie, nudging his sister.
"I mean the young albino. She's called *Chandar...*"
"Jess, what *are* you talking about?" laughed her father. "I think a lie-down's called for! Must be all that sea and sun!"
He pulled up in front of *Deer Leap*'s porch and everyone climbed out of the Land Rover. But before piling in through the front door they all peered once more into the dark depths of the forest in the hope of catching a flash of white. But all was quiet and still, except for the odd tinkle of early evening birdsong. Jessica looked disappointed but she knew that she would meet her *Chandar* again one day...of that, she was absolutely certain!

Within half an hour, picnic boxes and flasks had been washed and Jessica and Jamie were ready to explore *George* a little more before the sun disappeared.
"Now remember the golden rule!" called Mr Dawson as they made for the front door.
"Stick together!" chanted Jessica and Jamie, banging the back pockets of their jeans to make sure they'd got their folded maps.
"It's just gone seven," said their father eyeing the grandfather clock in the hall. "You've both got watches on, so I want you back here before dark. Nine o'clock at the latest! Understood?"
"Yes, sir!" they both beamed, checking their watches and giving their dad a playful salute.
He had the habit of sounding like a sergeant-major at times, but they knew he had their safety at heart. After all, *George* was a new frontier, unexplored territory, unlike the *Queen Mary* who they'd known like the backs of their hands. Scouting parties needed to be back before sundown, lest they fall prey to marauding indians or, worse still, marauding cannibals!

The sun shimmered low in the orange-pink evening sky as Jessica and Jamie galloped along the grassy track towards *George's* green and secret depths. Soon it would be dipping below the highest tree-tops, but, for now, the children's criss-crossing shadows followed them eagerly down the track, disappearing only when the children darted in amongst the tree trunks. Here the shadows were left behind as Jessica and Jamie leapt from one pine-needle drift to the next, delving deeper and deeper into the forest.

Jessica lead the way, her long coppery hair flowing behind as she dodged between the greeny brown trunks. She was intent on reaching the wall she had pictured in her mind since the day before. It all *seemed* very familiar, but she couldn't be absolutely sure.

Suddenly, she stopped. So suddenly that Jamie almost ran straight into her!

"Hey! What's up with you?" he exclaimed.

"Ssshh! Let me think! I'm sure I stopped here yesterday!" Jessica mumbled.

"You're right! Look at this, Jess!" shouted Jamie, fingering the tip of a rough twig just above his head. "It's hair! Long copper hair, like yours!"

A couple of long strands of hair gently swayed in the air like the silken thread of spiders at dawn.

"That's right!" gasped Jessica. "I remember! I had to stop here because my hair got caught up. That means the wall *has* to be around here *somewhere!"*

"Wall? What wall? What *are* you going on about?" asked Jamie.

"Never mind. Just follow me!" his sister hastily replied.

She walked slowly forward, scanning this way and that for any trace of those half-buried mossy stones. But none were to be seen, not even one single, solitary stone! She looked down-hearted, as her brother impatiently ran on in front.

"Jamie! Jamie! Hang on a minute!" she called. "Remember we've got to stick together!"

But then, just as she was about to sadly slump down at the foot of a tree and have a rest, Jamie's voice suddenly brought a smile to her face!

“Sis! There’s more of your hair here!” he shouted.
Jessica, with renewed hope, dashed towards him.
“That’s it!” she gasped. “I stopped *twice* yesterday because of my hair getting tang...*and look!! There’s the wall!!”*
Her face lit up at the sight of the old, mossy stones as she rushed over and sank into the ferns and pine-needles that lapped them.
Then, to Jamie’s amazement, she began looking into all the gaps between the stones, feverishly delving her fingers into one after the other.
“What’s up, sis? Have you lost something?” he asked curiously.
Jessica still thought it was best to say nothing about the musical horn notes from yesterday. Her brother would only laugh if she said anything!
“I..I’m just looking at all the different mosses on the stones!” she whispered. “Come and have a look. They’re beautiful!”

All the stones were covered with small velvetty cushions and silky carpets of mosses. Some flat and smooth, some quite bushy. Each stone seemed to have its own miniature field or forest of every shade of green. Jamie joined Jessica on his knees and they both investigated the cracks and crevices between the rough rocks.
A brightly coloured ladybird scampered across one of the lawns and shiny, black millipedes coiled and uncoiled like oily springs among the tiny bushes. Amber centipedes appeared from nowhere carried along by their waves of golden legs and armoured woodlice bustled in and out of dark caves. They were all in a tiny world of their own, perfectly undisturbed for years and years.
Indeed, the wall looked as if it had stood for centuries. Now half-buried in pine-needles, but once standing proud, dividing the desolate moors and giving shelter to sheep through many a long winter blizzard. But now completely forgotten with no use at all other than as a maze of secret caves and cracks for its creepy-crawly residents.
Gold tipped fern fronds, marking the onset of autumn, flanked the stones in both directions as the wall wound away into the forest depths, eventually dissolving beneath overhanging spruce trees.

"I wonder how far it goes," whispered Jamie, as he watched a tiny spider abseil a rocky cliff face.
"You remember dad showing us the map this morning," said Jessica. "*George* has miles and miles of walls and all those barns and little farmhouses."
"We could follow them like paths and then follow them on the map so we never get lost!" Jamie suggested."We might find they lead us to some super, secret, old ruins hidden in *George's* deepest, darkest depths..."

Jessica wasn't listening. She was sitting by the wall, her head resting on the mossy pillows like she'd done the day before. This time though, there were no sounds...no tinkly, musical notes...no haunting melodies from hidden horns. Perhaps they *had* been in her imagination after all. Perhaps the whole thing *had* been a daydream. Perhaps she had been having one of her *flights of fancy,* as her father called them.
She turned her head to one side and looked into the gap between the stones that were closest to her face. It looked very snug and cosy she thought, with a deep mossy carpet on the floor and a couple of pale green discs of lichen on the ceiling. A fragment of twig, a scattering of pine-needles and a small cone made up the furniture. Her fingers delved into the cave. She felt her knuckles graze against its rough, gritty walls. She sensed the cold, soily dampness in its deepest, darkest crevice. Then, thinking she may be disturbing a family of woodlice, she slowly withdrew her hand. But as she did so...a sudden, unexpected glint of light caught her eye! To her astonishment, a tiny droplet of silver rolled over the cave's mossy carpet...plummeted over the edge of the stone...and fell onto the pine-needle drift just below. Jessica, her eyes fixed on it, sprung to her feet. She stared at the gem, utterly entranced by it. It looked so out of place lying on the dull, tan coloured pine-needles, like a pearl in an ashcan.
"Jamie! Come and have a look at this!" she called, her eyes still glued to the silver droplet.
Her brother popped up from further along the wall on the far side.
"What's up, sis?" he asked, curiously. "Found a Roman coin or something?"

His sister squatted down and carefully picked up the speck of shining silver between her thumb and forefinger and placed in the middle of her open palm.
"I..I just pulled my hand out of a gap in the wall...and it just sort of came out with it!"
She slowly raised her hand and gazed at it more closely.
"It's beautiful!" she sighed, her face at last breaking out into a beaming smile. "It's the shape of a tiny, tiny drinking vessel...like a mug...a tankard I think they called them... like they used to drink ale from centuries ago...it's even got a carved pattern round the middle and on its curved handle!"
Jamie scrambled over the wall and he too was amazed by Jessica's find.
"It reminds me of one of the things hanging from one of those dangly bracelets girls have!"
"A charm on a charm-bracelet, you mean?" smiled Jessica. "You could be right, but how has it got here in the middle of nowhere, hidden in the depths of an ancient wall?"
Jamie shrugged his shoulders, looked at the wall and then knelt down and peered into more of the dark gaps between the stones.
"I wonder if there's anything else!" he gasped as he put his head into all sorts of weird positions trying to investigate the wall's mossy cracks and expecting hidden treasure in every one!
"Which one had the tankard in it, Jess?"
"That one!" Jessica pointed, still marvelling at her discovery. "The one with the twig and the little cone."
Jamie slid his hand into its cool darkness, his fingertips blindly probing the soily dampness.
"Jess!" he suddenly exclaimed. "There's something else here...if I can...just...get it...between my...fingers! It's wedged in!"
With a grim expression contorting his face, Jamie was determined to bring out his find.
He twisted and turned, looking as if the wall had grabbed him and he was trying to escape its grasp!

“That’s it! I’ve got it!” he gasped at last, as he slowly withdrew his black, soiled fingers from the miniature cave.
“It’s another silver charm!” he beamed, holding it out for his sister to see.
Jessica looked at it and couldn’t believe her eyes!
“It’s a horn!!...a tiny, curly, hunting horn!” she exclaimed. *“So that’s what I heard yesterday when I lost you!!”*
She instantly bit her lip and looked anxiously at her brother. She’d been determined not to say a thing about the sounds she’d heard, knowing that he’d just poke fun at her.
But now, she’d gone and blurted it out.
“Jess, *what* are you talking about?” asked Jamie, slowly looking up from the tiny horn into his sister’s eyes. “What *did* you hear yesterday?”

Chapter 5

Jessica told her brother the whole tale and how it had preyed on her mind ever since the day before. As Jamie inspected the two silver charms he shook his head from side to side looking puzzled.
"Perhaps it was a breeze blowing through the horn that made the sound," he suggested, as usual trying to explain everything in a matter of fact sort of way.
"But I heard *three different notes*!" insisted his sister. "As if they were being played deliberately. It couldn't have been the breeze!"
"Well it certainly is mysterious," admitted Jamie, "and, while we're talking mysteries, so is all that business with the rainbow band around the albino deer's neck!"
"What do you mean? You told dad you didn't see anything!"
"Well I *did*! But with dad saying he *didn't* I wasn't sure and thought it must be a trick of the light or something!"
"I tell you it was there alright!" whispered Jessica. "And even stranger was the voice in my head that spoke the name *Chandar*. Did you hear that too?"
Jamie shook his head slowly again and looked disappointed.
"No, sis, I didn't," he admitted sadly.
Jessica put an arm around him, glanced at her watch and looked up at the darkening sky.
"I tell you there's something magical and mysterious going on and I think we ought to do some more exploring before we go home. Come on,

we haven't got long. Let's follow the wall a bit further into the forest."

So, with the two silver charms safely tucked in her back pocket, Jessica lead the way along the side of the ancient wall as the sunlight began to fade. Almost with each step the forest grew darker and darker, and together with the low overhanging spruce branches, the going became difficult. Now and again they stopped to investigate a tempting gap between the stones in the hope of finding more treasure, but it was becoming too gloomy to see anything clearly. In one large crevice Jamie spotted a couple of half nibbled acorns and the purple, seedy remains of a bramble staining a patch of moss.

"But there are no oak trees or bramble bushes around here!" Jessica said. "It's just never-ending spruce trees!"

"Of course, that's how the charms got here!" burst Jamie.

"It's birds...probably thrushes...bringing stuff in here to eat from the edges of the forest!"

"But where would they find the silver charms to start with? And they're not exactly tasty morsels to the average bird are they, little brother?"

Jamie shook his head, looked pensive and then suddenly exclaimed,

"Got it! By *George,* I've got it!...joke there, sis!... By *George,* get it?" he laughed.

Jessica gave her usual look of disapproval at one of her brother's jokes.

"Got what?" she asked. "Quick before we have to go back!"

"Magpies, of course!" beamed Jamie.

"They're always pinching shiny things and....."

"Sssh! What's that?" Jessica suddenly interrrupted, grabbing hold of Jamie's arm and almost making him jump out of his skin!

“What’s what?” Jamie whispered.
“Sssh! Listen! I’m sure I heard a twig crack somewhere over there,” Jessica replied, nodding her head back in the direction from which they had come.
“You mean we’re being *followed*?” gasped Jamie, his green eyes growing bigger by the second, and *his* grip on his sister’s arm getting tighter.
They both froze and listened intently, their hearts pounding.
The twilight silence surrounded them.
No bird song. No breath of wind.
Just an eerie stillness.
Then...they both heard it...and saw it!
A grey squirrel jumping from one branch to another on its aerial highway!
They both sighed with relief.
“That could explain the squashed bramble!” smiled Jamie in the gloom, trying to sound as composed as possible and not at all scared by cracking twigs!
“But it still doesn’t explain the charms and the sound of the horn!” said Jessica. “Come on, let’s be getting back to *Deer Leap*. It’s after half-past eight and I can hardly see where I’m going!”

“Let’s just go on for another five minutes!” pleaded Jamie. “We can jog back home in no time. We’re only about quarter of an hour away!”
Jessica was easily persuaded, and fortunately the wall became simpler to follow, sometimes even allowing them to walk on its broad top, like stepping stones beneath the trees. Mostly, however, they scrambled over pine-needle

drifts on each side, battling through occasional clumps of fern. The going was toughest where the spruce trees grew closest to the wall with their lowest branches grabbing and grasping at them. But they fought on through, with Jessica managing not to lose any more strands of hair and eventually they came to a small clearing. The spruceland had come to an end and was replaced by tall, slender, pale green larch trees with no low branches at all. Here, there were hardly any pine-needles on the ground, but instead, their feet sank into soft, silky grass. And, whereas it had been growing gloomier and gloomier in the spruceland, unexpectedly, it became lighter. There were clumps of heather like they'd seen on the moors and even the sound of birdsong. It had been deadly quiet amid the spruce trees, but here the warm dusk was filled with the songs of chaffinches and greenfinches and the buzz of insects. The crescent moon and the brightest stars appeared in the twilight sky making silver birch trees look more silvery than ever and illuminating the woodland floor with a milky half-light.

Suddenly, ahead of them, they saw a great splash of red, scarlet and orange...like a bonfire on a November night. It was a huge, cascading rowan or mountain ash tree, aflame with masses of brilliant berries. It seemed like a fiery fountain frozen in mid flow, arching over the wall. As Jessica and Jamie approached its glow they could see that every branch was heavy with chunky, scarlet bunches of the tiny fruit, all ready to feed a host of birds.

Beneath the scarlet banquet lay the first break in the wall, bounded by two leaning, velvetty green gate-posts about four or five paces apart. Beyond the further post the wall relentlessly strode on and on into the forest. Jessica and Jamie dropped to the foot of each finger of stone, their heads resting on the soft mosses and their legs stretched out in front of them. This would be a suitable place to end the day's exploration. Tomorrow they could begin again at the gate-posts.

Jessica looked up at the moon and, with a hint of reluctance in her voice, said that it was definitely time to return to *Deer Leap,* although she wished she could curl up between the cushiony clumps of grass and sleep beneath the stars.

"I know exactly what's going through your mind!" said her brother, tracing the twinkling stars of the *Plough* with his finger. "You'd like to stay out all night, wouldn't you? Like we used to do in the *Mary*!"

Jessica nodded and smiled.

"I wish we could, too!" Jamie went on. "It's warm and dry...but...we can't tonight, that's for sure!"

"But what about *tomorrow* night?" beamed Jessica. "Let's ask dad when we get back! Agreed?"

"Agreed!" echoed Jamie, jumping to his feet and looking at the crescent moon cutting through the clouds.

"It looks like a huge tilted cereal bowl floating through the sky, doesn't it?" said Jessica, imagining an equally huge spoon scooping out cornflakes and milk pouring out of it.

"No, I reckon it looks like a giant toe-nail clipping flying through the sky!" Jamie laughed.

"Clip! There goes another one!" he chuckled as he pointed to another one skimming over the tree tops.

"It's *comets* that fly through space, *not* giant toe-clippings!" pointed out Jessica with a grin and springing onto the wall next to her gate-post. "Come on! Let's get home on time or there'll be no chance of dad letting us camp out tomorrow night!"

Suddenly, she stared at one of the flat stones beneath her feet.

"Jamie! Look at this!" she called, carefully bending down to look at what lay just in front of her toes.

Both of them gazed in amazement at the small splash of colour on the dark stone. It was as if the fiery fountain had dripped onto the wall.

It was a pile of scarlet berries from the mountain ash. Not a bunch, like

the ones in the tree...all attached to a single fallen twiglet...but they were all separated and piled into a small, neat pyramid. There must have been thirty or forty of them altogether, all shiny, round and smooth.
Jamie carefully picked one off the top of the pile, but as he did a couple rolled from the pile and plunged over the edge of the stone and into the soft grass below to join hundreds more that had fallen from the tree.
"That's funny," he said quietly. "All those on the ground are all crinkly and shrivelled up...but the ones in the pile are all...sort of...fresh and shiny, as though..."
"...They've just been picked and piled up like tiny apples in an orchard!" burst Jessica excitedly. "And *definitely not* the work of a squirrel or a magpie!!"
"And neither is *that*!!" exclaimed Jamie, pointing up into the rowan trees's fiery branches.
"*Just look at those*! *I can't believe it*!!"

Chapter 6

Crack!

The smooth, light brown shell split as Mr Dawson sliced the top off his boiled egg at the breakfast table. As he plunged his spoon into the golden yolk, Jessica put the all important question, her fingers crossed tightly beneath the table.

Luckily, the boiled egg was neither too hard nor too soft!

It was just right!

And so was her father's reply!!

"Of course you can!" he said, picking up one of his toasted soldiers. "You never came to any harm in the *Mary,* so I'm sure *George* will look after you just as well! But make sure you've got enough to eat and drink, and don't forget your torches! I've got piles of paper-work to catch up with, so I'll be glad of the peace and quiet for a day or two. And it'll give you a chance to get to know *George* a little better. When can I expect you back?"

He dipped his soldier into his egg and the yolk dribbled down the side of his egg-cup.

"Sometime late tomorrow afternoon, I should think," replied Jessica, spreading marmalade on a piece of toast and feeling the excitement bubbling inside her.

"Just in time for tea!" joked Jamie, his ginger mop of hair in its usual first-thing-in-the-morning-pulled-through-a-hedge-look!

"My heart goes out to you, Jess!" laughed her father. "Imagine having to wake up next to your brother in a tent, doing his wildman of the forest impression!"

"What about me having to put up with *her*?" grumbled Jamie, self-consciously pulling his fingers through his shock of unruly hair. "Can you imagine waking up to *that* face sticking out of its sleeping bag! It'll be like waking up next to the ugliest, mammoth, man-eating, wriggling caterpillar from..."

"OK, OK, Jamie!" said Mr Dawson. "All I can say is that I'm glad that I'm not wedged between you two in that tent of yours. Anyway, you might find a good ruined farmhouse to set up camp in, or snuggle down beneath the trees under the stars. The weather forecast's good and the ground should be dry. There hasn't been rain here for ages!"

As soon as they'd tidied everything away after breakfast and Jessica had driven all the washing-up soap suds down the plughole, they began to stuff their backpacks with all they would need for their expedition. The larder shelves were raided for food. Biscuits, crisps, cake, chocolate, dried fruit, tins of beans and fish would be enough. They rammed it all into their backpacks together with a tin-opener, a couple of forks, two bottles of water, a little gas-stove, matches and their torches. Waterproofs were stuffed on top, with a few plasters, a tube of antiseptic and emergency whistles in the side pockets. Sleeping bag rolls were tied beneath their packs and Jessica secured their little light-weight tent on the top of her pack, while Jamie threaded a couple of plastic mugs onto his straps.

At eight o'clock, having checked they had their maps in their back pockets, they were ready to go.

"And make sure you come back if the weather turns!" called their father as he

waved, energetically dancing in the porch to the rhythms of the *Rolling Stones*. "See you tomorrow!"
He watched as Jessica and Jamie made their way down the grassy track, dew glistening in their footsteps.
"Bye, dad!" they called with a final wave.
"Hope you can cope by yourself!" laughed Jamie.
"I'll manage!" called Mr Dawson with a final flourish before he vanished and the *Stones* faded away.

Once again, the sky was blue and, even at this early hour, the children felt the warmth of the sun on their bare arms and legs as they strode down the track, their bulky red backpacks gleaming brightly. But soon they were in the shade of the trees as they headed for the wall. This time they had no trouble finding it and soon they were having a welcome breather at the spot where they'd found the silver tankard and horn the evening before. Jessica felt in her pocket to make sure she still had them and Jamie marked the place on his map with a tiny cross and '*Charmstones*' written by it in his smallest writing. Then they slung on their backpacks and scrambled along the wall through the spruceland. It was even tougher going than the night before with the extra baggage, but they managed without too much trouble to push their way through the grasping lower twigs.

At last they came to the more open and green larches, and there, in all its glory, stood the mountain ash tree, blazing brightly in the morning sun. Excitement once again began to bubble in them as they both wondered whether or not the tree would still bear last night's mystery in its branches amid the thousands of berries. They rushed almost breathlessly over the soft grass, shook off their backpacks and propped them up against the gate-posts. Then they stood under the rowan and gazed up into its mass of scarlet.
Yes! They were still there!
All three of them, still hanging from near the end of one of the highest branches, glinting in the sunshine and joined by delicate spider threads glistening with droplets of dew.

Jamie found a long stick, jumped onto the wall by the second gate-post and began poking it up through the tree's branches as far as he could.
"It's...no good!" he strained on tip-toe. "I can't...reach...any of them!"
"Try and shake the nearest branch!" suggested Jessica from below.
Amid much rustling of leaves there was a sudden shower of whole clumps of berries which pattered onto the silky grass around the gate-posts.
And then...at last...one, two...and finally, the third silver fruit fell to the forest floor...quickly followed by Jamie who pounced on the treasure like a kitten on a ball of wool!
"They're tiny baskets!" he exclaimed, as he carefully picked two of them up and put them on the palm of his hand.
"They're charms again," whispered Jessica. "Probably off the same bracelet as the others even though these are much larger. Look how fine the woven silver strands are, and the lovely round handles. They're like wicker baskets."
She then fell onto the damp grass and peered at the third basket and its even more amazing cargo. For wedged inside were two scarlet rowan berries just beginning to wrinkle with one of them having a strange silver and deep red stalk.
"It looks like a dagger handle! It's a tiny dagger pushed into the berry up to its hilt!" exclaimed Jamie.
Jessica put the basket on Jamie's palm and he delicately pulled at the shining stalk.
Slowly, the sharp, silver blade of a dagger slid from the berry.
It was the most magical find so far.
Jamie's hunch was right. It was indeed a dagger with a beautifully scrolled handle embedded with a ruby no larger than a crystal of rock salt.
"But this can't be a charm," gasped Jessica suddenly. "It's the odd one out. There's no way to attach it to a bracelet!"
"And why is it plunged into a berry?" wondered Jamie, gazing at the tiny dagger that was no longer than the width of his thumb nail.

For a few minutes the two baffled explorers rested on the same flattened grass as the night before, leaning on their gate-posts. It was a lovely morning. Warm and peaceful with just the sound of birdsong silhouetted against the silence. In fact it was so quiet that when a jay flew slowly overhead through the larch tips they could hear its wing beats! The children's eyes explored the tranquility, but their thoughts were far from tranquil!

It was Jessica who broke the silence.

"Do you think there's a connection between the baskets and the freshly picked berries we saw last n...?"

"The berries! I knew there was something missing! The berries! They've gone!" called Jamie, loud enough to waken the dead, never mind cause dozens of birds to suddenly take to the air in alarm. "The pile of berries! There's not a single one left!"

It was true. There wasn't a sign of the neat, squat pyramid they'd seen the night before. Each and every scarlet berry had vanished!!

"Come on, Jamie!" gasped Jessica, as she secured the charms and the dagger in her back pocket and struggled into the straps of her backpack. "Let's get going along the wall and see what else we can find! We'll get to the bottom of this...or my name's *Little Red Riding Hood*!"

"And I suppose I'm the *Big Bad Wolf*!" laughed Jamie, putting on his deepest growl. "Oh! What big eyes you have!"

"I'm supposed to say that if I'm *Little Red Riding Hood*, not you, you twit!" insisted Jessica.

"OK, OK, clever clogs! *Fi-Fi-Fo-Fum!*" growled Jamie, as he pulled on his backpack. "Will that do, then?"

"All the better to see you with!" growled Jessica in reply as she peered into another likely looking crevice in the wall and Jamie quickly wrote *Ash Berry Gate* on his map.

The two intrepid explorers then delved beyond the gate-posts into unknown territory, keeping their eyes peeled for any glints of silver. Soon they left the larches behind and were once again in darker spruceland. At times the trees grew so close to the wall that it became almost impossible to follow it, but they battled on against the grasping branches until they came to a swathe of golden ferns where they encountered another wall. This one met their wall from the right and continued to the left, like a kind of crossroads. Jamie found the junction on his map and traced along the new wall to a place called *Old Soulsyke Farm*.

"That's the one to take!" he announced, as though he was Doctor Livingstone in the depths of the African jungle. "It passes what looks like a small quarry and another small building on the way...probably a barn or something."

"Right, I'll buy that!" said Jessica. "Lead on Macduff! I can't wait to see the old buildings, although I bet they're just tumbled down heaps of stone!"

After a few minutes they reached the old quarry. It was quite deep and overgrown with the wall following its top edge next to a steep drop into a cauldron of tangled ferns, bramble, nettle and gorse bushes which smothered the quarry's orangy-brown rock. Now and again, just the odd jagged tower of rock jutted through the tangle like giant, discoloured teeth.

"This must be where they quarried all the stone for the walls and the buildings," suggested Jessica as they made their way slightly nervously along the brink of the great hole. "Imagine, centuries ago, people here quarrying and building walls and barns and farmhouses!" She could almost hear the clinking of iron picks on the sandstone and see the horse-drawn carts filled to the brim with rough cut stones.

They left the hollow behind and plodded on towards *Old Soulsyke Farm*. Soon they came to the remains of the small building Jamie had spotted on his map. It was just a pile of moss covered rocks and thin, flat roofing slabs with ancient weatherworn wooden beams sticking out at strange angles. Just beyond the ruin, the wall was broken once again by a pair of leaning gate-posts, so Jamie jotted *Barn Gate* on his map. They decided to stop for a while and have a drink and a bite to eat.

The sun shimmered in a perfectly blue sky as Jamie perched on the wall and Jessica climbed on the rocky pile and found a comfortable slab. They nibbled ginger biscuits and swigged water from one of the lemonade bottles, glad to be free from their backpacks for a while. Jessica splashed a handful of water over her face to refresh herself, but as she screwed the top back on the bottle she sniffed the air curiously.

"Jamie...," she said quietly, "I'm sure I can smell wood burning!"

Her brother sprung off the wall and twitched his nose in the air as he walked over to the ruin.

"I can, too!" he gasped. "But there are no cottages for miles, and surely it's too hot today to have a fire indoors anyway!"

"Perhaps someone's burning garden rubbish and the smoke's drifted into the forest," suggested Jessica.

Jamie suddenly grabbed his sister's arm.

"Perhaps there's a fire *in the forest*!" he exclaimed. "It hasn't rained for ages and everywhere's as dry as dust!"

Jessica for the first time looked anxious as thoughts flashed through her mind of them both being trapped by leaping, licking flames and swirling clouds of choking smoke! They'd both seen raging, out-of-control forest fires back in Scotland and they knew how quickly they could spread! She quickly shoved the water bottle into her backpack and tied the draw cord, all the time nervously peering into the distant trees.

"Come on, Jamie! Let's get back to *Deer Leap*!" she panted.

But it was at that moment that Jamie pointed at the pile of fallen stones.

"Look, Jess! That's what it is!"

Curling and weaving upwards from between the mossy rocks was a single, slender plume of blue smoke.

"But there can't be a fire under there, surely?" said Jessica, her eyes now fixed on the peculiar wisp that wove into the air and faded away

to nothing. “It must be damp under the rocks and, anyway, the sun’s rays couldn’t get through that lot!” 
“Well, there’s no smoke without a fire! Or so dad’s always saying!” said Jamie, sniffing the smoke. “And have you smelled it? It seems...sort of...scented!”
“It’s like...roasted nuts!” said Jessica, dropping her voice to almost a whisper, and looking around the rest of the ruin half expecting to see more plumes of smoke rising into the air.
“That’s it! Roasted chestnuts at Christmas! How strange!”

But it wasn’t another wispy plume that suddenly caught her eye. It was something even more mysterious! Something lying near where the barn door had once been. Something half buried beneath the ancient tumbled stones.

Chapter 7

Trapped beneath a thick, decayed, wooden beam was a short bent tube of rusted metal with the remains of black rubber clinging to its tip. Jessica grasped the rubber and tugged at the tube, but it wouldn't budge. It was stuck fast. The black rubber crumbled in her hands and she could feel the rough, flaky rust.

"Let me have a go!" burst Jamie, flexing his muscles like a circus strongman. "I'll have it out of there before you can say *Jack Robinson*!"

"Oh, yes!" laughed his sister, making way for him.

Jamie grabbed hold of the protruding metal and pulled for all he was worth!

"*Jack Robinson*!...*John Robinson*!...*Jill Robinson*!...*Jessica Robinson*!....*Jamie Rob*...!"

"OK, OK! Clever clogs!" gasped Jamie, finally giving up and falling backwards in a heap. "Let's clear away some of these rocks and we'll have it out in no time!"

One by one, they lifted the heavy stones which surrounded the tube, and as they did so, they found that the tube was connected to a whole great knot of tangled metal underneath.

It was almost all solid rust, except for the odd shiny patch and some blue painted bits.

Each removed rock revealed more and more of the mysterious tangle...until Jamie suddenly realised what it was!

"It's a *tricycle*!" he exclaimed into the silence of the forest. "Look, there's the chain, the frame, the pedals and one...two...three twisted spoked wheels and their mudguards. The bit you saw first was the handle-bar with the remains of one of the rubber grips!"

The whole, mangled, metallic machine was at last freed from the weight of rocks that had pinned it down for years and years. Its three battered wheels were just about in tact but nowhere near round in shape. Their spokes were bent and broken in every direction, with their rubber tyres almost completely rotted into shreds.

The chain was an unmovable belt of solid rust and the tattered remains of the blue saddle fell apart when Jamie touched it.

It was almost like the skeleton of a once lively living thing. Once it would have carried a happy laughing boy or girl, been well oiled and looked after. But now, here it was, dead, buried and forgotten. The only thing missing was a bell on the handle-bar. Surely it had had one once. All tricycles did. It would have shrilled at the touch of a child's thumb, but now the body lay deadly silent, its voice gone forever.

"But who could have left it here, in the middle of nowhere?" wondered Jessica.

"To be squashed flat and buried when the barn eventually collapsed," added Jamie, imagining the machine as it once was...blue, shiny and gleaming.

Somehow, the sight of it lying there, dead and rotted, saddened both of them. They began silently to re-bury it, replacing the gravestones one by one, until not even the telltale handle-bar was visible.

Then they quietly slung on their backpacks, glanced at the still weaving wisp of mysterious smoke and headed away from the ruin, images rushing through their minds of who could have once ridden the trike, but then abandoned it forever. And it was Jessica, of course, who looked back and saw, as clear as crystal, a girl perched on the saddle of a shiny blue tricycle wearing a pretty, flowery, lace-necked frock with her brown hair in ribboned pig-tails. The girl smiled and waved her hand, as a boy wearing baggy, green corduroy trousers down to his knobbly knees and a striped, woolly, sleeveless pullover emerged from the fully restored barn.

He, too, smiled and waved, then tweaked the tricycle's bell with his thumb. It's shrill tinkle echoed in the forest, as Jessica's image quickly faded.

"What was *that*?" burst Jamie staring back at the ruin. "It sounded like a..."

"Tricycle bell?" suggested Jessica, biting her lip.

Jamie nodded, as puzzled as ever.

"It's just our imaginations playing tricks with us," joked Jessica a little awkwardly.

"But surely not with *both of us* at the *same time* hearing the *same thing*!" insisted Jamie, as he made his way alongside the wall, shaking his head and tossing his arms. Jessica just smiled to herself and followed. She reckoned it was best to say nothing more at the moment. She was sure that soon everything would be made perfectly clear!

The going got a bit tougher as the wall began to climb a ferny bank. Anxious to reach the farmhouse, Jessica and Jamie scrambled along the wall taking a side each, both tripping and stumbling beneath the trees in their rush to be the first to the top of the slope.

Jamie won the race and collapsed panting in a huge cushion of springy, purple heather. Jessica soon joined him and they both lay exhausted, their chests heaving and unable to utter a word between them. They just lay there catching their breaths and looking upwards through the overhanging branches into the blue sky beyond. There wasn't a breath of wind nor a cloud in sight, just the bright green stretching fingertips of the trees and the sounds of birdsong and buzzing insects. Their panting gradually slowed down as they rested in the dappled shade watching hornets and hoverflies amid the heathers' tiny purple flowers.

They were lying nearly at the top of the slope, but not quite. Jamie, when he had rested long enough, rolled over and clambered on all fours over the purple cushion and peeped through a final curtain of fern.

What he saw made him blink his eyes...and look again!

Yes! It was still there! He wasn't dreaming, but the view before him was so absolutely incredible and totally unexpected!
"Jess! Come up here and look at *this*!" he called over his shoulder.

They both parted the fringe of green and gold fern and gazed across the summit of the small hill they had just climbed. Instead of the unceasing ranks of slender pine trees they had battled through all morning, they were now lying on the edge of a beautiful small wood of giant broadleafed trees. Straight in front of them was a quartet of huge, grey barked beech trees, their thick branches clothed in green with just the merest hint of autumn gold. Their firm, smooth trunks looked like the legs of an outsized elephant rising from a deep, crinkly carpet of fallen leaves from countless years past. Beyond stood darker, twisted and gnarled oak trees and lighter coloured sycamore and birch. It was all so very different from the rest of the forest, with the great open, airy canopy of criss-crossed, thick, knobbly branches and swathes of broad leaves overlapping one another. It was wonderful and the birdsong was almost deafening!

Jessica and Jamie grabbed their backpacks and ran into the wood, stirring up the fallen leaves and weaving in and out of the giant trunks. The wall they had been following was all but completely buried in the leaves, but it eventually met another at a kind of T-junction almost overgrown with heather. They jumped over it and then they saw, straight in front of them, the jagged outline of the ruined buildings that made up *Old Soulsyke Farm*. They were there at last!

On the map, *Old Soulsyke* was bang in the middle of the crest of a small, round, flat-topped hill, surrounded by the last wall the children had met. The three farm buildings were made from

the same orangy-brown sandstone as all the walls had been and the ruined barn. But, unlike the barn, the buildings were still standing.
"Come on, Jamie!" called Jessica. "Let's have a look around. It looks like a super spot to spend the night...and it'll save having to put the tent up!"
"And we might even see the ghost of one of the old farmers' wives from centuries ago!" joked Jamie in his best spooky voice.
"Don't be silly, little brother!" replied Jessica. "But you *do* realise that we could be the *first* people to have visited this place for years and years! I wonder if the boy and girl who owned the tricyc..."
"How do you know it was a boy *and* girl" interrupted Jamie, looking suspiciously at his sister.
"I don't...it was just a wild guess!" laughed Jessica, again a little awkwardly, fingering an acorn nervously.
"I'm beginning to think you're holding something back," said Jamie quietly, but with a hint of annoyance in his voice. "There's definitely something you're not telling me! Next you'll be coming up with their names, like you know *Shandy's* the name of the albino deer!"
"*Chandar*, not *Shandy*!" Jessica snapped back. "And yes! I *do* know what the boy and girl are called, so there!"
"What then? Go on, tell me!" burst Jamie, now totally confused and not knowing whether to believe his sister or not.
"Jonathan and Jane!" announced Jessica. "There you are, I've told you! How I know, I've no idea. But I know they're called Jonathan and Jane and I saw them as clear as daylight back at the ruined barn!!"
"Do you mean when we heard the tricycle bell?"
"Yes, and I saw Jonathan ring the bell when he came out of the...."
Suddenly, Jamie, who was definitely beginning to think that the heat of the mid-day sun was starting to affect his sister, grabbed hold of her arm.
"Sssh! Can you hear that?"
"I can only hear birds singing!" replied Jessica.
"No, listen. It's coming from up in the branches of that tree...and that's *no bird*!" exclaimed Jamie, pointing to a nearby, towering horse chestnut.
Then Jessica heard it.

The same sound she'd heard by the wall the day before last!
The sound of notes from a horn...very faintly, sounding as though they were coming from miles away.
Jessica just couldn't believe her own ears.
"It's definitely coming from up in the tree!" whispered Jamie, peering upwards and straining to hear.
But then, the sounds stopped, as suddenly as they had begun.
Jessica gazed up into the branches.
"I told you I heard a horn the other day!" she smiled, somehow relieved that now her brother had heard it too. "Now perhaps you'll believe me! And what's more, I think the horn is something to do with the charms we've found...and the strange pile of berries..."
"And the rainbow colours round *Shandy's,* I mean *Chandar's* neck... and the smoke from the pile of stones...and the tricycle...and you knowing the names of the deer and the boy and girl at the barn!" said Jamie breathlessly. "Boy! Oh boy! This is turning out to be a *real* mystery!!"
"Come on, let's explore the farm buildings!" Jessica said excitedly. "I can't wait to see...
Hang on, what's that? I'm sure I saw something move near the top of the tree!"

Jamie looked up into the horse chestnut tree and then he, too, caught sight of a movement!...and then he exploded into laughter!
"It's a *squiggle*!"
"*Squirrel,* Jamie!" grinned his sister. "You called them *squiggles* when you were about *two-and-a-half*!"
Then she put a finger to her lips and looked into the branches intently.
"Listen!" she whispered. "There it is again.
The horn!"
"It *is* coming from the tree!" exclaimed Jamie, unable to control his excitement. "Wow! It must be a pretty musical squiggle!"

This time, there were three long, drawn out notes, each one starting loudly and then fading away to nothing.
"There must be some weird squiggles around here!" whispered Jamie. "You're sure you want to spend the night here, sis? We might be woken up at midnight by the whole *squiggle orchestra*!"
"Playing the *'Nut*cracker Suite', I suppose!" laughed Jessica, although she was certain that the horn notes were nothing to do with bushy tailed animals!

As the squirrel darted along its branch and vanished into lush foliage, the children couldn't help thinking that something strange and magical had occured. Even Jamie, with his doubts, was beginning to be drawn into the forest's mysterious spell. This had been no normal walk in a forest like the ones they'd so frequently enjoyed back in Scotland. *Mary* had a special enchanting beauty all of her own, but that had been all about the power of nature; the scenery and the wildlife. But here, *George* seemed to possess an altogether different power. A strange, magical force all of its own...and amazingly, although they knew there was no one else around for miles, they both felt that they were *not* alone...and that they were being watched at that very moment.
A shiver ran down both their backs and goose-bumps prickled on their arms...not because of fear, strangely enough, but because of an excited anticipation of what might happen next!

The old farmstead was clustered around a central yard which was a patchwork of giant uneven slabs of green stained stone separated by a lattice of straggly weeds. As the children became enclosed by the enticing buildings which seemed to beckon them to within their grasp, their hearts began to beat faster and faster.
But, although it seemed strange to be surrounded by buildings in the middle of a forest, the farm felt warm and welcoming.
There were a couple of barns, one with a roof and one without, an open topped stable and the farmhouse itself with square, dark, gaping holes for windows and a rectangular hole where a front door had once been.

The roof of the house seemed to be intact and even its chimney stack stood erect against the blue sky.

Suddenly, a streak of pure white flashed out of the doorway like lightning, sped across the paving stones and vanished into one of the barns. Jamie's knees instantly turned to jelly and Jessica stifled a scream as they both stared open mouthed into the dark hole where the streak had bolted. They were not alone after all.

The ancient farm had a cat. A sleek, white cat with enormous green eyes.

"A ghost cat in a ghost farm!" joked Jamie nervously in a quivery voice.

"Then we'll call him or her... *'Spook'*!" said Jessica, trying her best not to sound shocked by the cat's sudden appearance.

"You're sure you don't know it's name already?" muttered Jamie with a touch of sarcasm.

Jessica scowled at him with one of her dismissive looks, but decided to say nothing. Instead, she tiptoed across the stone slabs to *Spook's* barn and peered inside.

"Completely disappeared!" she said.

"Yeah, ghosts have a habit of doing that sort of thing!" replied Jamie with a grin.

They dropped their backpacks in a dry stone trough by the doorway of the farmhouse and Jamie looked through one of the window holes with its rotted wooden frame.

"It's pretty gloomy inside!" he called, his voice booming around the empty groundfloor room.

Jessica gingerly stepped through the doorway and into the damp darkness. Although the sun was shining brightly, hardly any light entered the house. At first she could hardly see a thing but gradually her eyes became accustomed to the murky black. There was just one room with patches of plaster clinging to its rough stone walls. Wooden beams crossed the low

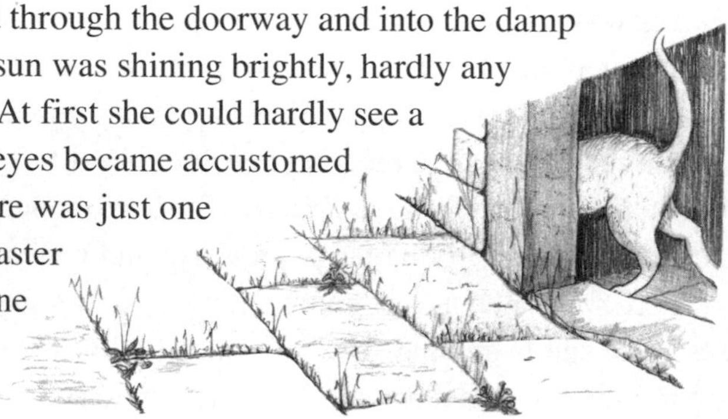

ceiling which had a square hole on the far side, probably for a ladder thought Jessica.
Opposite the doorway was a rocky fireplace and hearth where she imagined a log fire's dancing flames warming the lower room and sending heat up to the loft which would have been the bedroom.
Jamie followed his sister into the farmhouse and shone his torch into the room's darkest nooks and crannies. The shadows cast from the wooden beams seemed to make the ceiling move as he shone the light around. Rusty hooks, like talons, clawed the air from the middle beam. From one, a long length of rope dangled like a snake caught by a bird of prey. It was coiled below on the dusty, stone-slab floor, looking as if it hadn't been disturbed for years. The torch beam then fell upon an oblong, white pot sink sat on chunky stone supports.
"It doesn't have any taps!" noticed Jamie, as he wrote his initials with a finger in the thick grey grime that coated the inside. "I wonder where they got their water from?"
"There must have been a well or something in the yard," suggested Jessica, "or one of those handpump things you yank up and down."
"If we can find a water supply, this place'll make a super den to come to at the weekends!" enthused Jamie, beginning to feel at home.
"We'll have a look around after we've had a bite to eat," said Jessica. "I'm starving!"
"Me, too!" agreed Jamie. "Let's sit on the stone trough outside and get warm again. It's a bit chilly in here."

Thoughts of themselves being watched by hidden eyes gradually vanished as they tucked into great chunks of fruitcake and ginger snaps. It was a beautiful day and here they were in the middle of their own perfectly secret wood with its own perfectly secret hiding place. Bird song filled the air and the warmth of the sun made them both feel like setting up camp at the old farm instead of delving deeper into *George's* depths. And they didn't even need a tent! The loft would do nicely!

During the afternoon they explored the other buildings and looked for a well but with no luck. They didn't even see *Spook* again. The cat seemed to have vanished into thin air!

Getting up into the loft proved to be quite a challenge, but with the help of the coiled rope and an old ladder they found, Jamie at last managed to poke his head through the square hole in the ceiling and pull himself up. Jessica tossed up his torch and a moment later the loft was flooded with light.

"I wonder how long ago there were people sleeping up here?" asked Jamie as he shone the torch beam around.

"Well dad said the pine trees were all planted back in the 'Nineteen-fifties', so I suppose that's when all the farms were abandoned," replied Jessica from below. "So that's about half a century ago!"

Like the lower room, fallen plaster littered the floor revealing the ancient stones again. There was a dividing wall across the middle made of newer stones and wooden boards, probably to make two bedrooms. One of the rooms even had the tatty remains of flowery wallpaper clinging to some of the plaster. The white-washed roof beams still seemed strong and firm, although there were one or two missing roof tiles which allowed rays of sunlight to slice through the darkness.

"It's great up here!" called Jamie. "We've even got a bedroom each! Come up and have a look!"

Jessica climbed the ricketty ladder and she, too, was delighted with the den.

"I'll have the bedroom without the hole in the floor if you don't mind!" she decided. "Then if we get attacked by wolves in the middle of the night, you can pull up the ladder!"

Jamie howled like a wolf with toothache, pulled out his imaginary sword and fought back the ferocious invaders.

"What? You? Single-handed?" Jessica giggled. "You couldn't hold back a pack of cards never mind a pack of wolves!"

"You don't know what I'm capable of doing once I'm roused and angry!" retorted Jamie, still swishing his sword. "Anyway we'd have the ghosts of your *Jonathan and Jane* to help, wouldn't we?" he taunted.

Jessica once again gave her brother one of her frowning scowls as she began to clear away chunks of fallen plaster to make a flat place for her sleeping bag. Most of the pieces were small and easy to move to one side, but one particular piece was as big as a large door mat. It had somehow fallen from the wall and landed with its pink, flowery wallpaper facing upwards. It reminded her of the wallpaper in her new bedroom back at *Deer Leap*, with its hedgerow flowers and rambling roses, but, of course, it was nowhere near as fresh and new looking. The pattern had faded and there were brown stains probably caused by dripping water from the roof. As she tried to lift one end of the plaster slab, the paper began to peel away. She couldn't resist trying to peel more and more of the damp paper from the plaster. It had suddenly become a challenge to get the whole lot off in one sheet!

It came away quite easily, revealing the greyish white, crumbly plaster beneath...but also some strange, thick, jet black lines on the back of the wallpaper. As she carried on, more and more lines appeared.

"Jamie, come and have a look at this!" she whispered quietly, sounding puzzled.

Jamie scrambled over and shone his torch on the creamy, blotchy paper that looked almost like ancient parchment.

"They're sort of...pencil marks...done with a thick, chubby pencil!" he suggested. "And look, you can see the same lines on the plaster, but much fainter! I think someone's drawn on the plaster when it was on the wall...."

"Then it was wallpapered over...," added Jessica, "and now it's coming off onto the paper as I peel it off!!"

Gently, Jessica carried on as carefully as she could...and slowly, the wallpaper curled off the slab of plaster into a roll. Now it really did look like an ancient piece of parchment with its mottled brown stains and crinkly edges!

Then she began to slowly unfurl the roll and, between them, they managed to flatten the paper and stop it from curling up again.

It was covered in a complete maze of the thick, pencil lead lines, but what excited Jessica and Jamie most were several words written with the same blunt, black pencil. They were hardly readable mainly because they were all back to front like mirror writing, but gradually they made out the words *'farm'*, *'gate'*, *'low field'* and *'high field'*.

"All the lines must be *walls*!" burst Jamie suddenly, at last beginning to understand the jagged pattern. "And look! There's the barn where we found the tricycle!"
He pointed to the word '*barn'* on the map and then traced the wall that lead from the ruined barn to the farm - the one they'd walked beside only a few hours before!
"And look at *this*!!" exclaimed Jessica, pointing to the largest and blackest word printed on the very edge of the paper. "It says '*well'*!!"
"That's it then!" said Jamie. "It's a map showing the walls and fields around the old farm...and for some unknown reason, the '*well'* seems to be the most important!"
"But why would anyone want to draw a map on their bedroom wall in the first place?" wondered Jessica. "And why is the well so important?"
Jamie hardly heard what his sister was saying as he pored over the map, inspecting its every detail.
"Perhaps there's something special about the well?" Jessica went on in a world of her own.
Just then, Jamie shot up in the air, nearly knocking his sister flying!
"Look! Look at that!" he pointed excitedly at the bottom corner of the map.
"It's a year! And two capital letters!"
Quickly, Jamie traced the numbers backwards.
"*Nineteen...Forty...Nine*!" he exclaimed. "And the two letters are...."
"*J*... and ... *J* !" whispered Jessica, her face beaming with excitement.
"*Jonathan*... and ...
Jane!!"

Chapter 8

Just one hour after their startling discovery, Jessica and Jamie collapsed into a soft bed of fern fronds at the junction of two walls much deeper in the forest beyond *Old Soulsyke*. They had followed a wall on the mysterious map firstly down the other side of the farm's heather crowned hill and then along a shallow valley. It had been hard going for most of the way through more spruceland with low hanging branches and deep pine-needle drifts, but at least they were travelling light with just one backpack between them which they carried in turn. It was wonderfully light, having left all the provisions back at the farm base-camp. They'd decided just to take waterproofs, half a bottle of water, some biscuits and their torches. Jessica carried *'J' and 'J'*s map rolled up in her hand and Jamie had the rope from the farmhouse wound round his body and over his shoulder like a mountaineer!

The hot afternoon sun had weakened and it felt cooler as shadows lengthened. Nevertheless, they were both tired as they rested beneath the waving ferns.

"It can't be too much further to the well from here," said Jamie as his sister unrolled the map.

"I feel like a pirate on a desert island looking for buried treasure!" laughed Jessica as she spread the ancient looking parchment on a patch of soft grass.

"Now then, Jamie, lad!" she croaked in her best pirate's voice. "I reckon we 'eads due north sixty paces, then nor'west twenty paces. Then we starts a' diggin'!"

"Right ye are, Cap'n!!" echoed Jamie. "Then we's be the richest sea-dogs on these 'ere 'igh seas!" He broke off a fern, sprung to his feet and used it as another imaginary sword to fend off *Blackbeard's* cut-throats who were storming his faithful tub!
"Returning to dry land for a moment, Jake...I mean, Jamie!" laughed Jessica. "I think the well's only a few more steps along that wall over there!"
"C'mon then, skipper!" urged Jamie, still all at sea. "Let's get to ye olde booty!"

They scrambled through the ferns and then along the top of the moss covered wall. Everything was going well...until Jamie came to a sudden halt and pointed ahead.
Not far in front was another pair of leaning gate-posts, but it was not the posts that had made Jamie suddenly stop...it was what was on top of them!

Perched on each post was a magnificently coloured bird. They were identical and about the size of a small crow, with browny pink breast feathers and wings with black and white patches and wonderfully iridescent, gleaming streaks of blue. And, as if to add just a touch more glamour, they both had pink and black spotted crests standing proudly on their heads.
"Jays!" whispered Jamie.
"They're beautiful!" replied Jessica, as both birds preened their glorious plumage, completely unaware that human eyes were upon them.
"They've probably never seen people before, being so deep in the forest," whispered Jamie, as, amazingly...two more...then a third...then a fourth...flew beneath the spruce trees showing off their magnificent colours, especially the blue wing flashes which shimmered in the late afternoon sun. It was almost like

being on the tropical island they had imagined held pirates' treasure, with parrots in the treetops!

As Jamie took a cautious step forward, the two birds on the gate-posts fluttered upwards in alarm, making an awful screeching sound that didn't go at all well with their splendid feathers! Then, in a wild flurry of blues and pinks all six birds vanished into the depths of the forest.

Jessica and Jamie, for a moment or two, stared into the emptiness and felt strangely alone. The first real colour the sprucelands had shown them had gone.

"That's *ten jays* altogether!" announced Jessica, breaking the silence.

"*Ten*? How do you make that out?" queried Jamie. "I only counted *six*!"

"The six flying jays...plus the two *'J's* on the map...plus us two!" replied Jessica with a grin as they walked towards the gate-posts.

Beneath each giant finger of stone were dozens of the blue, shimmering jay wing feathers. But instead of being scattered any old how, they were neatly heaped into four tidy mounds.

"It's as though they've been collected into piles!" whispered Jessica, crouching down to look at the small glinting heaps. She carefully picked up a couple and put them on the palm of her hand. They shimmered like miniature rainbows or drops of oil on water.

"They remind me of the neat pile of berries we saw beneath the mountain ash!" said Jamie, as he glanced into the crevices in the wall by the gate-posts hoping to see a glint from yet another silver charm.

"I'm going to wear a feather for luck and to remind me of those jays!" said Jessica, choosing one and weaving it through the laces of her trainers. Jamie did the same and they both admired the splendid blue flashes on their feet. Jessica then sprawled on the grass and unfurled the map.

"The well should be somewhere near these gate-posts," she said, "and, according to this, there should be a track heading in both directions from here."

If they hadn't have had the map they would never have noticed it...but, very, very faintly...winding away through the trees, and well covered with light green grass, lay the track. It was about as wide as a horse-drawn cart and humped along the middle where wheels had never rolled. Jessica gazed along the track and pictured a trundling wagon pulled by a pair of chestnut horses with long manes, driven by a bearded, old peasant wearing a simple, brown smock. Then she saw an elegant, finely dressed woman riding side-saddle on a pure white Arabian stallion. Had fleeing highwaymen galloped to safety at *Old Soulsyke* and passed through these very gateposts? Or had a flying mailcoach once called in at the farm to water its four-in-hand?

Jessica lay back in the grass and let her mind wander into the past...one of her favourite pastimes, but she was almost immediately jolted back to the present!

"Come on, Jess! It's going to take *both* of us to find it!" complained Jamie, as he kicked around in the undergrowth looking for any sign of the well. The trouble was, he didn't really have any idea what he was searching for! The only kind of well he had seen was the sort in fairy tales, in story books from when he was younger...ones with little red roofs, low circular walls, buckets dangling on ropes with winding handles!*...ding, dong, dell, pussy's down the well* sort of thing!

"There's nothing here!" moaned Jamie.

"You can't give up yet!" Jessica called back, snapping out of her daydream. "It took ages and ages for Egyptian treasures to be found using ancient maps! You've got to have patience!"

"You've got to have a sister who helps!" retorted Jamie, dropping down glumly in the ferns and watching Jessica search for the elusive well.

"I thought you said *both of us* had to look!" she called from under a large spruce tree. "Come on, let's see a bit of action, or I'll come and get you!"

"Come on then, bossy-boots! Come and get me! I'm having a rest!"

Jessica ran across the track, grabbed Jamie's arm and, amid lots of protest, pulled him to his feet.

But, as she pulled, Jamie's heel skidded on the grass and tore the thin turf away from the rock beneath. Dropping her brother in a heap, she looked at the soily scar and felt the smooth stone they had uncovered. "*This is it*!!" she cried at the top of her voice. "We've found it!"

Jamie sprung to his feet and together they tugged and pulled at the grass above the flat stone. The soil was so thin it came away easily to reveal more and more of what seemed to be a slab of smooth rock, square in shape and almost as large as one of the paving stones back in *Old Soulsyke's* farmyard.

As they dug, the sun dipped below the trees and darkness began to fall. The air became cooler and the earth felt moist. Insects stopped buzzing and birds stopped singing. And, although both said nothing, each knew what the other was thinking as night-time approached, well away from *Old Soulsyke* and even further away from *Deer Leap* and dad! They'd spent many nights camping out back in Scotland, but there, they'd known every nook and cranny and felt safe. Here, it was all new and unfamiliar, but the excitement of finding the buried stone slab and the thought of a well shaft being under it, somehow pushed fearful feelings away.

As their fingers reached the four edges of the stone, they realised that it was resting on more slabs beneath, but they also found that the top stone was quite thin, not much thicker than a floorboard.

"Let's try and lift it!" gasped Jamie, as he wedged his grubby fingers under one of the edges. Jessica joined him on his side of the slab and together they slowly raised the stone, their hearts thumping with excitement.

It was like a trap-door being opened in the forest floor...opening for the first time in maybe fifty years! Jessica's skin began to creep and the hair on the back of Jamie's neck bristled, as, slowly...a black, square hole appeared beneath the slab.

They managed to steady the stone on its edge, and then, with a gentle push, it fell with a thud onto the soft grass, upside down. Woodlice and beetles scurried in every direction looking for shelter, their

peace shattered by the sudden upheaval of their dark, dank, secret world.
Jessica and Jamie stared at the void that had opened before them.
The well.
'J' and 'J's well.
They'd found it!

The hole was blacker than the blackest blackness of the night. A damp, musty smell rose from its depths. It was as though the well had held its breath for years upon years, and now was breathing out, relieved to have fresh, cool air rushing into it, at long, long last. The children stood slightly back and wondered how deep the hole plunged. Jamie kicked a cone over the edge. They waited for a sound............but heard nothing. Then he shone his torch into the gaping mouth, like a dentist looking for a rotten tooth. The beam lit the well's circular, crumbling stone walls, which were draped in dripping moss. But then the beam fell on something totally unexpected! Something that made Jessica and Jamie look at one another in amazement! Each knew exactly what the other was thinking!
The real adventure was about to begin!

There, just a few wall stones down the shaft, was the first of many rusted metal rungs of a ladder leading down into the gloom. Jamie stepped closer and shone his torchbeam down the ladder as far as he could, but the bright beam faded into darkness after about

twenty rungs. Then, as he swung the beam around the shaft, he spotted what looked like a ledge opposite the ladder with a gap in the wall stones above it.
"It looks like a passage leading off from the well!" he gasped.
"We've just *got* to get down there and explore! Come on! I'll lead the way!"

Jessica grasped her brother's arm and shook her head. Although she, too, couldn't wait to climb down into the unknown, she thought it wiser to go down at first light after a good night's sleep at *Old Soulsyke*. She glanced up through the treetops into the sky. It was almost as black as the well except for the odd twinkling star. Night-time had crept up on them quickly and cast its cloak over the forest.
"Mind you, it's going to be tricky finding our way back in the dark...!" she said, peering through the ranks of tree trunks.
"Then let's get down the well!" insisted Jamie. "It's as dark down there as it is up here!"
"Tell you what!" suggested Jessica, hoping a compromise would be the solution. "Let's sleep here under the ferns instead of going back to the farm. Then as soon as the sun comes up we'll climb down! OK?"

Jamie reluctantly agreed and together they made their nests for the night under the stars. A pine-needle drift by the wall made a comfy mattress, and soon they were snug under their waterproofs, nibbling the last of the biscuits.
As Jessica looked up through the silhouetted treetop branches into the dark sky, she traced with her finger the stars that made up the giant *'W'* of Queen Cassiopeia. Then she dared herself to look into the great square emptiness of Pegasus. Would she see more magical images within its vast picture frame? Would the leaping albino deer be there again? Or the enormous candle?

This time there was nothing but a blank, black canvas. But something told her that she had arrived at the place where she was meant to arrive. She felt strangely content as she glanced at the thin crescent moon hanging motionless in the sky. She thought of the horn sounds she'd heard first by the wall near *Deer Leap* and all that had happened since. Now, she was here, in *George's* deepest, darkest depths beneath the trees by yet another wall...and next to a mysterious well...with a ladder plunging down into...who knows what or where!

An owl hooted softly in the distance. She touched the charms which were still snuggled safely in her back pocket. Then she looked back into Pegasus. This time the magic was with her. Once again, a vast, broad, white candle appeared, its base embedded in a mass of pink, glassy crystal and its flame burning brightly, smoothly and strongly with no hint of flutter or flicker. Then an enormous pair of human eyes appeared behind it, illuminated by the flame and each holding a reflection of the flame in their bluish pools.

A face began to form...an elderly face...whiskered, bushy white eyebrowed, sunken cheeks, lined forehead. Slowly, thin lips appeared and the face smiled, the eyes burst into life...and then...the lips broke into words. Jessica heard them clearly. The voice was warm and deep.

"*The flame is called 'Lumina'...and she welcomes you*!"

Then, almost instantly, the image vanished...it had completed its task. Its magic had found the person it sought. And once again, Jessica knew the magical image was for her eyes alone. She gazed up at the stars and smiled.

"Jamie!" she whispered. "Are you awake?"

There was no reply.

She could just hear his soft breathing. He was already fast asleep!

It reminded her of when they slept in the same room back in Scotland, what seemed like a long, long...long.....long time ago....

Her eyes slowly closed...and Jessica, too, fell into a deep, deep sleep....

A few hours later, Jamie's eyes shot open wide!

Directly above his staring, frightened eyes, clouds had covered the inky blackness, starshine and moonshine blotted out.

It was pitch black. Darker than ever.

He couldn't even make out his bedroom window.

His bedroom window?

Of course he couldn't see it, he suddenly remembered!

He was sleeping in the middle of the forest, under the ferns, by a wall...and near the wonderful well!
His sudden bout of panic left him as his eyes became accustomed to the dark and he heard his sister's reassuring shallow breathing.
Why, though, had he woken so suddenly?
After all, it was so deadly silent!
An owl hooted in the far distance.
That was it, he thought, as he rolled over and curled up in his pine-needle bed.
Then...he heard a sound that made his stomach turn and his spine tingle.
Crack!!
A twig snapped to his left.
Crack!!
Another snapped to his right.
Jamie froze!
He could hear his heart thudding in his ears.
He dared to inch his fingers blindly over the pine-needles to grab his torch.
His fingertips crept away, searching anxiously in the dark.
Where *was* it? He was sure he had left it on the forest floor, just an arm's length away.
At last his fingers felt it and in one movement, he drew the torch towards him, pointed it upwards...and switched it on!
It's white beam pierced the darkness and lit the high overhanging branches.
Slowly, he lowered the beam down one of the eerie, green trunks...
CRACK!!
Louder than ever! This time from just behind him on the other side of the wall!
He felt like yelling and waking his sister!
But he couldn't...his mouth felt stifled and gagged.
As the beam moved lower and lower, his heart beat faster and faster.... and then....

he saw them!!!

Chapter 9

Pairs of bright lights, twinkling jewels, sparkled in the torchlight. Seven...eight...nine...ten pairs, as the beam panned the forest like a searchlight.

Very bright, like low-level stars encircling him.

Then, as his eyes became used to the dark, he made out the shapes of heads...slender bodies and legs...and *antlers*!

He gasped a sigh of relief!

They were deer! Standing perfectly still like statues, just as he'd seen them back at *Deer Leap*. And again, in the midst of them was the young albino, its white fur and ruby eyes gleaming in the torchlight, and around its graceful neck the shimmering rainbow. Jamie peered at the band of colour, then he quickly shone his torchbeam onto his own feet and the greeny-blue, iridescent feather he had threaded through his laces.

It was incredible!

The albino's rainbow was a chain of the same woven jay wing feathers! Dozens of them!

"Jess!" he whispered as loudly as he dared. "Jessica, wake up!"

His sister stirred and mumbled, and then propped herself up on one elbow and rubbed her eyes.

"What's the matter?" she whispered. "Why are we whispering? There's no one around for miles!"

Jamie swung his torchbeam across the forest.

"There!" he said, pointing into the trees. "Look!"

"You've woken me up in the middle of the night to show me a load of green tree trunks!"
"But...but...they were there a second ago!"
"What were there? What are you talking about?"
"They've disappeared into thin air!"
"*What's* disappeared?" asked Jessica, becoming a little agitated and more than a little alarmed.
"*Deer*! A whole herd of them! Just like at *Deer Lea*...!"
"Ssshh! Listen!" burst Jessica, scrambling to her feet.

Jamie switched off his torch and the two children listened to the silent stillness of the night. The owl hooted again in the far away distance...but then...they both heard it...a long, single note from a horn! Then came another...and another...even longer and louder than the notes they'd heard from the horse chestnut tree back at *Old Soulsyke*. This time the notes seemed echoey and almost next to them, not distant and faint.
"*The well*! *The well*!" exclaimed Jessica suddenly, almost making Jamie jump out of his skin. "The sounds are coming from *the well*!!"

In a flash they were both crouched by the well's black, gaping mouth. For a moment all was quiet, but then the horn began again...one long, echoey note after another...each note starting faintly, becoming louder and louder, and then fading away to be replaced by another and then another. It was as though several horns were being blown in turn!
Then, a final, eerie, especially long note faded...and silence followed.
"We've just *got* to get down there!" urged Jamie at last, dying to discover the well's secret.
"*Then let's go*!!" replied Jessica, brimming over with excitement.
Jamie could hardly believe his ears! Was this Jessica, his sister, talking? Normally she was the ultra-cautious one, needing to think everything through dozens of times! But this time it seemed they'd both been bitten by the same bug! They just *had* to discover the secret of the well!!

Jamie shone his torch down into the black throat and they both knew what was to be the first target...the ledge!
They quickly secured one end of the rope to one of the nearby trees and threw the loose end down the well. It reached way past the ledge, dangling by the rusty ladder.
Moments later, Jamie sat with his legs also dangling into the hole, as though he was going to make a parachute jump from a plane. And he was no less nervous!
Slowly he turned from a sitting position into a kneel and lowered his left foot tentatively into the spooky emptiness, feeling for the first rung of the ladder. Gradually, he put his whole weight onto it, gripping the rope tightly, just in case!
"It's OK, Jess! It's strong enough!" he gasped, with just his head and shoulders protruding from the well.
Slowly, his head disappeared into the hole as he stretched for the next rung.
"This one's OK, too!" he called back to his sister, his voice echoing.
"Do you think they'll take my weight?" asked Jessica nervously.
"I think they'd take a *baby elephant*, but I'm not sure about *you*!!" laughed Jamie, feeling more confident.
"Charming!!" muttered Jessica, as, she too, began her descent into the unknown.
Jamie tried the next rung and then the next. Soon he was level with the ledge, with Jessica just above him. He shone his torch for the first time into the gap in the wall.
"Jess!" he shouted. "*There's a door, just inside from the ledge*!"
Without even thinking about the drop below him, Jamie stretched a leg over to the ledge and pulled himself over into the small passageway that lead to the door. There was just enough headroom to sit, and soon his sister was perched next to him, watching the torchbeam shining up and down into the gloom of the well.

Shuffling around to inspect the mysterious door was a bit tricky, but after a few moans and groans they both managed to turn round. It was only about half the height of a normal door but about the same width. It was made from vertical planks of rough, knotted wood with a mossy, green tinge. Its sides were straight, but the top was arched. A small, rusty, round iron handle was on the right, about halfway up, with a large keyhole just below it.

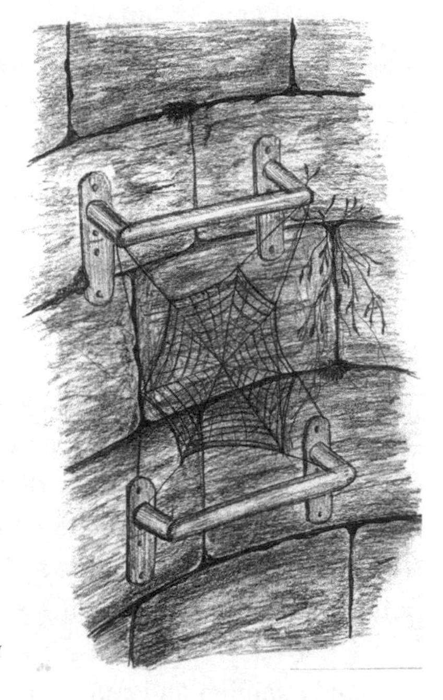

"It's bound to be locked!" grumbled Jamie, sounding like an expert on ancient, subterranean passages. "Mysterious doors always are!"

"You never know," said Jessica, optimistically. "We might just be in luck! After all, why would anyone want to lock an underground door miles from anywhere. You're not really expecting buried treasure, are you?"

Jessica reached with stretching fingertips to touch the gnarled, old wood...and to her astonishment...it moved! Not much, just an inch or so...but the fact that it had moved *at all,* totally surprised them both!

A moment later, they were shuffling up to the door taking care not to bump their heads on the low, arched ceiling carved into the bare rock.

Jamie pushed the door again...and once again it moved, this time with a short, sharp creak which sent shivers of fear and anticipation racing up and down their spines as the crack of darkness became wider and wider.

As they both pushed again, the door jerked steadily open until there was just enough of a gap through which Jamie could shine his torch.

The beam lit a wall of solid rock, vertical and smooth, not made of blocks of cut stone like the farm, but more like a sheer cliff face.

The wall was bare except for what looked like rusty, curved iron candle brackets fixed into the rock. Each one held the remains of a chubby, creamy coloured wax candle encrusted with frozen drips of melted wax. They were linked together with drooping, dusty hammocks of old cobwebs.

"After three! OK?" called Jamie, bracing his shoulder against the door and bursting to set eyes on the rest of its secrets.
Jessica nodded, placing the palms of her hands flat against the wood.
"One!....two!....three!" they chorused, and then they shoved at the door with all the strength they could muster.

With an eerie, creaking growl, the door swung open. Then with a final whimper it came to a grinding halt. Jessica and Jamie fell forwards in a heap and found themselves in what seemed to be some kind of cellar cut out of the solid rock beneath the forest. Jamie shone his torch into the room, and as they watched and followed its beam, their eyes widened with amazement as light fell upon the unexpected, enchanting world beyond the door!!

They were both speechless as the torchbeam explored the secret room and illuminated its magical contents. They just couldn't believe what lay before their eyes!

The floor was absolutely jam packed with scores of brilliantly shining and colourful *toys*! Not plastic and electronic toys from the present day, but chunky metal toys from the past. All standing there as though they hadn't been touched for years, yet without a single trace of dust or cobwebs to be seen! It was as though each and every one of them had been polished and cleaned every day since they'd found themselves entombed in the mysterious forest cellar.

Jessica and Jamie were totally amazed by the sights that filled their eyes. The colours were so bright and vivid, especially in the middle of the floor where the toys formed a wonderful fairground around a beautiful carousel. The carousel itself was the largest and most colourful of all the toys with its glowing white horses on their golden barley-sugar pillars frozen in their circular canter. Silver edged mirrors shone under their galloping hoofs and small brightly dressed figures clung tightly onto the horses' reins.
A Ferris wheel, the size of a car tyre, loomed above the fairground giving its miniature passengers a bird's eye view of the busy roundabouts, dodgems and side-shows. A green steam-engine with huge red wheels and a tall black chimney looked as if it would hiss and rumble into action

at any moment, steered by a stiff, top-hatted gentleman who was about the height of a matchstick.

Just beyond the fairground there were old fashioned racing cars with dashing, goggled drivers with determined expressions set in their moustached faces. There were one-man-bands frozen in mid-clatter, with dancing monkeys about to crash silver cymbals, crowded red London double-decker buses all on their ways to either Hyde Park or Oxford Street, laughing clowns and smartly uniformed, saluting soldiers. Marmalade cats played with hoops, spotted dogs gnawed on enormous white bones, while chugging harbour tugs and vintage cars and vans stood by a tall green and yellow striped helter skelter.

A couple of leopard skinned, bearded strongmen looked very strained and uncomfortable as they lifted heavyweight dumb-bells and a fierce looking lion-tamer wielding a chair and a whip stared grimly at a fully maned lion perched on a stool.

Just behind them was a troupe of acrobats all painfully posed mid-action in a variety of contortions. Beyond them was the small circular track of a railway with brightly painted signal boxes and a station. A maroon coloured steam engine had just left the platform, pulling six green and cream carriages with tiny open windows.

Everything was so colourful, alive and so full of detail, yet everything was still and lifeless, as though they had all stopped dead as soon as the cellar's ancient wooden door had been pushed open!

Jessica and Jamie, still unable to utter a word, crawled further into the secret wonderland and just gazed at the magical collection of toys. Jamie wondered whether or not he should dare touch anything in case the magic suddenly ended and the toys vanish, but he eventually plucked up the courage and touched one of the racing cars...a long, green one with a yellow number eight on each side, metal tyres and spoked wheels and driven by a mean looking ace-driver with his green scarf trailing stiffly behind in an imaginary wind.

"It's as cold as ice!" he whispered, quickly withdrawing his hand.

"Everything's made of tin, I think," suggested Jessica. "That's what toys were made of before plastic. I think you had to wind them up with a key to make them work."

"That's right! *Clockwork* they used to call it." whispered Jamie, looking around for any keys. "Dad's always on about it.

He had a few when he was a kid."

Jamie picked up the racing car and fingered a small key-hole on its side.

"That's where you put the key, I reckon," said Jamie, pretending to wind an imaginary one. "It sort of wound up a spring inside that would drive the wheels."

"Just imagine this lot all working together!" beamed Jessica, picturing the carousel and the Ferris wheel spinning round. "It must have been terrific!"

"But whose are they? And why are they here?" asked Jamie, as he picked up a bright orange, metallic air balloon and its basket floating by clouds and rainbows attached by wires.

"That reminds me!" burst Jamie, suddenly remembering the herd of deer that had woken him. "The albino fawn was there, and this time I definitely saw the rainbow around its neck!"

"You mean *Chandar*?" smiled Jessica.

"And guess what the rainbow was made from!" said Jamie. "Feathers! The same as the ones we found near the top of the well..."

"You mean jay feathers...all strung together into a necklace?" queried Jessica, curiously inspecting her trainers with the shimmering flashes of blue threaded between the laces.

"But how could a wild deer have a daisy-chain of feathers around its neck?"

Jamie shook his head and carefully stood up.

"It's one mystery after another' sis!" he muttered. "Do you think we'll ever get to the bottom of it all?"

"What? The mysteries or the well?" laughed Jessica, also getting to her feet, but having to keep her head slightly bowed because of the low ceiling.
"Both!" replied Jamie. "And the bottom of the well is the first target!"
"Yes, but not yet!" insisted Jessica. "Let's look further into this place. How far does the cellar go back into the rock? I can't see an end wall."

Half a dozen thick wooden beams stretched across the low ceiling, separated by greenish, crumbly plaster with scattered cushions of moss. Jamie crept along the side wall under the candle brackets, and then shone his torchbeam into the darkness beyond the fairground and the railway. First, there was a gap of bare, rocky floor...but then...the exploring white wand of light fell upon...the most amazing sight in the whole cellar!!

Standing alone in the far corner, where the ceiling was slightly higher, was the most splendid house imaginable! It was a dolls' house but like no other Jessica nor Jamie had ever seen! It was magnificent! The back of the house faced them with the complete rear wall and windows removed and propped up against the cellar wall.
It had five floors each with six or seven rooms all connected by passages and staircases and, as Jamie's torchbeam danced from room to room, the furnishings and decoration in each one was fantastic.

There was a kitchen with wooden shelves and cupboards, a large square table in the middle with chairs around it with plates, knives and forks arranged as if for a meal. A large pot sink stood by one wall with long-handled pans hanging above it. An ornate dresser was crammed with floral crockery and cooking tools.
There was a giant black fireplace with open oven doors at each side, its mantel shelf lined with shining brass candlesticks, plates, tankards and toasting forks. A black kettle hung above its wood stacked grate just waiting to bubble and boil. There was even a washing line sagging across a corner of the kitchen loaded with pegged clothes drying.

Jessica and Jamie crept closer until their faces were almost inside the rooms of the wonderful house, their eyes mesmerised by the amazing detail, especially in the house's grand lounge. This was the largest of all the rooms and was richly decorated with polished furniture, soft suites, carpets, framed oil paintings and even a grand piano with a velvet topped stool and sheets of music awaiting a maestro of the tiny ivory keys to fill the room with Mozart. Chandeliers, alive with drops of crystal, tumbled from the delicately moulded ceilings and one wall was lined with shelves crammed with leatherbound, gilt titled books with a ladder to reach the highest volumes.

There was a school-room on the top floor with a blackboard easel, a bench of desks with lids and hinged seats, inkwells and quills. On the master's desk was a globe about the size of a necklace bead and a colourful abacus frame for counting lessons. Jessica peered at tiny chalk writing on the blackboard wishing she could make out what it said, but it was too small. Next door was a children's playroom with rocking horses, dolls, a fort, toy soldiers and even a dolls' house! A dolls' house inside a dolls' house, and by it stood a red and white striped puppet theatre with Punch and Judy hand-puppets lying lifeless on a yellow stage.

Beneath the attic floor were the bedrooms. One, the grandest, had a large, comfortable looking, four-poster bed draped in lush folds of lace edged, red velvet with tasselled drawcords.

The other bedrooms had brass bedsteads, each covered in blankets and eiderdowns with pure white pillows. There were panelled wardrobes and ornate dressing-tables scattered with handmirrors, hairbrushes and perfume bottles. Each bedroom even had a floral water jug and basin for washing and a tin bath with tiny sponges and loofas.

The detail in the house was amazing, but it was the fact that everything was was so clean and so neat and tidy that surprised Jessica and Jamie even more. But then again, *all* the toys in the cellar looked brand new, shining and gleaming, as though they'd never been played with, fresh out of their boxes!

They could hardly tear themselves away from the dolls' house, but eventually Jamie nudged his sister and beckoned to her

to head back to the cellar door. There was still unfinished business to see to down the well!
They turned from the house and Jamie shone his torch back over the fairground towards the small door. It was then that yet another curious sight was revealed by the wandering beam!

The wall near the door was just bare rock, featureless except for the rusty candle brackets. But above the door was a large rectangular hollow carved into the rock to make a kind of deep shelf...and along the shelf was a row of full size drinking tankards.
"They're exactly the same as the charm we found in the wall...but a *hundred times bigger*!" exclaimed Jessica. "And look! There's a dagger standing up against the back of the shelf! And that's just the same as the tiny dagger we found in one of the baskets hanging from the mountain ash tree!"
Tip-toeing between the clockwork toys, they made their way over to the shelf and gazed up at what it held. Indeed, the tankards and the dagger were identical to the charms except they were rusty and tarnished.
Jamie stretched up and carefully grasped the dagger, and, although it was badly corroded, the ruby gemstone in its handle gleamed brightly in the torchlight. Beneath the greenish tarnish he could feel the dagger's delicately worked carved patterns and its blunt blade. As he returned it to the shelf, his hand bumped against another object tucked away in the dark shadows at the back of the rocky shelf.
There was a sudden tinkle of metal.
Jamie's fingers groped blindly about behind one of the tankards...and then they grasped something cold, smooth and rounded. His hand grasped the hidden object and slowly he drew it to the edge of the shelf.
The children gasped and looked at one another as the torch beam lit the mysterious find.
It was a blue painted bicycle bell!!
"It's the same blue paint that was on the tricycle we found at the ruined barn!" said Jamie.
He gave its ringer a tweak with his thumb.

The metal grated at first, but then, when he gave it another tweak, the shrill trill of the bell filled the cellar.
As he put it back on the shelf, he realised, as did Jessica, that things were beginning to fit together in a way that didn't exactly solve the mysteries, but at least clues were starting to make some kind of sense. The shapes of the charms and the objects on the shelf and now, the tricycle and the bell...with the map drawn by *'J' and 'J'* somehow linking them.
"We've got to decide what to do," said Jessica calmly. "Do we go further down the well? Or do we return to camp?"
"There's no contest!" Jamie exclaimed. "We've *got* to carry on with the journey and find out where the horn sounds are coming from!"

So, with a last swish of the torchbeam around the magical cellar, the two intrepid explorers crawled back through the door and onto the ledge. They pulled it closed behind them and then, as its creaking echoes faded, they sat on the edge of the ledge, their feet dangling down the well.
"I'm sure I can feel a warm breeze coming from down there!" remarked Jessica, gazing into the blackness.
Jamie wafted his hands in the dark and felt the same warm air flowing through his fingers.
"I can, too!" he said. "And it smells sort of..."
"Scented?" suggested Jessica, sniffing the breeze.
"Come on!" said Jamie, impatiently. "Let's get going! I can't wait to find out what's down there!"
"Do you think the ladder rungs'll be safe?" wondered Jessica, a little anxiously. "I think we'd better take the rope. Just in case."
"OK. I'll go up and get it," said Jamie, as he shone a weakening torch beam on the opposite wall. "And I'll get your torch, mine's beginning to fade."

He lay his torch on the ledge, stepped over to the metal rung and a second later he'd vanished up the well. Jessica perched in the darkness pondering on the findings in the cellar and the origins of the strange, warm, scented breeze. It was so completely dark that she could hardly tell whether her eyes were open or closed. But her mind's eye feasted on the welcome blank canvas and soon pictures were painted across the black emptiness. Once again the eyes and the aged face appeared illuminated by candle light. Its mouth smiled and then the thin lips spoke words which Jessica heard as clearly as last time.

"Lumina knows you are coming.
Make haste and may your journey be a safe one,
for all our sakes. You are our saviour."

The image faded as jerking flashes of fresh torchlight from above spilled across the blackness. Jamie was making his way back down the well. Jessica sat there on the ledge, for a moment stunned by what she'd heard. She shook her head and then touched her ears. Had she heard the voice or was it all in her imagination? Uncertainty made her head spin and she began to feel dizzy, her legs dangling in limbo, seemingly between one world and the next. The jerking flashes from above made her even more confused. She slumped forward and was on the brink of a fall that would end all hope of her being a saviour. Her head spun faster and faster. She felt as though she was plunging through space! Down...down...through banks of wispy, swirling cloud littered with flocks of jays with blue wing flashes, flying wildly around her, all panicking and trying to save her.

"*Jessica*! *Jessica*! *Wake up*!" suddenly came a familiar voice, and hands pushed her backwards onto the ledge.

Jessica's eyes sprung open and she squinted into the glare of torchlight.

"What's the matter? Where am I?" she yelled, her trembling screams echoing down the well below her.

"It's me, Jamie! You must have nodded off! You were about to fall!"

Both their hearts thumped in unison, both gripped by fear.

"Any sign of the deer?" mumbled Jessica drowsily, rubbing her eyes.

"No, but it's a lot cooler up there than it is down here!" said Jamie.

"No wonder you fell asleep with the warmth and that peculiar scent in the air. Perhaps we ought to rest for a while. We've had a long day and hardly any sleep!"

"No! We must carry on. We're *wanted*, we're *needed*!" burst Jessica.
"Sis, what *are* you talking about?"
Jessica looked into her brother's eyes and for a moment she wondered whether she was doing the right thing. She would never forgive herself if he came to any harm. But somehow, some kind of determination was burning within her. She *had* to go down the well and answer the call of *Lumina* and the horns. It was too late to back out now. They knew she was coming.
"What about you going back to the top of the well and I'll go down alone?" she suggested.
"*No way*!" laughed Jamie, swishing his imaginary sword. "I'm up to my neck in all this as much as you are, sis! And besides, you might need protecting from whatever's...."
"There's nothing to protect me from, I can assure you," insisted Jessica, slowly shaking her head. "I tell you, we're *needed*! Someone or something is *guiding* us down here with some kind of magical power."
Jamie looked at his sister and somehow understood...but not quite. Whatever she meant was probably right, and soon everything would fit into place and make sense. He had always trusted her and now was to be no exception!
"Anyway, remember what dad said!" he suddenly pointed out.
"We've got to '*stick together*'!"
They both smiled and thought of their father back at *Deer Leap*.
It seemed as though he was hundreds, if not thousands of miles away, and, for a moment, they sat there on the ledge, lost in their own thoughts of their cottage, their father, but most of all about what may be waiting for them in the dark, deep depths that lay tantalisingly beneath their feet!

Instead of tying the rope to a ladder rung, Jamie looped it over the one opposite the ledge and let two equal halves hang down the well. Although the length would be shorter, it would save climbing up each time to untie the knot and then climbing back down again without a safety rope in place.

"Now remember to get hold of *both* ropes if you need to!" warned Jamie.
"Yes, sir!" laughed Jessica, trying to salute in her cramped position.

So, they left Jamie's fading torch on the ledge and set off downwards into the unknown. Even with the much brighter beam of Jessica's torch shining down the well, they still couldn't see the bottom. The circular stone wall which surrounded them just carried on and on, down and down and vanished into the gloomy blackness. Three times they had to stop when they reached the dangling rope ends. Each time they pulled the rope through from the top rung and then threaded it over the next rung, ready for the next part of their descent. And all the time, the air became warmer and warmer.
"Are you sure we're not coming to the centre of the Earth?" joked Jamie.
Jessica, her hair blowing in the breeze, sniffed the air.
"The sweet scent's getting stronger, too!" she remarked. "Perhaps there's a secret marshmallow factory down..."
Just then, Jessica shouted so loudly that Jamie almost lost his footing on a rung.
"Jamie! Look down there now! I can see a faint glow!"
"That can't be right! It's your eyes playing tricks!" called Jamie, steadying himself.
"Look! It's there! Look!" insisted Jessica.

As they rested, clinging onto their rungs and the rope, they both began to make out the faint glow from below. Or *was* it their imaginations? They both began to wonder. Perhaps they were seeing things! After all, they had virtually had no sleep and it had been a long day. And it *was* the middle of the night! Was the whole journey a dream? Were they really both curled up in their beds back at *Deer Leap*?
No! Surely two people couldn't be having the same dream at the same time!
"Are you in *my* dream?" whispered Jamie, his eyes fixed on the mysterious glow.
"Are you in *mine*?" replied Jessica, her eyes also glued to the hypnotic light.

"Tell you what!" suggested Jamie. "I'll turn the torch off for a second and then we'll be able to tell whether or not the glow's really there!" With a flick of the switch, they were both plunged into silent, pitch black. But then, as their eyes became accustomed to the gloom, they could see one anothers' faces dimly lit in the pale, milky light.
"How peculiar!" whispered Jessica. "It's as though we're going to come out at the other side of the world!"
"Then I hope the natives of Australia are friendly!" laughed Jamie, bursting into song. "*Tie me kangaroo down, sport! Tie me kangaroo down!*"
"OK, OK, Rolf!" said Jessica. "You just make sure you hang on to that rung or you'll be landing in the outback faster than you think!"

Jamie switched on the torch and they began to descend again. As they delved deeper and deeper beneath the forest floor the faint glow became a hazy disc of light...and it grew larger and larger as they climbed down step by step. It almost looked like a pale full moon in a starless night sky. It was as though they were space travellers moving closer and closer to a distant moon-base.
Gradually they could see that they were coming to the end of the well shaft and it was that which was forming the disc from the peculiar light beyond it. But how could there possibly be light so deep underground? Deeper and deeper the children climbed until they began to make out strange rocky shapes within the glow...crags of bare, whitish and pink rock just beyond the perfectly round end of the stone shaft. And winding through the rocks was what seemed to be a narrow glistening ribbon just inches across.
"It's moving water! It's a stream!" called Jamie, pointing and squinting into the increasing brightness.
It was not at all what they had expected. They had both imagined a dismal, dripping, dank, damp end to their journey, perhaps wading through a wide, cold, babbling subterranean stream in pitch darkness or some kind of perilous pond of unfathomable depths. But instead, here they were looking down upon a strange, milky, glowing, almost inviting place...with a sweet smell and a warm breeze!

"There's not much water in the stream!" said Jamie, looking at the thread of glinting water. "Surely not enough to supply a farm!"
"Perhaps once it was much bigger and provided enough water," suggested Jessica. "But why does everything glow? And what *is* that sweet smell?"

By now, Jamie had reached the very last rung of the ladder, with the drop into the enticing, magical landscape directly beneath him. From where he was to the pearly stream's gravelly shore was only about six feet or a couple of metres.
The jump itself wouldn't be too bad thought Jamie to himself...the problem would be getting back up to the well's last rung when they returned. They decided that the only solution was to do what they had done all the way down the well...dangle the rope in two halves from the last rung. That way they would be able to pull themselves up from the stream into the well when they were ready to leave.

So, with the rope dangling in position and the torch wedged into his back pocket, Jamie teetered on the final rung, ready to push himself off backwards and fall into the strange valley below. It seemed even more like jumping out of an aircraft than it did when they were sitting at the top of the well!
"I can't wait to get down there and explore!" called Jamie, as he shoved himself away from the ladder. "Wish me luck, sis! See you in fairy land! Here *g..o..e..s*!!"
A moment later he had gone.
"Good luck, Ja.....wait, hang on, *hang on*! *What's THAT*?" screamed Jessica, as she suddenly noticed a swirling, sparkling mist creep menacingly across the hole.
But it was too late!
Her brother had jumped.
The mist thickened and swirled and curled even faster!
Jamie vanished.
The whirling vapour had swallowed its victim!

Chapter 10

"*Jamie, Jamie*! Are you alright?" called Jessica into the thickening mist, her voice echoing spookily up the stone shaft. "I can't see you!"
There was no reply.
"*Jamie*! *Where are you*?" she called again, her mind instantly flashing back to when he disappeared in the forest near the wall the other day. Panic and fear once again began to grip her. She could hear her heartbeat thumping in her ears. The warm air was beginning to make her hands feel clammy as she tightly gripped her rung.
"*JAMIE*!! *ARE YOU THERE*?? *CAN YOU HEAR ME*??"

Jamie had landed with bended knees and a crunch on the gravel below. He'd stood up and looked around...and then gazed, awe-struck at the scene before him. This just *had* to be a dream!
The fine gravel by the stream was not gravel anymore! It had become drifts of smooth, white pebbles! And the stream wasn't just a narrow, winding, ribbon either! It had become a wide, fast flowing river, so wide that its opposite bank was only just visible!
A couple of seconds before, he had been a small leap away from a tiny trickle of water, just inches wide...but now, as he peered upwards, it seemed as though he had been miles away...like he really *had* jumped out of an aircraft! But it had only taken him seconds to land...not minutes!

Way, way above him he noticed clouds of soft white mist lapping the roof of what seemed to be an enormous but staggeringly beautiful crystal cavern. Its sheer size left him spellbound, with its towering, mountainous white and pink sides speckled with glistening crystals. Giant pointed pillars of white rock soared upwards from the banks of the river and smaller sharper icicles of rock plunged down from the roof through the mists.

Other than the sound of babbling water, there wasn't a sound to be heard, but he could still feel the gentle, warm breeze and smell its sweet scent. It all made him feel quite relaxed and calm, not at all fearful or anxious. He just stood and stared at the magnificent cavern which stretched as far as his eyes could see in both directions, its almost sheer walls broken by hollows and ledges, and all the way arching over the river which now seemed to have a luminous green tinge instead of being milky white.

The only thing that puzzled him was the rope. The two dangling halves were there, coiled on the bank just a short distance away from him. Its thickness was just the same as before, but it was its length that mystified him! The two strands soared up and up into the swirling mists, both swaying gently in the breeze. He knew that, somewhere up there, it was looped over the last rung of the well...which, in turn, lead up the ladder to the real, everyday world!

Was Jessica still up there?

Would she jump?

Could *she* see *him*?

Of course she could, he thought. After all, she was only a few feet away! But what about the clouds? If he couldn't see her, then perhaps...

"*Jess*!" he shouted.

His voice seemed tiny in the vastness of the cavern, although it echoed again and again as it bounced between its sides like a pin-ball.

He glanced at his watch in an attempt to do something normal, something he would do in the real world. Two minutes past two in the middle of the night. Surely he was in bed and this was a dream!

"*JESS..I..CA*!!" he shouted again, this time a touch trembly, as a bolt of fear struck through him for the first time since jumping from the last rung.

His heart pounded as he stared up at the swirling clouds, longing for a gap to appear to show the bottom of the well with his sister still clinging there, waving and ready to jump.
Suddenly, he heard...or thought he heard... a faint voice, a distant voice coming from where the rope dissolved into the mists.
Yes, there it was again! But it was so faint and weak!
"Jamie!! Where are you? Can you hear me?"
Instantly he was back in his bedroom a couple of nights ago listening to his sister's calls through the wall...but the images vanished as quickly as they'd arrived...as suddenly, and with no warning, he had the shock of his life!!
It happened so quickly!
Out of the mists, way, way, above him, two crushingly enormous shapes appeared, like a pair of giant, alien spaceships, but looking like two gigantic blue footprints. Their deep, angry zig-zags filled the sky and instantly, Jamie felt like an ant beneath a threatening footstep.
He cowered and raised his arms over his head...only to watch, to his relief, the great soles shrink as they rushed towards him, followed by shrinking socks, legs, yellow T-shirt...and then a familiar plume of flowing copper hair. It was like a punctured inflatable giant emerging out of nowhere from behind the clouds and then shrinking as the air rushed out of it. One second enormous...and then...a moment later...there was his sister crunching onto the pebbles and tumbling into a heap next to him!
Jessica sat up, rubbed her eyes and peeped through her fingers at the wonders around her. She was absolutely speechless as she slowly got to her feet and gazed open-mouthed into the depths of the cavern.

They both appeared to be the same size as usual, but whatever was beneath the well...had grown...and grown...and grown!! But on the other hand, it also appeared that the cavern had remained the same size and it was *they* that had shrunk! There was no way of telling! The trickle of water had become a river, the gravel had become pebbles, yet Jamie had witnessed before his very eyes his sister becoming smaller and smaller as she'd jumped from the bottom of the well! It was all very

peculiar. Very peculiar indeed! But as they gazed up and down the magnificent valley, thoughts of understanding were dissolved by the incredible beauty that surrounded them.
Both ways glowed the same pinkish white, and they could easily see into the misty, milky distance filled with endless, steep, creamy rocky cliffs, giant boulders, ledges and forests of soaring pillars with the plunging rock icicles stabbing down from the mist lapped roof.
It was a magical landscape with its soft light seeming to come from the rock itself.
"Stal-ac-tites!" whispered Jessica, pointing into the sky.
"Pardon?" replied Jamie, thinking his sister had suddenly burst into some foreign language.
"Stalactites!" repeated Jessica. "That's what they are...hanging down from the roof. Those things that look like icicles!"
"They look more like giant, pink carrots to me!" said Jamie, with a grin.
"And those bigger ones reaching upwards from the ground are called *stal-ag-mites*! And they're all made of the same rock as everywhere else!" Jessica went on.
"Sis! I don't care if they're made from *sugar and spice*; all I want to know is...*are we really here*?"
Neither of them had imagined that such a place could possibly exist...but, here they were in the middle of it! They could touch the pebbles on the shore. They could hear the river water lapping. They could see the stalactites and stalagmites, and they could even smell the sweet breeze! They *had* to be there! This was *real*!
Jamie picked up a small, smooth pebble and gently tossed it into the clear, greenish water. With a splash it disappeared beneath the waves...together with the children's fears and questions. The place was so calm and beautiful that it just seemed to hold the two of them in its gentleness. They almost felt at home in a new world...far from the bottom of the well...far from the magical forest cellar...far from the dark sprucelands...and even further from *Old Soulsyke* farm...and *Deer Leap* and their father! They'd been shipwrecked on a distant shore. But thoughts of rescue didn't occur to them. Neither did survival nor shelter.

The only thought that was beginning to push its way to the fore and distract them from the marvels of the world they'd fallen into, was the exciting thought of...*exploration*!

It was Jamie who urged Jessica to follow him along the shore upstream. They left the rope to the Upper World behind and slowly walked over the drifts of white and pink pebbles, both of them marvelling at the ever changing scenery before them. The cavern's sheer sides were strung with narrow ledges beaded with small gaping cracks and caves. The stalagmites seemed like a never ending forest of tapering stone pillars stretching into the distance, mirrored by the smaller stalactites springing from the cavern's roof. But it was the countless millions of twinkling crystals that captivated the children the most - their incessant winking almost befriending the explorers! One great boulder they passed was packed with them, each as big as a cricket ball and each as clear as glass with a faint, warm, milky pink glow. Each crystal almost looked as though it had been somehow planted into the boulder and then blossomed into its half a dozen shimmering, glassy faces. Some had even merged together into solid glassy bouquets, each a beautiful miniature world of crystal mountains and valleys.

As they wandered on, Jessica turned and looked downstream. Already the rope was some distance away, reaching high, high into the clouds, looking like some mysterious thread connecting one world to the other. But as she turned back to follow Jamie, she noticed a patch on the giant boulder free from crystals. There were scratch marks on the patch. Carefully, Jessica traced them with her finger, and suddenly her heartbeat began to race as they formed a distinct pair of familiar letters!

"*J and J*" she whispered to herself.

She traced them again. Perhaps it was her imagination. After all, the scratches were quite rough and jagged. They could be anything... just random scratches. But as her finger traced the two thin grooves, she noticed below them four more scratches in the pale pink rock!

Her finger jumped to them in a flash as though it had a mind of its own. Slowly it traced a '*1*', then a '*9*', then a '*5*' and then another '*5*'*!!*

"J and J !!" she suddenly burst, "It's *Jonathan and Jane* again! They were here in *Nineteen-Fifty-Five*!!" 
Jamie rushed back to the boulder, felt the scratches himself and then excitedly searched around the boulder for any more empty patches.
"It *has* to be the same 'J' and 'J' who drew the map back at the farmhouse*...but six years later!"* exclaimed Jamie.
"And that was the year *George* was planted according to dad, and *Old Soulsyke* and the other farms were abandoned!" recalled Jessica.
Jamie looked into Jessica's eyes. He could tell exactly what she was thinking.
"You don't think that your *Jonathan and Jane* came down here when they were forced to leave the farm?" wondered Jamie, a little uncertainly.
Jessica gazed at the scratches in the rock and then looked back into her brother's eyes.
"I do!" she said slowly, "and what's more...I reckon that they're still..."
Suddenly, a sound they both knew well came echoing through the cavern.
It sounded so loud and near that Jessica and Jamie both darted behind the crystal boulder.
Until now the sound had always been tiny and distant...but now it seemed to be almost on top of them, surrounding them with its haunting single note.
More, even louder notes followed, pressing Jessica and Jamie closer together into a fearful huddle behind the boulder.
Their eyes opened widely and stared frantically into the cavernous heights.
Their hearts began to beat faster and faster as the sound began to swamp them.

Several notes suddenly chorused together in a triumphant crescendo, and Jessica clamped her hand to her mouth to stifle a scream.
She had seen something move on the opposite bank of the river!
She nudged Jamie and pointed.
Shivers shot up and down their spines and goosebumps tingled on their arms.
Their hearts pounded even faster...as long, dark shadows crept slowly and menacingly along the cavern wall.
Jessica and Jamie were not alone!

Chapter 11

The shadows were cast from an orangy, red glow behind a large boulder on the other bank. There were three of them, creeping along the wall as though their owners were moving away from the flames of a hidden fire. Each, unmistakably, belonged to a human, dressed from head to toe in a long, flowing cloak.

Suddenly, all three shadows lifted horns from their sides, and raised them, together with billowing sleeves, towards their hooded heads.

Jessica and Jamie gazed across the river hardly able to believe their eyes...and then their ears...as the most eerie and yet beautiful music filled the cavern. One horn played alone to begin with and then the other two joined in to create a strange, magical mixture of feelings within the hidden listeners. At one moment fear was swamped by joy, and then the next moment, joy was drowned by fear. But it was the haunting music, the sweet breeze, the quietly lapping water and the soft glow of the rocks that eventually calmed the children and drove away all traces of fear. After all, this *had* to be a dream! It just couldn't be real!

The same thought had just drifted through both children's minds when, as suddenly as it had begun, the music stopped.

The last notes faded away up and down the cavern as the shadows shrunk and vanished while the orangy, red glow dimmed and died. The three hornblowers had disappeared. Or at least their shadows had!

Jessica, with newly found courage, stepped from behind the crystal boulder and walked to the very edge of the river. She removed her trainers and lemon socks, rolled up her jeans...and then cautiously tested the water with a big toe. It wasn't icy cold as she had expected, but hot! Not boiling kettle hot but comfortable bath hot. Perhaps very warm rather than hot.

"Jamie, come on!" she called. "It's fantastic! I'm going for a paddle. It's brilliant!"

As she waded into the river shallows, she could feel the current between her toes. Pale green, frothy rafts of bubbles swirled between her legs as she waded deeper and deeper. Soon she was up to her knees and enjoying every moment, her jeans soaked.

Suddenly, something a long way upstream caught her eye. It was a large square of breeze-filled, yellow cloth, and beneath it was what looked like...no, it couldn't be!...the bouncing, golden prow of *a sailing ship*? It reminded her of a Viking or Roman galley she'd seen in history books, but this one was there for real, plunging through the froth and bearing down upon her at a fantastic speed borne out of the current and breeze. Bigger and bigger the yellow square of cloth grew, filling more and more of the cavern. If she stood there much longer she would be swamped by the swash, or worse...but as the craft neared, stiff oars were lowered on each side into the waters, the sail was dropped and the majestic ship slowed and veered to the opposite bank where it glided ashore where the hornblowers' shadows had been.

Jessica crouched in the warm water with her hair flowing behind, and watched as sweet smelling froth swished around her face. One by one, three hooded and purple cloaked figures stepped from behind the huge boulder on the far bank and seemingly glided towards the slowly bobbing ship. Jessica could just about make out their faces in the pale light. They were silver bearded, with drooping moustaches, which could have made them appear severe, but instead each wore a broad smile...and each held a horn, exactly the same shape as the charm they'd found in the wall. Soundlessly, the three figures glided up a plank onto the golden craft.

Nobody else was in sight. It was as if the boat was crewless, although Jessica knew that couldn't be true as, silently and effortlessly, the yellow sail unfurled and climbed the golden mast. Next, the banks of oars plunged into the water and the vessel inched backwards from its mooring and nudged into the current. Jessica crouched even lower, her head hidden in a raft of froth, and watched as the boat floated away downstream with its oars withdrawn. She peered at the rows of portholes hoping to catch a glimpse of an oarsman, but, once again, there was no sign of any crew. Then, the golden boat picked up speed and soon its sail and stern had faded into the distant mists.

Jessica emerged from the warm froth and waded ashore dripping from head to toe...but to her astonishment, her clothes were already drying in the breeze!

"Jamie!" she called. "Did you see the ship?"

There was no reply.

In fact, there was no sign of Jamie at all!

"Jamie! Where are you?" she called again, as she pulled on her socks and trainers and then ran over the pebbles to the crystal boulder.

He surely can't have wandered off, she thought. Not deep below the forest, in a mysterious cavern, with her up to her neck in the river?

"Jamie, where are you? I hope you're not playing one of your..."

Suddenly, her heart skipped a beat as she stared into the half-light behind the boulder...for there, just beyond where they had been hiding...stood two cloaked and hooded figures...and standing between them...was Jamie!

"*JAMIE*!!" she shouted in disbelief, lunging forward to grab her brother, but before she'd taken a couple of steps, she froze as the figure on the left raised his hand and calmly spoke.
"Welcome to our world, Jessica. We have already met your brother and greeted him. You are both safe here...as, indeed, we all are!"
Jessica was speechless as she gazed at the trio. They were standing on the bottom step of a stone staircase cut into the cavern's wall. It climbed and twisted up into the mists like some kind of stairway to the stars! The two mysterious figures turned and began to climb the rock steps. Jamie followed, not saying a word, but beckoning his stunned sister to follow. And, as though in a trance, she, too, walked over to the staircase and followed.

Underfoot, the steps were smooth and alive with twinkling, friendly crystals. The slope was gentle and soon Jessica and Jamie could look down upon the flowing water below and across to the opposite shore where the hornblowers had been. They came to a short, flat terrace with a rough, wooden table in the middle with several three-legged wooden stools gathered round. Set in the centre of the round table was a crystal candle-holder with a thick, white candle; its flame flickering in the breeze. The two figures gestured to their guests to sit and rest.
Jamie at last whispered to Jessica from behind a cupped hand as though he didn't want to be noticed.
"He's called Quentin," nodding towards the taller of the two strangers, "and he's Toby," giving the shorter, plumper one a sideways glance. "They introduced themselves while you were having your little dip in the river!"

Jessica smiled and whispered back to her brother, "Nice to see you've made a couple of friends! But I've *already* met Quentin...and the *candle flame*! She's called '*Lumina*'!"
Jamie stared at his sister with such an astonished look on his face that Jessica almost burst into a fit of the giggles, but at the last moment she composed herself and put a finger to her lips.

Quietly and calmly, their two hosts sat down and swept back their hoods. Quentin, who looked the older, although they both looked *very* old, had a silvery, grey beard and large pooly, blue eyes under bushy, silver eyebrows and a wispy thatch of matching hair. And, although his skin was sallow and pale, he had a lively, youthful sparkle about him, mainly because of his twinkly eyes. Toby, if anything, looked even more sparkly. He had a silver, bristly chin and the top of his head was balding and shiny. Between was a rosy, round face with even more twinkly blue eyes. In the dim light their cloaks appeared a sort of heathery purple tied round their ample middles with golden rope-belts. Both wore sandal like shoes which seemed to be made from beaten tree bark and plaited grass!

As the candle flame danced and was reflected in their blue eyes, Jessica and Jamie waited for them to speak.

It was Quentin who spoke first.

"Once again we would like to welcome you to our world. You must find it very different in many ways from your own world above..."

Jessica just *had* to interrupt, although her nerves made her stutter.

"W...what do you mean? '*Our world*' ...a..and '*Your world*'?" she asked.

Toby, with his arms folded within his baggy sleeves, replied with a broad smile.

"Let us start from the beginning," he said, after a deep breath, and a raising of his eyebrows to his companion.

"A very good place to start!" nodded Quentin, with an equally broad grin. "Mind, if I may say so, a far more suitable place to begin than the end!"

"I agree," said Toby. "For if we did that, we would finish our tale at the beginning and nobody wants to hear the end before the beginning...so as I was saying, let us start from the beginning!"

He took another deep breath, while Jessica and Jamie began to wonder whether or not they'd followed a girl called Alice down a rabbit hole, rather than climbed down a well!

"Our story," began Toby, "is one that is hard to believe, but other visitors have all come to understand..."

"Do you mean other people have come down here, too?" chirped Jessica, a little more confidently, though not mentioning *'J' and 'J's* visit.
"Yes, a few have made the journey, but more of that later," said Toby calmly, and obviously keen to relate his story. "Let me continue."
He paused and took another deep breath.
"It all started over four long, long centuries ago in your world's time, in the days when the King of England was a man by the name of Henry Tudor..."
"You mean Henry the Eighth?" chipped in Jessica as politely as she could. "The King who had six wives...?"
"And chopped the heads off some of 'em!" added Jamie, with a glint in his eye and a playful blow on the table with the side of his hand.
"Yes, yes, that is so," said Toby, slightly impatiently, "but his marital habits are not of our concern just now. Our story began because Henry Tudor had certain religious beliefs...and he hounded all those with, shall we say, *different* views!"
Toby paused and his face took on a grimmer look.
"Many were killed," he said slowly and solemnly, "and many great abbeys and small churches alike were destroyed by this all too powerful Henry! Many people fled for safety, hiding in remote parts of the kingdom, miles from anywhere and miles from danger!"
Toby paused again, and for once, the twinkle in his eye seemed to fade.
Quentin put a reassuring hand on Toby's arm and took up the story.
"Some sheltered in caves," he began, looking intently at each of the visitors in turn, "and some even fled underground and lived like moles!"
Jamie was just going to ask about the well, but Quentin raised a finger, and went on.
"Have you come across *Soulsyke Farm*?" he asked.
Both children nodded and looked at one another.
"And it's well?"
The children nodded again.
Toby carried on, having recovered his composure.
"*Soulsyke* attracted hundreds as a safe-house in those troubled times.

Beneath the farm were secret cellars sometimes packed to overflowing with men, women and children. The well even had a secret hiding place as you will have discovered for yourselves!"
"You mean the cellar with the door down the...?" burst Jamie.
Toby nodded, and carried on in the same breath. "Some fearful souls even delved *deeper*...!"
This time he did pause and his blue eyes stared at the flickering candle flame.
"They delved deeper...and *never returned*!!"
Jessica glanced at Jamie and they both had the same thought. Quentin and Toby quickly sensed their concern and Quentin smiled.
"They never *wanted to return,* you understand! Once they had discovered *Aqua Crysta*!!"
"*Aqua Crysta* is the name of your world?" asked Jessica, gazing around at the magnificence of the cavern.
"Yes, indeed. It means the *Crystal Water*!" replied Toby. "And every person who has ventured here has stayed with no thought of returning to the *Upper World*...and, what is more, every single person who has arrived here had been deeply unhappy with their lives above."
Quentin continued.
"The last to come were our friends, Jonathan and Jane..."
Again, Jessica and Jamie knowingly glanced at one another, but without saying a word.
"You know of our friends?" enquired Quentin, with a smile.
The children shook their heads.
"After all, it would not be possible!" he went on. "For they arrived *half a century* ago, in your Upper World time!"
"Then it *must* be them!" burst Jamie, unable to control his excitement. "So *'J' and 'J' are Jonathan and Jane!* We found their initials on a boulder by the river and on a map to the well...!"
"*A map to the well*??" exclaimed Quentin in an alarmed tone for the first time. "But no map exists! This *cannot* be true!"
"It's at the top of the well in our backpack...our bag!" Jessica explained nervously. "Where we made camp...when we found the well."

"Then it has to be found and destroyed before it falls into the wrong hands!" retorted Toby as calmly as he could. "The secrecy of *Aqua Crysta* has to be kept at all cost, or our world and its magic will disappear *forever*!"
Jessica and Jamie both began to feel uneasy, thinking they had done wrong. It was Quentin who put them at their ease again.
"We thank you for discovering the map, but it will *have* to be destroyed and the well headstones closed again. It will take a full expedition force to the surface to complete both tasks. At least twenty in the party!"
"Why as many as that?" enquired a puzzled Jamie. After all, it was only a smallish backpack!
"I'm sorry. I do apologise. I thought you both realised!" said Toby. "Do excuse us!"
"Realised what?" asked Jessica, beginning to worry again.
Toby slowly went on.
"Everyone who has travelled to *Aqua Crysta* throughout the past Upper World centuries has not only never returned to the surface for good, but they have dwelt here contentedly in our timeless and shrunken world!"
Jessica and Jamie were speechless!
Quentin got to his feet and walked over to the children and sat on another stool closer to them.
"We have no Sun here, nor Moon. So we have neither daytime nor night-time. Magically and wonderfully, life here is almost endless, eternal, with no time as *you* know it. Without the daily rising and setting of the Sun and her sister Moon, we know no days and nights, no weeks, no months, no seasons...no years! My grandfather was one of the first to travel here, in the Upper World year, *Fifteen Hundred and Forty-Eight*. He died in the year *Seventeen Hundred and Forty-Seven* aged *One Hundred and Ninety-Nine* Upper World years!! His son, my father, died aged *Two Hundred and Twenty-Five*!! And I, myself, was born *Two Hundred and Ninety Four* years ago! Toby, here, is forty years younger!"
Jessica and Jamie just could not believe their ears!
The men who were talking to them were more than *two centuries,*

nearly three centuries old... but they seemed to be no older than their own grandfathers!
"But how do you know your age if you live in a timeless world?" asked Jamie.
"We count the harvests," replied Toby. "Once every Upper World year we send food collecting parties up to the surface to gather berries, nuts and the like."
"In fact," said Quentin, casting his eyes upwards, "a party is up there at this very moment."
"You mean that is all you eat, and you live to such great ages?" asked Jessica.
"We grow fungi in the cavern, but the food we collect from above does not decay and lasts for a whole year, from one harvest to the next!"
"But surely it must rot!" remarked Jamie. "Freshly picked berries can't last for that long!"
Quentin shrugged his shoulders and slowly shook his head from side to side. "It is, indeed, a mystery, but it is thought that the magic that preserves the berries also preserves us!"
"We hardly decay either!" smiled Toby. "Whether it be the water, the rock, or the air we breathe, no one has discovered why...but we are all grateful for the magic!"
"You still haven't told us why it takes so many of your people to do such small tasks as fetching our map or replacing the well's headstones." mentioned Jessica.
"Follow us!" said Toby, rising from his stool. "We will show you!"

The quartet left the candle burning and continued up the next flight of steps cut into the crystal rock, Quentin and Toby leading with their mystified guests following.
Jessica whispered to her brother, "Whilst they were talking I was watching the candle!"
"Yes, I noticed it, too!" whispered back Jamie. "The wax wasn't melting! Never-ending candles! I wonder if everything here lasts forever?"
"I think I understand what they mean by their *timeless* world," Jessica whispered. "But what's this *shrunken* business all about?"

The staircase climbed on and on, higher and higher above the river and then began to twist around a great crag of glowing crystal studded rock. The scenery was magnificently beautiful. The pale pinks and creamy whites of the sheer, twinkling cavern walls soaring high above the milky green river far below with its boulders and pebble strewn shore. It was difficult to imagine that all this lay below *George's* endless ranks of trees and drifts of pine-needles, up there, beyond the swirling mists that lapped the cavern's roof.

Toby stopped and beckoned the children to follow. Jessica and Jamie caught up with him and rounded the next corner...and then they saw before them the most amazing sight of their incredible journey so far! So *this* is what Quentin and Toby meant by their *shrunken world*!!

Chapter 12

Ahead was the gaping mouth of a cave, packed to overflowing with enormous red berries - mountain ash berries - the same as the ones Jessica and Jamie had found piled upon the wall beneath the fiery boughs of the rowan tree in the forest. But here, there were hundreds of them. It was like some kind of berry warehouse, high above the cavern floor, crammed with the giant, smooth, scarlet fruits...each one twice as big as the globe on Miss McDougal's desk back in Scotland!!

As the two children stared in disbelief, Jamie nudged his sister as three purple cloaked figures approached the entrance of the cave and slowly signalled to Quentin and Toby with raised arms. After returning the signal, Quentin and Toby took the last few steps towards the cave followed by the completely astonished Jessica and Jamie.

It was as they stepped into the cave mouth that they really sensed the size of the rowan berries. A single berry was almost waist high, and a couple on top of one another were easily taller than Jamie! They were certainly real enough - hard, red and shiny. Suddenly, the unbelievable was becoming frighteningly believable! The neat piles of berries they had seen back in *George* must have been the work of the harvest expedition party that was still up there! That would account for the silver baskets...the dagger...and the horn sounds! They must have been alarm calls to warn the party of approaching Upper World folk...Jessica and Jamie, themselves!

Things were at last beginning to fall in place...but it was all still totally incredible! Here, next to them, were the same berries, once no larger than peas in a pod, that were now big enough to climb up and sit on! The question was, had the berries become larger, or had Jessica and Jamie become smaller? It was becoming clearer and clearer that it was definitely the children who had shrunk! And, surprisingly enough, any anxiety they felt was quickly dispelled by the wonder and magic that surrounded them. So much so, that they both felt, somehow, happy and safe in this amazing, subterranean land.

They were politely introduced to the three Aqua Crystans, who turned out to be around a hundred years younger than their two hosts. In fact, the man, Lepho, and the two women, Greta and Merry, had just returned from a forest expedition and were inspecting their harvest. The cave was apparently known as the '*Larder Cave*', and as they ventured further into it they saw gigantic, juicy brambles towering above them, not to mention even larger acorns, walnuts and slices of toadstool. Smaller caves branched off from the main one, and, these too, were full of berries and nuts, each cave with a passage along one side with just enough room to pass. Lepho explained that all the collected food was stored in this part of *Aqua Crysta* because it was near to a long and winding tunnel that wound through the solid rock to the Upper World - the '*Harvest Passageway*', as he called it. The people of *Aqua Crysta* all lived down by the *River Floss*, he explained, in one of the two townships - *Pillo* and *Galdo* - one at each end of the long cavern.

Jessica and Jamie, by now totally bewildered by everything they saw or heard, just followed the five, heathery cloaked Aqua Crystans. They were even feasted on delicious wafer thin slices of walnut and juicy scoops of rowan berry washed down with fizzy bramble wine. And, as they were being told all about life in the incredible cavern, they discovered, as they had suspected, that they had, indeed, been spotted in the forest by the harvesters. Firstly at the *Charmstones* near *Deer Leap*, then at the fiery, crimson ash tree and then once more beneath the towering horse chestnut at *Old Soulsyke*. The notes blown on the horns *had* been alarm signals...and even the ghostly trio of hornblowers by the Floss had heralded the arrival of Jessica and Jamie. It seemed that they had been expected, just as Jessica had thought!

Lepho, they discovered, was to lead the next expedition to the surface and there was already talk of finding the map and closing the well-head. News of the map had certainly travelled quickly, not to mention the arrival of the Upper World folk with the strange, bright clothing!

Nothing surprised Jessica and Jamie anymore. Even when they were offered a sip of oak-leaf tea from tankards which were exactly the same as the charm they'd found in the wall and the full sized ones they'd seen on the shelf in the cellar, with their delicate patterns and curved handles. Amazement and wonder had become the order of the day. The magic was becoming ordinary and expected. They were strangely beginning to feel at home!! Or would they suddenly wake up at the foot of the forest wall near the well, have a bite to eat and be back at *Deer Leap* for tea? The cottage and their father seemed so far, far away!

Jamie drained his tankard's last drop and looked at his watch.
He blinked and looked again. It was *two minutes past two*!!
The same time that he'd landed in the cavern after his jump from the well's last rung.

"*My watch has stopped*!" he called out, much to the surprise of the Aqua Crystans. "It's never done that before!"

There was so much interest in his watch that he unstrapped it and passed it round for everyone to inspect. It was something they'd never seen before.

"What time will it be?" asked Jessica. "We've got to be home later today. We promised dad we'd be back by the late afternoon!"

Toby poured a little more refreshment into the tankards of his companions and honoured guests, and, as Lepho offered everyone a slice of hazelnut, Quentin cleared his throat with a gentle cough.
"I feel we ought to explain a further miracle of our realm," he said, with his usual smile. "We described our world as being *timeless*. By that we do not only mean that we are without day and night, without Sun and Moon, without aging and decay. But, for reasons unknown, time itself stands still. In no way does it seem to pass in our underworld. So while you have been here there has been no time. *It is still precisely the same Upper World hour as the moment you fell into our world from the bottom of Soulsyke's well*!!"
Jessica and Jamie, once again, looked at one another in astonishment.
"Y..you mean...that time...has *stopped*?" trembled Jessica, with a quiver in her voice.
"You mean it is *still* two minutes past two in the middle of the night?"
Quentin nodded and Lepho handed the watch back to Jamie who stared at it as though it had sprung to life rather than stopped dead.
"But, my friends," Toby continued, "when you return to the Upper World...that is, *if* you return to your Upper World...it will be the *same time* as when you *left it*!"
The little word 'if' suddenly sent shivers of fear racing down the spines of Jessica and Jamie.
"What do you mean... '*if we return*'?" they chorused.
"Be not alarmed," reassured Toby. "The answer is simple. You may find, like all the others who have travelled here, that you find peace and happiness in *Aqua Crysta*. Wait until you have visited Pillo, sailed on the Floss, seen the beautiful Lake Serentina, explored Galdo...!"
"But you said that everyone who has come here has been *sad and unhappy* with their lives in the Upper World," Jamie interrupted, glancing up at the rock ceiling. "We're not! We love our new cottage! We love our father and our lives up there!"
Toby gently placed a hand on Jamie's shoulder.
"Listen," he said softly and calmly. "There is more to tell. Listen carefully, both of you, and try to understand."

He paused, and while the others silently sipped their oak-lef tea, Jessica and Jamie looked into Toby's twinkling blue eyes, wondering what was coming next!
He began.
"The last people to come here were two children about the same age as yourselves...Jonathan and Jane...as I have already mentioned.
They arrived at a time when the land above *Aqua Crysta* was in great turmoil. Scores of Upper World men with monsters of iron changed forever the nature of our peaceful harvestlands. Many, many ancient trees were uprooted to make way for the new *Great Pine Forest* with saplings stretching for miles in all directions from a small patch of beautiful woodland the men thankfully left standing on *Soulsyke Hill*. Heather moorland, too, was churned up and destroyed by the iron monsters and along with it all our supplies of delicious wimberries and our beloved, almond fragrant, gorse blossom!"
He paused again, seemingly lost in his memories, but then he resumed his tale.
"Then, having done their worst, the men went, along with their iron monsters, leaving desolation and despair above our realm. Mercifully they did not discover the well, but they had destroyed our rich and plentiful harvestlands. Fortunately we have survived with the fruits of the remaining woodland of *Soulsyke,* but the rest of their new forest has given us nothing. It yields no food, just acres upon acres of dark, dismal ranks of pine trees, and their almost useless cones and needles! All our sustenance comes from *Soulsyke Wood*!"
He stroked his bristly chin and looked gratefully at the hoard of fruits and nuts that surrounded them.
"Now, it was just before the men and machines began their destruction that Jonathan and Jane came to us by means of the well, in the same way that you came here. They told us of what would happen one day in the Upper World future. They told us that the saplings would grow and perhaps in half a century they, too, would all be destroyed by even more men with even greater monsters of iron! Once again the peace would be shattered, the well could be found and *Aqua Crysta*

discovered, or at the very least, the woodland of *Soulsyke* taken from us!"
Once again he paused and recovered his calm with a sip of tea.
"And, it is our belief," he went on, "that the time Jonathan and Jane spoke of... is *here*...and that *you* are our warning...and, hopefully...our *saviours*!"
"But what makes you so sure?" asked Jessica, instantly recognising the word.
Quentin answered.
"You have been drawn to our realm by magical forces that we, ourselves, cannot even begin to understand. The spirit of the ancient woodland is somehow with you and has guided you here. It has lead you with signs which you have found and followed. It is said that even the spirit's timeless, enchanted young deer has revealed herself to you! That, indeed, is of great significance! And, it is also said, that by magical means, she made her name clear to you!"
Jessica slowly nodded her head and closed her eyes.
Quentin swept back his baggy cuffs, and Jamie and the others watched, as the old man wrote in the dust on the table top with a long, boney finger.
On and on the finger wrote while Jessica's eyes kept tightly closed.
At last a word of seven letters was written for all to see except Jessica.
"Tell me, my friend," said Quentin, "without opening your eyes, what is the name of the young albino deer that belongs to the ancient spirit of the woods?"
All eyes were fixed on Jessica as she spoke.
"The deer called herself... *Chandar*!" she announced confidently.
The other Aqua Crystans burst into excited whispers.
"Open your eyes, my friend," said Quentin, "and look at the name before you!"
Jessica opened her eyes and looked at the letters in the dust. The name she had spoken was there, staring at her. It was all she needed to convince herself that she and her brother had fallen into something greater and more magical than they could ever understand.

“And I know that I have heard your voice and seen your face on our way here!” said Jessica, looking into Quentin’s eyes. “You told me the name of your sacred candle flame...the one that has burned for hundreds of years without melting the wax that feeds her!”

She once again closed her eyes and Quentin wrote a name in the dust.
“Speak now, my friend!” Quentin whispered. “The eternal flame. What is her name?”
Jamie and the rest of the Aqua Crystans gazed open-mouthed in silence as Jessica uttered the word,
“*Lumina*!”
Jessica opened her eyes and nodded knowingly while another explosion of excited whispers filled the larder caves.
“And there’s more!” said Toby. “Look at your feet! Both of you, look at your feet!”
Jessica and Jamie looked at their trainers...and then something else clicked into place. Of course, the jay feathers...the same as the albino fawn had worn around her neck!
“The feather of the jay bird has always been regarded as a sign of good fortune and prosperity by our people,” explained Toby, “and it is also a symbol of the spirit of the woodland. They are prized by all, and you, by wearing them, will, we are sure, bring us the good fortune we will need in the troubled times ahead!”

Jessica and Jamie looked at one another. It felt strange to be a *warning*. Even stranger to be *saviours*! But they had no regrets. They felt calm and happy. Wanted! Honoured! They *had* to help in any way they could! There was no doubt about it, this magical, secret world they had stumbled into, *had* to be protected and saved from the eyes of the Upper World! If they could help, then they surely would!

Without another word, for somehow, a silent understanding had been reached, everyone finished their oak-leaf tea and Lepho lead the group back into the main larder cave. As they walked by the piles of giant scarlet berries, a cloaked figure standing at the mouth of the cave raised his horn to his lips and blew three short notes.
"The *Goldcrest* is here to take you upstream to Pillo," announced Lepho. "I will escort you and soon you will meet our last newcomers, Jonathan and Jane, and you will see their happiness for yourselves!"

As they gazed beyond the cave mouth and into the cavern below, Jessica and Jamie couldn't help thinking what lay ahead. A voyage along an unknown river to an unknown township deep beneath the night forest! And a meeting with the other *'J' and 'J'* in whose footsteps they seem to have followed into this magical, mystical, timeless, shrunken world!

Nothing seemed real, yet it was. All that seemed certain was that they had been mysteriously drawn into the magic and that they were determined to help the inhabitants of *Aqua Crysta* in whatever way they could!
But, if they had only known what perils and catastrophies were awaiting them, they would have most certainly realised that this was no living *dream* but rather, the beginnings of a living *nightmare*!!

Chapter 13

Quentin and Toby bade farewell to their guests from the Upper World and wished them luck. Greta and Merry shook their hands and pointed to the *Goldcrest* moored way, way below by the Floss, looking like a tiny model. Between the children and the golden ship lay the long and winding rocky staircase which clung tightly to the twinkling cavern walls. The tiny vessel seemed distant but at least the journey to it would be easier going down, than coming up!

The trio began their descent. Lepho walked in front, his cloak trailing behind. Before rounding the first corner, the children turned and waved back to Quentin, Toby, Greta and Merry, who all gently returned their farewell, behind them the amazing hoard of scarlet berries. Once around the corner, the larder cave disappeared from view and the full glory of the magnificent cavern unfolded before them. Jamie checked his watch again. Still only *two minutes past two!*

"Dad's always saying that the longest dreams only last seconds!" he whispered to Jessica with a grin. "*This* has to be the proof!"

The landscape was like nothing in the *real* world. It was pure fairytale with its glistening pinks and whites and its countless, winking crystals set like stars in a cloudless, milky sky. Masses of long, pointed stalactites clung from the misty cavern roof, some short, some long.

"They still look like a worm's eye view of a carrot field!" joked Jamie as he gazed upwards.

"You watch where you're going!" warned Jessica, just behind. "One slip now and you've had it!"

The drop to the cavern floor was almost sheer, and with no handrail and worn, slippery crystals underfoot, the descent seemed more nerve-racking than the climb had been. They were glad when they reached the level terrace with its wooden table and three-legged stools...it was such a relief for a few moments not to watch every footstep! The candle flame was still flickering with, once again, not a drip of melted wax to be seen!

Lepho sat down and rested his feet on one of the stools. He unfastened a plaited grass bag from his belt and placed it on the table. "Sit down and take the weight off your feet!" he said. "Somehow it always seems more wearing on the soles on the way down the *Larder Steps* than on the way up!"

Jessica and Jamie already liked and trusted their guide. Although he was a century younger than Quentin and Toby he looked around the same age. He, too, had blue eyes set in a bristly, bearded face, but his hair was ginger and curly and he wasn't as talkative as his elders. It was his smile that warmed the children to him. In that art he seemed to be well practised with deep smile lines etched in his face below his ruddy cheeks. But it was the fact that he smiled with his eyes as well, that captivated Jessica and Jamie. He somehow reminded them of their mother.

From the bag he took out a sort of leathery bound book and a fine crystal nibbed wood carved pen and a small crystal pot of purple liquid.

He introduced the book as though it was a valued and precious friend. "My *Journal* !" he announced proudly. "Our *Journal* ! The *Journal of Aqua Crysta* herself! Within its pages is the history of our realm and I have been long entrusted with its keeping and writing. Nearly one hundred volumes reach back to her birth. This is but the latest."

He carefully opened the book, dipped the nib into the ink, which looked like bramble juice, and looked intently at the eternal candle flame.

"She burns strongly and brightly now," he said. "The Guardians of *Lumina*...Quentin and Toby...will be pleased and relieved. They were sure that she was dying because she sensed *Aqua Crysta* was doomed. But we can see that in your presence, Jessica and Jamie, hope has returned. Look how boldly she plumes!"

Lumina almost seemed to be listening as she soared upwards, squatted for a moment and then soared again, even higher, like a pirouetting ballerina.
"She has danced since our World began!" said Lepho, averting his gaze to Jessica and Jamie.
"And it is *you* who will keep her alive!"
He turned the pages of small, neat, purple script until he came to the last words he had written during his latest harvest expedition. He pointed with the slender, smooth crystal tipped pen, and invited Jessica to read them.
Jessica felt strangely honoured and privileged. She whispered,
"*...if she dies...we die...the magic will be no more...*"
Lumina soared once again as Lepho wrote with his steady hand:

'*The magic lives on....our saviours have come*!
Our beloved realm is safe in their hands!'

Then he lifted the page towards *Lumina's* warmth, watched the words lose their gleaming wetness and become woven forever into the history of *Aqua Crysta*.
At that very moment, as if the words had been carved in stone, Jessica and Jamie felt the power of the magic that had drawn them to the mystical cavern coursing through their veins. Determination became etched on their faces as they looked at one another. Jessica put her hand onto Jamie's on the table and Lepho closed his on top. A union had been forged. A union which would see them through to the end...of whatever... lay ahead!

As the trio slowly descended from the terrace, the shimmering Floss gradually became closer and closer and wider and wider, with the river's floating rafts of froth easily visible. Soon they could hear the gurgling water as it splashed through the cavern...but there was *something* not quite right!

It was Jamie who spotted it first.
"The river!" he suddenly called. "The river's running in the opposite direction!"
It was true. The rafts of froth were moving *upstream*...or was it *downstream?* Then Jessica noticed the breeze was blowing back to front as well! Lepho paused, then he turned and smiled.
"All will be explained later," he said. "For now, just enjoy the journey... and come to understand that this is not the Upper World and the nature of things here is somewhat..."
"*Different*?" suggested Jessica with a return smile.
"Jonathan and Jane will be expecting you soon," said Lepho, as he turned and carried on down the steps. "We had better be getting down to the *Goldcrest*. Captain Frumo will be awaiting our arrival!"

As they rounded a bend they could see the golden galley moored by the shore, gently bobbing in the shallows, and reflecting the shore's white pebbles and lapping waves in her shimmering bows. She was a beautiful sight and Jessica and Jamie could hardly wait to get on board. As they crunched over the pebbles beyond the last step, they noticed a slender, wooden plank glide effortlessly from a gap in her side and come to rest on the shore. And, like the last time, when she had picked up the three hornblowers, there was no sign of any crew! She looked deserted!
But suddenly, a solitary figure appeared in the gap at the end of the plank...a purple cloaked and hooded figure, with his arms raised in a gesture of welcome. Slowly, he lowered his arms and then swept back his hood, revealing the face of a much younger man, clean shaven and with a mass of curly, jet black hair.
"That's Captain Frumo!" whispered Lepho. "Walk up the pathway and greet him!"
Jamie stepped onto the narrow plank followed by Jessica, and the two of them walked up the slope towards the beaming captain.
"Welcome aboard the *Goldcrest*!" he hailed and shook first Jamie and then Jessica warmly by the hand. "We shall be sailing as soon as you are at the prow so that you have the best view of the voyage!"

The children stepped onto the ship and immediately saw the invisible crew - dozens of purple clad figures manning the oars on each side beneath a sort of narrow deck which ran around the ship with a long hollow in the middle. With Lepho, they made their way to the very prow of the galley, while the great, yellow sail was hoisted and unfurled into all its dazzling glory. The oars were extended until their blades dipped beneath the swirling waters of the Floss and the *Goldcrest* gently nudged into its current. The voyage had begun!

The great square sail billowed in the breeze as the oars lightly fingered the Floss and Captain Frumo took the wheel. A moment later, the children felt a sudden thrust of speed as the golden vessel was swept forward in the fast flowing mainstream. The oars were withdrawn and the oarsmen, maybe two dozen of them, dashed up onto the deck and took up positions along the rails, anxious to enjoy the voyage as well! And what a voyage it was!

With the warm breeze and the fine spray from the Floss, Jessica and Jamie marvelled through squinted eyes as the splendid scenery of the journey unfolded before them. The towering cavern walls and boulder strewn shores rushed by as the *Goldcrest* picked up speed. The beauty was breathtaking as they gazed high into the pink ceiling mists swirling around giant, pointed stalactites, like pink icicles in candy floss. Caves, paths and staircases filled every glance, some down at shore level, some way, way up near the top of the cavern walls. More and more people came into view, all heathery cloaked, some in groups on the shore, some climbing staircases, some sitting at tables on flat terraces. All waved and cheered as the golden galley glided by, and the crew joined the children and Lepho waving back. Jessica and Jamie were really beginning to feel like *honoured* guests. News of their arrival had certainly got around!

Gradually, the cavern and the Floss widened and the current slowed down together with the breeze. Instead of rushing by, the scenery merely drifted by. The crew manned the oars, plunging them into the still waters, and heaved the vessel toward what appeared to be a distant and very different shore.

"Pillo!" smiled Lepho, pointing ahead as the ship's prow cut through masses of floating froth. "That's Pillo, our destination!"
In the distance the children could just make out an incredible jumble of windows, doors, roof tops, stairways and towers climbing in a tangle from the purple fringed shore...all crowned with the most glistening, pink and white, crystal studded rock they had seen so far in the magical realm. Pillo looked magnificent, reflected in the almost mirror like Floss, and awash with bright crystal light. A huge underground village, no, more of a town...the home of hundreds of Aqua Crystans!

As the ship veered to the right and headed for the pier, Jessica and Jamie could see what appeared to be the end of the cavern just beyond the town. A vast, smooth towering wall of rock swept around the end of the Floss to form an enormous solid crescent, topped with a dark, narrow shelf which ran along its whole length. The wall seemed to glisten with water rather than crystals, and thin, tumbling waterfalls reached from top to bottom, trickling from the dark shelf into the Floss.
The children's eyes wandered back to the fast approaching purple shore beneath the maze of houses...and, by now, they could make out what the purple was! It was a solid, bustling throng of excited, waving Aqua Crystans all lining the shore, waiting for the arrival of the visitors from the Upper World. As the ship edged towards the pier, the children could hear the sounds of cheering and clapping drifting across the silent water. It was strangely echoey and eerie, although it made them feel like popstars arriving at an airport as they waved back to the crowd! Somehow, between *two minutes past two* and...*two minutes past two* in the middle of the night, they had become celebrities!!

By now they could see that all the houses behind the people were cut into the cavern wall itself...pink and white rock houses with scores of dark square windows and rectangular doorways. They all seemed to be built on top of one another, connected by a maze of winding paths and staircases.
The *Goldcrest* glided majestically towards the welcome and came to rest by the short, wooden pier that jutted out from the shore. Her oars were

withdrawn and she was tied to a stumpy post by several of the crew who had jumped ashore. Lepho beckoned to Jessica and Jamie to follow him, and with Captain Frumo leading the way with the rest of the crew behind, the little procession trooped down the plank onto the slightly ricketty pier.

The excited, noisy hubbub of the crowd was almost deafening, but it faded as a large, imposing figure stepped from the sea of smiling faces and walked slowly up to Captain Frumo. A figure this time dressed in a much darker purple cloak than the children had seen so far. And not only was his cloak different, but around his neck was a gleaming gold chain with a large gold medallion glinting on his chest. As the figure approached, Lepho whispered that he was called Merrick...the Mayor of Pillo.

Captain Frumo bowed, shook hands with him and then introduced the children. Jamie also bowed and shook the Mayor's hand, followed by Jessica, who managed a small curtsey, thinking it would be the thing to do. Merrick smiled warmly and gave them both a welcoming hug. Jessica knew it was rude to stare but she couldn't help gazing at the features of the Mayor's face. He had the most piercing blue eyes she'd ever seen, set beneath two enormous, bushy, snow white eyebrows that had almost knitted together into one! Together with his matching huge beard and moustache and rosy cheeks, he could have been mistaken anywhere for Santa Claus...especially if he'd been wearing red rather than deep purple!

"He's the only person," whispered Lepho in Jessica's ear, "in the whole of *Aqua Crysta* who is over *three hundred harvests old*!!"

Jessica looked in amazement at the Mayor.

"Then he's even older than Quentin!" she gasped.

"Yes, he's the oldest inhabitant of *Aqua Crysta*! He was born in your year *Sixteen-Fifty-Six* in London, and travelled here as a boy having escaped that city's Great Fire and Plague ten years later!"

"Welcome to Pillo, the chief town of *Aqua Crysta*," said Mayor Merrick, at last. "You have both travelled far from the Upper World. I hope that you have been made welcome!"

Jessica and Jamie nodded and the Mayor continued.
"I also hope that you have a pleasant stay with us, and I know that there are two particular people who are looking forward to meeting you... Jonathan and Jane. I am sure you will have heard of them by now!"
"And we're looking forward to meeting them, too!" chirped Jamie.
"Lepho here will take you to their home. I believe a celebration is being prepared for your arrival, so be on your way. I will speak with you later!"

With that, Mayor Merrick turned and the procession followed, the crowd parting to let it through. Jessica and Jamie just could not believe what was happening. Not only the magical voyage and the moviestar welcome, but now they were actually on their way to some kind of party! Jonathan peeped at his watch...yes, just as he expected! Still *two minutes past two*!!

All the heather hued folk carried on cheering and waving as the procession wove away from the shore. Jessica and Jamie shook scores of outstretched hands and returned the beaming smiles of the Aqua Crystans. Everyone seemed to be so happy and carefree! Many looked as old as Quentin and Toby, but many were much younger, and some, wearing knee length purple smocks instead of cloaks, seemed to be children...although each, no doubt, was a century old, at least!

Soon they came to what seemed to be a market place with rows of brightly coloured stalls each piled high with all sorts of strange looking goods. Some had ornaments and trinkets made from pinky white rock and crystal. Some had shoes made from plaited grasses and beaten bark, while others stocked cloaks, rolls of cloth, wooden toys, foods and drinks. All the time, the crowds of Aqua Crystans danced along with the procession, still clapping and cheering.

Just beyond the market they passed the glowing embers of a fire where, according to Lepho, its tenders were roasting slices of acorn and horse chestnut.
"Can you smell that smell?" whispered Jamie to his sister.
"It's the same as the smoke at Barn Gate where we found the tricycle!" replied Jessica, sniffing the air. "Perhaps we're underneath that part of *George*...and *that smoke* was from *this fire,* and it's travelled up through cracks in the rock!"

It was certainly difficult to think that up there was the quiet, night time forest they'd been exploring during the afternoon, and now they were beneath it in a magical, crystal lit township surrounded by hordes of laughing, cheering people! But, somehow, thoughts of *George, Old Soulsyke*...and even *Deer Leap* and their father...seemed to be melting away in the magic. Strangely, they were both beginning to feel very much at home! The thought made them both happy and sad at the same time...their enjoyment of it all tinged with a strange inkling of guilt, as though they shouldn't be there at all! Were they really strong enough and capable enough to be *saviours*? Would they let everyone down?

They came to a path that began to climb towards the houses which were stacked high upon one another along ledges and terraces. All of them seemed to be more or less the same with hollowed, open, paneless square windows and wooden front doors. All the doors were differently carved and stained, some with numbers, some with names.

At last, they saw ahead of them...at the end of a widish terrace with tables and benches...a house that definitely stood out from the rest! Well, it wasn't so much the house that was different, it was all the rows of tiny, triangular, red and blue flags that were festooned all over it, not to mention a long, yellow banner strung between its upstairs windows, with the word 'WELCOME!!' printed in bold, purple letters. As Jessica and Jamie approached the house, its mottled brown door slowly opened and out stepped two very different figures...very different, indeed, from anyone else the children had met in *Aqua Crysta*.
No purple cloaks nor smocks here!
Instead, one was wearing green, baggy corduroy trousers down to his knobbly knees, with a striped, woolly, sleeveless pullover, a checked, long-sleeved shirt, rolled down, grey socks and black, scuffed leather shoes! The other wore a pretty, flowery, lace necked frock, and on her feet, white ankle socks and brown open-toed sandals.
They were Jonathan and Jane!
And they were still children...nearly fifty years after arriving in Aqua Crysta!!!

Chapter 14

Mayor Merrick stopped and beckoned Jessica and Jamie forward. Silence fell upon the procession and all the onlookers and neighbours as the strange quartet met...Jessica and Jamie in their bright, fluorescent twenty-first century clothes, and Jonathan and Jane dressed in the 'Fifties' fashions of the previous century!
In the sudden, expectant silence of the terrace overlooking the Floss, the two pairs of children stepped forward. Then their faces burst into broad smiles, they shook hands and hugged one another as though they were long lost friends meeting after years and years apart! They almost felt as though they somehow knew one another although, of course, they realised that *that* was impossible!

Once again, the clamour of celebration around them grew with all the curious Aqua Crystans laughing and talking about the long awaited encounter. Everyone seemed delighted with the meeting, as the dark haired Jonathan and Jane led their guests of honour into their small house, along with the Mayor, Lepho, Captain Frumo and most of his crew.

Inside, in the cramped couple of rooms, the guests were treated to a whole, scrumptious array of foods, all washed down with the most wonderfully flavoured drinks. Jessica especially enjoyed a sort of cool, bramble jelly with buried chunks of crunchy hazelnuts, topped with a smooth toadstooly cream. Jamie's favourite was round, roasted slices of acorn with a dip made from crushed fern fronds, but they were both eager to try a little of everything. It was all so tempting, and, after all, they were a little peckish after their journey!

The walls of the two small rooms were studded with crystals so there was plenty of light despite the small windows. Cupboards and shelves were crammed with all kinds of foods and ornaments and there was no fireplace because of the constant warm breezes. Mossy matting covered the floors and the cosy chairs were made from walnut shells with cushions of plaited grasses. But, most wonderful of all, was a huge glistening blue-green jay feather which stood propped up in a corner. It was so long that its end curved along the ceiling like some kind of creeping plant. Jonathan explained that most houses had one or two to bring good fortune. Full sized feathers were apparently collected on harvest trips into the forest every year and shared among the Aqua Crystans. Jays it seemed were almost like sacred birds and had lived in the forest for centuries, so Jessica and Jamie decided to present their hosts with the feathers they had threaded into their trainers. They were gratefully received, as Jamie threaded his under one of Jane's sandal straps and Jessica wove hers into Jonathan's black shoe laces. All four of them were delighted and their friendship was now complete as they sat on a pile of mossy cushions under the giant feather and began to get to know one another better.

Jonathan and Janes' parents had died during the bombing of London in the Second World War and, as babies, they had been sent to live with their uncle who farmed sheep on the Yorkshire moors. He'd treated them terribly and when they'd discovered the forest cellar down the well they used it as a secret hiding place. For over six long years they'd visited the hidden room, never once daring to climb further down the well. Then one summer they began to hear horn sounds coming from its dark, mysterious depths. It was around the time the great pine forest was planted and their nasty uncle had been ordered to abandon *Old Soulsyke*. He vanished one night and never returned, leaving the twelve year old Jonathan and his eleven year old sister to fend for themselves.

"But what about all the clockwork toys and the dolls' house in the forest cellar? Where did they come from?" asked Jessica.
"Our uncle owned them all! Each and every one!" said Jonathan, looking out from under his brown fringe. "They were his pride and joy. He used to collect them and keep them locked up in one of the barns. Not that *we* ever got to play with them! They were too precious to play with! Strictly out of bounds!"
"So when he disappeared we broke into the barn and took them as fast as we could to the forest cellar," laughed Jane, her dark pig-tails coming to life. "We even had to take the dolls' house to pieces to get it down the well and through the cellar door!"
"It was a sort of happy time and sad time all mixed together," Jonathan carried on. "We didn't know what to do. We liked the farm and the ancient wood around it, but we hated our uncle. He'd made our lives a misery for over ten years, but we had the idea that if we hid in the cellar for a while and waited until all the forest planters had gone, then we could perhaps go back and live at *Old Soulsyke* ourselves..."
"But it was *then* that we heard the horns from down below!" beamed Jane, her brown eyes suddenly sparkling. "We decided to climb down the well...we jumped off the last rung..."
"And we've been here ever since!!" finished Jonathan with a beaming smile.
Everything was, at last, beginning to make some sort of sense, although there were still many things that still puzzled Jessica and Jamie.
"What about the map you drew?" asked Jessica. "The one on the wall at the farm?"
Jonathan smiled again.
"I must have only been about five or six when I drew that on the bare plaster of our bedroom," he said.
"We *both* got a terrible beating for it though!" remembered Jane.
"Luckily for us, our uncle couldn't make head nor tail of it and quickly covered it with some cheap wallpaper!"
"*I'll spank your backsides raw if you touch that wallpaper*! he told us,"

recalled Jonathan, suddenly looking sad. "He was always yelling *I'll spank you backsides raw*!!"
"And he often did!" said Jane sadly, grasping tightly one of the corners of a cushion.
Jessica and Jamie looked at one another and Jamie quickly changed the subject.
"But how come all the toys in the cellar are all so *new* looking? They're all so clean and gleaming after all this time!"
"That's because the cellar is part of the *Harvest Passageway*...the passage that leads from the larder caves up to the Upper World," explained Jane, more cheerfully. "So every harvest, different collecting parties do a bit of cleaning to keep everything nice and prim and shipshape!"
"All the Crystans call the cellar, the '*Palace of Dancing Horses*', after the beautiful fairground carousel which stands in the middle," added Jonathan.
"Wow! It must be fantastic travelling through there being as small as you all are!" laughed Jamie. "Everything must be *full size* to you!"
"That's right!" said Jane, "You can sit on the horses on the carousel, sit in the racing cars, climb aboard the railway carriages and explore all the rooms in the dolls' house!"
"There's only *one* problem!" said Jonathan glumly, looking at his sister.
"What's that?" asked Jessica.
Jonathan and Jane suddenly became awkwardly quiet.
"Have another slice of roast acorn!" burst Jane, thrusting a wooden platter under Jamie's nose.
"What's this problem you're on about?" repeated Jessica, grabbing hold of Jamie's hand which was hovering over the tasty morsels.
"It doesn't matter now!" insisted Jane, fiddling with the red ribbon on one of her plaits. "The Queen will tell you all about it when you..."
"The *Queen*!!" chorused Jessica and Jamie. "You mean *Aqua Crysta* has got a *Queen*!!"
"Yes," said Jonathan, slightly taken aback. "Has nobody told you? She's called Queen Venetia!"

Jessica and Jamie looked at one another again, and both took a slice of acorn, completely amazed by yet another revelation. They nibbled like a couple of mice as Jane went on.
"She's lovely. You'll be meeting her later, when the Floss changes direction again and Captain Frumo can take you to Galdo where she lives. She's beautiful and very wise. You'll like her!"

The two visitors sat quietly for a while eating more of the delights in front of them, while their hosts passed round trays of food and drinks to all their guests. Having spotted them by themselves, Mayor Merrick came over and sat down on the cushions, carefully arranging his ample, dark purple cloak as he slowly lowered himself down.

He told them all about his escape from London when the Plague and Fire struck the city back in the year *Sixteen-Sixty-Six*. He sadly remembered his friends and relatives, one by one dying from the Plague and how he looked back upon England's ancient capital city in flames as his family trudged northwards. His mother and father died on the harsh journey, but after nearly a year, he and his two younger sisters found themselves in the small harbour village of Whitby on the Yorkshire coast. A ship-builder and his wife took them in and then they went to live with a sheepfarmer at *Old Soulsyke*.
But, like Jonathan and Jane, three centuries later, they had a terrible time with the *Master of Soulsyke,* as he was known. After his beloved sisters mysteriously drowned near Whitby, Merrick decided to run away and hide in the secret cellar he and his sisters had discovered down a long forgotten well on the desolate moors. With him he took dozens of silver tankards, daggers and horns which the *Master* used to trade in the local towns. He hoped that he would be able to sell them later.

For months he lived in the cellar and then one morning he saw the *Master* and some of his cronies building a stone wall near the well-head. The wall became longer and longer, and then others were built dividing the moorland into great fields. Merrick felt trapped in the cellar, only feeling safe to hunt for food at night. It was after many weeks of this wall building that he decided to explore further down the well. On his first trip down he saw the wonderful crystal light beyond the last rung and some magical force compelled him to jump into the strange world. But first, he returned to his cellar and threw down the well every single silver tankard, dagger and horn. Then he climbed down to the last rung expecting to see a heap of silverware piled high amid the milky white rock...but it had all vanished and an eerie mist swirled about beneath his feet.

At first he had second thoughts about jumping, but the magical power forced him onwards. He plunged into the unknown and found himself on a white, pebbly shore surrounded by the *Master's* work and staring around at a wondrous cavern. At first he felt scared and alone but he was soon welcomed by the monks who had dug the well in the first place, and carved out the cellar, over a hundred years earlier when King Henry Tudor was destroying all the Abbeys of England, including the one perched on the clifftop above Whitby.

"So *that* explains the tiny charms we found in the forest!" exclaimed Jamie. "Over three centuries ago they were full size...and you threw them down the well where they shrunk in *Aqua Crysta*!"

"And they've been used by Aqua Crystans ever since!" said Jessica, feeling the carving on her tankard of fizzy bramble and imagining the ruins of the Abbey they'd seen back in the Upper World just the other day.

"But what about all the other people here?" asked Jamie, glancing at all the guests and the excited crowd on the terrace. "Where did they all come from?"

"Many people were here when I, myself, ventured to these parts." Merrick explained, stroking his white beard. "Many families had been driven here by King Henry Tudor, and, although no one remains from that time, their descendants are all around you! And, of course, many sad travellers have reached our world since the time I arrived. Indeed, all the way through the Upper World centuries, many have found happiness here. The last to venture here were our young hosts, Jonathan and Jane...and now...you have ventured here!"

"Were you never worried that the *Master* and his wall builders would find the well-head slabs and follow you down here?" asked Jessica.
"Whenever folk have found their way to the well, they have always closed the slabs behind them. Then, to be certain of their secrecy, a party would climb the *Harvest Passageway* and cover them with soil and moss until the entrance was hidden."
"But how did people find the well who wanted to come here?" asked Jamie, nibbling a chunk of seed cake.
Merrick looked at them both with his blue eyes twinkling brighter than ever.
"That," he said, "is one of the great unsolved mysteries of our realm! All we know is that if someone needs to come then they will find us by whatever means. You found us by stumbling upon a map, I believe, long forgotten by Jonathan and Jane. And we all know that you will bring good fortune to our world. How, we do not quite know...although you will find that Queen Venetia, in her wisdom, will have an idea as regards that matter! For the moment, let us all put it down to the magical, mysterious force of *fate,* which you, too, have in your Upper World. Things will happen if they are intended to happen!"

With that, the Mayor slowly rose to his feet and said farewell to the children and wished them well on their journey to Galdo. He thanked Jonathan and Jane for their hospitality, and as he majestically walked over the doorstep, he turned and gracefully waved to the children. Then, he was gone.
"We must be on *our* way, too!" announced Captain Frumo. "We will meet you on board the *Goldcrest* when the tide turns. Jonathan and Jane, make sure that our guests are down at the pier in good time!"
"We will!" assured Jane, as the Captain waved goodbye, and marched smartly from the house followed by his crew and Lepho.

The house was suddenly quiet with just the four *J's* sitting in one of the snug rooms. Jonathan and Jane began to tidy up, helped by their guests, who were really beginning to feel at home!
"How will we know when the tide changes?" asked Jessica, as she collected all the wooden platters and dishes from the table.

"Come out onto the terrace and we will show you," invited Jane, and the four of them trooped out of the house onto the rocky balcony beyond the doorstep.
The view was magnificent, and completely unexpected!

Way below, the Floss had all but disappeared, leaving the *Goldcrest* leaning, high and dry, by the pier! Instead of the great mirror of a lake, the floor of the cavern was bejewelled with a litter of small pools and ponds, each shining brightly, reflecting the milky white crystal walls of the cavern. The sweeping, smooth curtain of rock that was the end of the cavern still glistened and its slender cascades and trickles still plunged over its face. But there was hardly a trace of the wide, flowing river they had expected to see!
Jamie noticed a huge, broad pillar of rock just in front of the end wall, which seemed to run from the cavern ceiling almost down to the floor.
"What's that great rock column over there?" he asked, pointing towards the end of the cavern.
"It's not a solid column of rock," laughed Jonathan. "It's the pipe that leads up to the water-pump at the barn near *Old Soulsyke*! It looks like solid rock because it's become encrusted with crystals over the years. Didn't you see the pump when you passed the barn on your way to the farmhouse? I'd love to see it again. We used to keep our tricycle in the barn and have great fun riding over the field before the forest was planted!"
Jessica and Jamie looked at one another, not saying anything about the sad old crushed wreck they'd seen. They just shook their heads.
"N..no, we didn't," said Jessica. "I don't remember passing a barn at all!"
"When we came here," Jane went on, "we couldn't really bring the tricycle so we left it in the barn and just brought the bell as a kind of memento. It's up in the *Palace of Dancing Horses,* but it's high up on a shelf. We haven't touched it for half a century!"
Jessica and Jamie once again knowingly glanced at one another...then Jessica changed the subject.
"What I can't understand," she said, gazing dreamily out over the cavern, "is where you got your water from when you lived at the farm?"

"Sometimes we used the barn pump, but it kept running dry as you can imagine," answered Jane, pointing to the base of the great column of rock, "and the water was always warm!"
"It was super for having a wash in, but not very nice to drink!" recalled Jonathan, screwing up his face. "We often used to go to the barn in winter and have lovely warm baths in the big trough under the pump spout. I can see all the clouds of steam in the cold air now!"
"So you used another well for drinking water?" asked Jamie.
"No, but I wish there had been!" replied Jonathan. "Our job every day was to take buckets to a nearby beck and fill them with fresh water, then carry them back to the farm and either fill the sink in the kitchen or the trough in the yard. Every single day we did that from when we were both big enough to carry a couple of full buckets each!"

Jessica and Jamie were beginning to understand what life must have been like for their new friends when they lived with their uncle...and what a relief it must have been when he disappeared and they found *Aqua Crysta*!
Suddenly, Jessica grabbed Jamie's arm.
"Listen!" she shouted, "I can hear singing!"
"The tide's about to change and people are singing in celebration!" beamed Jane.

Aqua Crystans appeared from every doorway, nook and cranny and joined in the singing. The shore below was soon packed with folk all singing the most wonderful notes at the tops of their voices. Not singing words, but just melodic notes like monks used to chant in abbeys in the past. The music gradually filled the cavern. It was beautifully awesome, the power of it spine tingling.
"It's a custom from way back in time when the first monks came to *Aqua Crysta*," explained Jane and soon all four of them were joining in the celebration of the coming waters.

The wonderful, harmonic chanting became louder and louder until it reached a tremendous and thrilling climax...and then, just as the singing was at its greatest possible volume...a huge roar came from the end of the cavern, so loud that it drowned the singing completely!

Jessica and Jamie held on to one another in fear. It was as though a giant, underground dragon had been awakened from sleep...but still, the music went on and on, almost trying to compete with the roar. The whole cavern was filled with the deafening noise mixed with the incessant chanting of the Aqua Crystans.
Jessica and Jamie felt crushed by the sound and just *had* to put their hands to their ears. The peaceful tranquility of *Aqua Crysta* had been destroyed in a few moments. The children couldn't believe the change and how quickly it had happened!

Then, as the terrace almost began to shake beneath their feet, Jessica and Jamie stared upwards in disbelief at the dark curved shelf above the endwall of the cavern.
Something *was* stirring and waking on the lofty ledge!!
Its size was absolutely incredible...even out-matching its terrifying roar!
Jamie grabbed hold of his sister, whether for his own sake or his sister's he wasn't sure, but as his whole body shook and his teeth chattered, he suddenly wished he was back in his bed at *Deer Leap*!
The monster of the dark ledge...was on its way...and it was *angry*!!

Chapter 15

The monster that had awoken stretched along the whole crescent of the dark shelf, writhing and churning. One moment it filled the gap between the curved ledge and the cavern roof, the next it had plunged headlong down the endwall, engulfing the slender cascades, and falling like a gigantic white curtain, crashing onto the cavern floor!

It was an enormous, roaring waterfall, like a great dam overflowing, and pouring into an unsuspecting, dry valley below. At the foot of the fall the angry water churned and bubbled even more, giving birth to vast islands of floating, pale green froth, which followed the swirling, surging flood as it engulfed the myriad of helpless, tiny pools and ponds, drowning them all.

As the swash of the flooding tide lashed against the shore below the terrace, Jessica and Jamie feared the worst...that the whole township of Pillo would be destroyed!

They watched in horror as the *Goldcrest* was lifted and tossed like a piece of driftwood, straining and tugging at her mooring rope and the fragile pier. Surely she couldn't withstand the power that had been unleashed so suddenly into the calm and peace!

But then, the terrifying roar began to fade, the water began to settle and once again the chanting of the Aqua Crystans could be heard in all its glory. The waterfall carried on incessantly, but the water had reached its deepest in the wide cavern at Pillo and was now flowing along the rest of the cavern as the newly born River Floss.

Jessica and Jamie sighed with relief as they gazed over the magnificent lake reflecting the whites and pinks of the cavern roof like a huge mirror.
"So that's where all the froth comes from!" gasped Jessica over the gradually fading chanting. "But where did the water come from?"
"And where does it go?" asked Jamie, watching the calm Aqua Crystans getting on with their everyday lives after the celebrations.
"It flows down to Lake Serentina at the other end of the cavern," explained Jonathan, "then sinks through cracks down and down through the rocks where it becomes hotter and hotter before it's forced back up..."
"And becomes the Galdo Falls...!" said Jane.
"Ah, I've got it!" chipped in Jamie. "Then the water flows back to Pillo, sinks through the rocks, becomes hot..."
"And then it's forced up to become the Pillo Falls!" added Jessica. "And then it all happens again, and again!"
"And again and again, forever and ever!" laughed Jane.
"So the Floss flows both ways for the *Goldcrest* to link Pillo and Galdo and also gives you warm water and air!" said Jamie.
"And, most importantly, the magic bubbles in the froth which we all believe lead to our everlasting lives and our shrunken world!" smiled Jonathan.
"You mean the whole magical existence of *Aqua Crysta* is because of the bubbles in the froth made by the two waterfalls?" asked Jessica.
"To be honest, nobody knows for sure," replied Jane. "It's always been a mystery, ever since the first settlers arrived."
The children looked down upon the ever calming waters as the singing finally disappeared and the Aqua Crystans got on with whatever they had been doing before the Falls had erupted.

As the vast curtain of water continued to pour into the magical froth, the four of them headed for the pier where the *Goldcrest* was gently bobbing, awaiting her voyage while the tide was at its highest and strongest. The market stalls were still busy and people were playing games and dancing to the music of flutes made from hollowed twiglets. Again, everyone seemed so happy and content, all waving and cheering as the quartet headed for the shore.

The *Goldcrest's* yellow sail was already unfurled and filled with breeze as the children stepped aboard and were greeted by Captain Frumo and Lepho. Moments later the ship glided away from the shore and was soon in the strongest midstream current heading down the awesome cavern.

It was an even faster journey than the first time, with the cavern walls speeding by in a blur as the four children hung onto the rails of the bouncing bow. The crystal boulders near the Larder Cave staircase sped by and then Jessica and Jamie caught sight of their long, dangling rope stretching from the pebble shore up into the lofty mists. They both knew that it lead to another world...to *George, Deer Leap*...and dad. Jamie checked his watch...still two minutes past two! But what time was it up there? Was dad still asleep in *Deer Leap*? Or was the sun rising over the treetops and the smell of bacon wafting from the kitchen? Or was it mid-morning, mid-day...or even later? There was no way of telling!

Jonathan and Jane pointed out as much as they could as the cavern galloped by. There was a beautiful hanging forest of pinky white stalactites just beyond the rope and then came the giant *Meeting Hall* cave shaped like a Roman amphitheatre with banks of seats cut into the cave walls. Then there was the *Cave of Torrents,* a long, narrow cave leading off from the main cavern with dozens of tiny, step waterfalls disappearing into the distance.

More and more crystals seemed to be embedded in the cavern's soaring walls as the *Goldcrest* plunged on and on through the frothy waters... until, as had happened when they'd approached Pillo, the Floss began to widen and become more sluggish. Soon, the oars were out and Captain Frumo was at the wheel steering his vessel between hundreds of tiny, uninhabited islands, each a mass of glowing, twinkling crystals.

"There's *Galdo*!" called Jane, pointing ahead, her face full of wonder and amazement, even after years and years of seeing the magnificent sight.

The massive, tapering pillar of rock rose sheer from the swirling waters of Lake Serentina, like the remains of a thick stubby candle or the stump of a fallen tree. Its sides seemed almost verical, unclimbable, but as the *Goldcrest* neared the island, Jessica and Jamie could make out spiral staircases winding upwards with ledges and houses strung along them like beads on strings. Crystals twinkled in the pale pink rock giving a feeling of warmth and welcome. It was a splendid sight, but most magnificent of all was the summit. At its tapering peak was a magical maze of turrets and towers like something out of a fairytale. Each round tower was dotted with windows and capped with a round, pointed roof like a Chinese hat.

From the ship's bows, Jessica and Jamie stood spellbound as Galdo grew and grew before them. Purple dots became waving islanders and windows became filled with smiling faces and fluttering flags. Closer and closer the *Goldcrest* glided to the spiring island until she came to rest by a quay built out from the rock into the lake's lapping waves.

The children disembarked, this time leaving Captain Frumo, his crew and Lepho on board.

Like at Pillo, crowds had gathered to greet the travellers, all, once again, in their heathery hooded cloaks and smocks. And the welcome was just as friendly with lots of waving, cheering and good wishes. But, this time, without much of a shore to speak of, the people seemed closer and even more excited...that is, until suddenly, the noisy hubbub faded and stopped as though someone had thrown a switch.

All at once, the eager crowds parted like theatre curtains...and there...centre-stage...stood the most amazing person Jessica and Jamie had met...Her Majesty, the very noble Queen of *Aqua Crysta*...Queen Venetia herself!

Just as when they had met Mayor Merrick at Pillo, Jessica and Jamie stared, open mouthed. They both knew it was bad mannered but they just couldn't help it, however much they tried! For standing before them in a radiant purple gown braided with strands of gold, a long train elegantly flowing behind and a simple band of gold on her head, was a lady of exquisite beauty. With deep green eyes and a pale smooth skin, she appeared to be almost too young to be a Queen.

As Jessica and Jamie gazed upon her light, straw coloured hair cascading over her shoulders to well beyond her waist, she gently spoke.
"Welcome, Jessica and Jamie, to the Island of Galdo. We are pleased to greet you and hope you enjoy your stay."
Jonathan bowed his head and Jane curtseyed, so Jessica and Jamie nervously did the same.
"Follow me," she continued, "I will show you inside Galdo and you can enjoy its many delights."
"*Inside* Galdo?" whispered Jamie to Jonathan. "What's she talking about?"
"You'll see!" whispered back Jonathan with a gleam in his eye. "It's *Aqua Crysta's* greatest treasure!"
Queen Venetia turned, elegantly swished her gown's train behind her and gracefully glided away from the quay towards an archway which lead into a low, orangy glowing passageway. The four children followed, cheered on by the crowd which was packed like sardines along two sloping staircases above the archway. The passageway was quite narrow, just allowing the children to walk through in pairs. Small closed doors lined each side, and ahead they could see a bright red glow that marked the end of the tunnel. Waving figures silhouetted against the warm glow beckoned them on, and as the Queen reached them, she turned and raised her arms as if to introduce her visitors to something very special... something very special indeed!!
With their hearts beating faster than ever, Jessica and Jamie emerged from the end of the passageway...and, once again, they could hardly believe what lay before them!
Galdo was completely hollow!

It was like being inside a vast, rocky tube or a tunnel on its head, gradually narrowing to an arched roof, above which must have been the towers with their Chinese hats. It was as though the island had been turned outside in, with more spiralling staircases and ledges dotted with windows and doors climbing to dizzy, breath-taking heights. But, whereas on the outside of Galdo the windows all faced Lake Serentina, on the inside they all faced one another, joined by an amazing network of dozens of long rope bridges which spanned the hollow like swaying, sagging hammocks.

The Queen lead the four children across the wide, marbly floor and towards her own small *house*...not a palace, as Jessica and Jamie had expected.

As they wound across the smooth, rosy pink floor they waved up at more cheering Aqua Crystans who were appearing in all the doorways and skipping along the aerial rope ways. Market stalls similar to those at Pillo were scattered over the floor and there was a sort of indoor-outdoor carpentry area where folk were busily making tables and chairs and stools from a variety of nutshells. Then came a kind of public park with families enjoying picnics amid a forest of everlasting toadstools. These had apparently been grown from seed-dust accidentally brought down from the Upper World on the soles of harvesters' boots!

Queen Venetia followed a winding path through the gnarled, old fungi forest which lead to the steps of her surprisingly small house...which appeared, from the outside, to be just the same as every other house in *Aqua Crysta*! There was certainly no sign of sentry boxes nor guardsmen on parade! As she glided up the three steps, she turned and beckoned the children inside for cups of pine-needle tea and something to eat. So with a final wave to all the sight-seers watching from the tangle of bridges spiralling upwards towards Galdo's dizzy heights, the children eagerly entered the Queen's home.

If it had been similar to all the other houses in *Aqua Crysta* on the outside, it was certainly a *very different* story on the inside! Even Jonathan and Jane, who had visited the Queen's home before, stood with mouths wide open as they marvelled at the beauty. The rooms were about the same size as they were accustomed to, but it was the walls that made them appear enormous.They were almost solid crystal, like masses and masses of cut diamonds, all shimmering and reflecting in the pinkish light. Their colours constantly changed as the children slowly walked into the room. It was like being inside a kaleidoscope with every colour of the rainbow appearing and disappearing as the children moved. Crystal ornaments were everywhere, as too, were great bunches of full sized jay feathers reaching from the floor and curling along the crystal ceiling.

The Queen gestured to the children to sit on a long, soft cushion in the centre of the room while she slipped into the other room. She soon returned with a tray containing a grand, tall, glassy, crystal teapot in the shape of the island of Galdo, matching cups and saucers and plates of sliced sweet chestnut. She set the tray on a hazelnut table, poured the tea and then sat on a nearby cushion. As her guests politely sipped their tea and nibbled their chestnut slices, the Queen swept back her cascade of golden hair and spoke, her soft voice captivating Jessica and Jamie.

"Since becoming Queen," she began, addressing the newcomers, "I have wished to fulfil a solemn promise I made to the last travellers to arrive in *Aqua Crysta*. You have met Jonathan and Jane who arrived many harvests ago. They told of a secret hoard of magic in the well's hidden cellar...a secret hoard of magic that all the people of *Aqua Crysta* long to see come alive and thrill them in a way that not one of them could even imagine!"

Jessica and Jamie looked puzzled.

"That's right!" interrupted Jonathan, a little humbly in the Queen's presence. "It's wonderful when everything is moving and the music is playing. It's a whole fairground, but with trains too, and racing cars and...!"

The Queen raised her hand before Jonathan became too excited and smiled at his enthusiasm. Then she calmly continued.

"I know nothing of these things called trains and cars, but I do know that all comes to life with the help of the *Seven Silver Keys of Sigmund* which lie in *Sigmund's Cave*."

She paused as if she was suddenly upset.

"Where is *Sigmund's Cave*?" politely enquired Jamie.

The Queen gathered herself and carried on although her voice seemed sad.

"Sigmund, for many happy harvests my beloved husband, died in a tragic mishap when the *Silver Keys* were being hidden in a cave just off the Harvest Passageway..."

She paused again and reached for a handkerchief to dab her moist eyes.
"...The keys were very burdensome. It took a dozen men to lift each one as they were taken from the *Palace of Dancing Horses* to a secret place of safe keeping. When the seventh, and last key was being rested in the cave, it slipped from their grasp and Sigmund died under its great shaft along with two of his companions."
She stopped again and dabbed her eyes.
"When I became Queen of *Aqua Crysta* I promised Jonathan and Jane, my people and my husband's memory, that the *Seven Keys* would once again bring life to the forest cellar...but they are so, so heavy that I fear my wish can never be fulfilled. Even if we can carry the Keys to the Palace, how can they be made to work their magic? Jonathan and Jane tell me that they must be turned with great power and strength to bring the magic and music...and we cannot summon the forces needed.
It would be impossible!"
"If we can help in anyway, just tell us how!" burst Jessica, wondering what was coming next.
The Queen smiled and her face beamed again like the sun coming from behind a dark cloud. Her eyes twinkled to match the crystal walls.
"It has been suggested that you accompany Lepho and an expedition party to the Upper World to retrieve the map you discovered before it falls into the wrong hands. First of all, are you happy with this plan?"
Jessica and Jamie nodded, the thought of climbing the Harvest Passageway and then seeing the magical world of the forest cellar as tiny Aqua Crystans saw it filled them with excitement.
"But how does that help you with your wish to bring the toys to life in the *Palace of Dancing Horses*? We still won't be able to turn the clockwork keys!" said Jamie.
The Queen looked at her guests one by one and then continued.
"You are aware, I believe, that everyone who has travelled to our realm has been disenchanted and unhappy with their lives in the Upper World. Indeed, you are the first visitors to come here who are happy and content and in no need of escape from sadness or evil."

Jessica and Jamie once again nodded and glanced at each other with puzzled faces.

"If you wish to return to your world, I will understand. But if you do, I pray that you will never, never, as long as you live, tell other Upper World souls of the existence of *Aqua Crysta* and its people."

"As long as we live, your Majesty!" promised Jessica. "We would never ever dream of doing such a thing. We would never say a word!"

"You may, of course, still change your minds and come to live here, and you would be very welcome...but if you decide to return to the Upper World, then there is one other request I would like to ask of you."

"Anything you wish, your Majesty!" insisted Jamie. "Just tell us how we can help!"

The Queen poured some more tea and handed round a crystal bowl of delicious, crispy, dried wimberry skins.

"The only way of returning to the Upper World and changing back to your Upper World size is to return by the way you came, by means of the well. But the problem is, for two reasons, no one in the history of *Aqua Crysta* has *ever* made the return journey! Firstly, because no-one has ever *desired* to return, and secondly because, up until now, such a journey would have been *impossible*!"

"But how is it suddenly *possible*?" asked Jessica, nibbling a piece of the purple, dried wimberry.

"Your *rope*, my friends!" replied Queen Venetia, her eyes twinkling more than ever. "You are the first visitors ever to have dangled a rope from the last rung of the ancient well's ladder. Everyone else has simply jumped with no thought of return! And, believe me, there is no other way of reaching the bottom of the well. The cavern's walls are unclimbable, and besides, the bottom of the well is in the middle of the cavern's ceiling! It would be impossible to reach even if someone wanted to!"

"So you think that if we climb the rope," said Jamie, "then we will eventually pass through the mists and reach the last rung...?"

"And by that time, we should be back to our Upper World size!" added Jessica.

"But, your Majesty!" suddenly exclaimed Jane, leaping from the cushion. "Surely you cannot let our new friends risk such a journey! Not only is there the danger of the climb, but then there is our ignorance of what may happen in the mists!"
"The journey has not been attempted before!" added Jonathan, agreeing with his sister. "How do we know they will change back to their Upper World size even if they reach the mists?"
Before the Queen could reply to the heartfelt outburst, Jessica answered her friends' concern.
"We both realise that there are risks...but we are both prepared to take them. After all, we promised dad we'd be back for teatime!" she laughed.
"Then if *you go, we* go!!" insisted Jonathan, full of admiration of his friends' bravery and determination.
"But you said it was too dangerous a moment ago!" said the Queen. "Surely *you* don't want to return to the Upper World to stay? You are happy here!"
"No, we don't want to *stay* up there!" said Jane, glancing up at the Queen's crystal ceiling. "We just want to travel with our new friends and see where we *used* to live!"
Queen Venetia smiled and shook her head in amazement.
"My children, I am in wonder at your courage and friendship, and if you can climb the well and enter the forest cellar in your Upper World size, then you will be able to easily turn the *Seven Silver Keys* and bring the magic my people have so longed to see!"
"Then first we must take the keys to the cellar from *Sigmund's Cave* on our way up the Harvest Passageway on Lepho's expedition to retrieve the map!" said Jessica, beginning to bubble with excitement about what lay ahead. "Just tell us when the *Goldcrest* leaves for the Larder Steps, and we'll be on our way. I can hardly wait!"

Indeed, a noble and venturesome plan had been hatched...but would it proceed as arranged? The best laid schemes often go wrong! Who knows about this one? And what about the doom sensed by the candle flame, *Lumina*? Would that soon show itself?
Only time would tell!

Chapter 16

“Farewell, and may good fortune favour your venture!” said Captain Frumo as he shook each member of the young quartet firmly by the hand and patted Lepho on the shoulder.

“Look after my good friend! He is getting on in years, though not in spirit!”

Lepho laughed and shook the Captain’s hand.

“Worry not, my friend, I shall be in good company! Long live *Aqua Crysta*!”

“Long live *Aqua Crysta*!” echoed Captain Frumo as he made his way up the plank and ordered the oars to gently nudge his beloved vessel away from the shore.

Slowly and gracefully, her great sail was unfurled and the *Goldcrest* was once again captured by the breeze and borne away towards Pillo. The children watched until the yellow, billowing square vanished into the distance, and then silently followed Lepho between the crystal boulders to the foot of the stone staircase.

“Ready for the climb again?” he smiled, his hood swept back revealing his ginger hair and freckly, rosy face.

“We’re ready for anything!” beamed Jamie, looking like Lepho in miniature with his mop of matching hair and equally freckled face.

“Well, there’s certainly a long climb ahead!” Lepho warned. “What with the staircase and *then* the Harvest Passageway!”

“Don’t worry!” laughed Jamie. “We’ve both climbed Ben More in Scotland dozens of times. This’ll be a piece of cake!”

"There you go again, talking about food!" said Jessica, smiling at her brother. "One of these days you'll be able to say something without mentioning things to eat!"

So, with thoughts of the delicious nibbles they'd tasted in *Aqua Crysta* keeping them going, the party began the ascent to the Larder Caves. Soon they were resting on the rocky terrace with its table and stools, and the eternal candle flame, the spirit of *Aqua Crysta,* still soaring strongly. It seemed like days ago since Jessica and Jamie had first seen her, when Quentin and Toby had lead them there. Jamie glanced at his watch. *Still two minutes past two*! This minute was so full it would soon explode he thought to himself as he followed the rest onwards and upwards into the mists.

Speaking of Quentin and Toby, it was they that met them when they eventually arrived at the yawning mouth of the first Larder Cave at the top of the staircase. Many other Aqua Crystans were there too, all excited about the adventure ahead with much spirited talk about how, sooner or later, the *Palace of Dancing Horses* would come to life for all to enjoy. Lepho shook many hands and lead his party through the amazing cave with its bounty of luscious brambles and berries, hazelnuts, acorns and walnuts all ready for the market stalls of Pillo and Galdo.

Just beyond a small side cave where juice was being squeezed from brambles by a group of heather smocked children, Lepho pointed to an arched wooden door which seemed to be the end of the main cave. Before opening it, he suggested they rested at a small table where they were served the delicious bramble juice in the familiar tankards. As they sipped, they were joined by the Aqua Crystans who were to make up the party to carry the *Seven Silver Keys of Sigmund* to the forest cellar and rescue the map. All told, there were twenty of them, soon enjoying the tasty juice and chattering about the tasks ahead. Gathered around were dozens more Aqua Crystans, mostly relatives of the ones chosen to be in Lepho's expedition. Many hugs and kisses were exchanged as well as blue strands of jay feathers which were meant to bring good fortune on any journey, but especially on journeys to the Upper World, where many dangers could be encountered.

When the tankards had been drained of every drop, Lepho opened the wooden door and the party, with the children at the fore, just behind Lepho, walked through the archway into the Harvest Passageway.

Jessica and Jamie had become accustomed to the bright light of *Aqua Crysta,* but once through the door it became much more gloomy, mainly because there were suddenly no crystals embedded in the walls. The rocks still glowed but only dimly...so dimly, in fact, that people just became dark shapes without faces to tell one from another. The way ahead could only just be seen...until Lepho suddenly veered off to the right and lifted the lid of what appeared to be a large wooden chest standing by the wall.

As the lid slowly opened, the passage was flooded with brilliance! Faces were lit and once more shadows danced on the walls and ceiling. The chest was filled to the brim with dazzling crystals like a coal bunker filled with coal...its glinting, gleaming mountain of crystals alive with light and warmth!

Lepho instructed everyone to help themselves to one or two crystals to illuminate the way ahead. Some were lashed to sticks to use like medieval flame torches, some were on rope loops to wear round the neck like diamond pendants, while others were set on plaited bands to wear on the head like solitaire tiaras.

When everyone was adorned with crystals, Lepho closed the lid of the chest. Although the brightness in the passage faded like a giant lamp being turned off, the effect of all the crystal lanterns was remarkable. Now, the tunnel before them could easily be seen as the troop of glow-worms marched along its rough, sloping floor. The going was fairly easy with the slope occasionally broken by small flights of steps with plaited grass handrails.

The children, with their crystal torches and head bands lead the

way with Lepho, who, although mostly quiet, now and again spoke of his life in *Aqua Crysta*.

Born in Pillo nearly a hundred and seventy harvests ago, just after the time a young Queen Victoria had come to the throne in the Upper World, he had lead a life of bliss...enjoying his harvest journeys, exploring *Aqua Crysta's* every nook and cranny, eating, drinking, dancing, crystal carving, playing chess. He seemed to know everyone in Pillo and Galdo, and was looking forward to one day becoming Deputy Mayor of Pillo, and then perhaps even the Mayor himself.

"But my favourite pastime, without doubt, is playing a satisfying game of '*Sanctum*'!" he beamed.

"We have chess up there," said Jamie, "but I've never heard of '*Sanctum*'!"

"It's a wonderful game, my friend!" Lepho enthused. "And one that you definitely will *not* find in the Upper World. It was invented in *Aqua Crysta* around two hundred harvests ago.We play with crystal pieces on a crystal board, and my ambition is to become victor of our 'All Comers Grand Harvest Championship'! Young Hiolle Twig has been our champion for two successive tournaments! It is time for a change! Nobody can win it *three times*! Although it has to be said that it was Hiolle's own father, Folf, who won three victories over a hundred harvests ago! His achievement is still celebrated in all parts of our realm!"

"I'm sure you will equal his record one harvest!" smiled Jessica, amazed at Lepho's enthusiam for the game. "Are the pieces like the ones in chess?"

"They are in a way, but we have ones called warriors, archers, priests, sages and fools! And they are coloured differently on each side, so when you capture one, you turn it round and it becomes one of *your* men! Instead of being taken off the board, as in chess!"

He delved into one of his pockets and brought out a small figure delicately carved from crystal.

"This is one of the fools from my set of pieces. I always carry him to bring good fortune!"

Lepho placed it on Jessica's palm. Its exquisite detail gleamed beneath her crystal torch.
It was decorated like a medieval minstrel in a chequered suit of pale pink and white on one side and deep red and white on the other.
"It's even got one of those funny, droopy three-cornered hats with bells on the ends!" laughed Jamie.
"Games are of the greatest importance," said Lepho. "They give our people...how should I put it?...something to enjoy and....talk about!"
"Like we have the weather, football and soaps!" smiled Jessica.
"Soaps? How can you talk about soaps?" wondered Lepho, curiously.
"Surely soap is soap, its function is to just keep one clean! You need pleasure and stimulation in life! How can soap give you such things?"
Jessica and Jamie grinned at one another and were just about to launch into a description of twenty-first century soaps, when Lepho produced five tiny dried clay cubes from one of his other pockets like a magician.
"Take *'Quintz'* for example!" he beamed. "These give endless enjoyment. See how they all have different letters on each of the faces. Shake them, toss them on a table between friends and you have endless pleasure and exercise for the head at the same time!"
Once again he placed one on Jessica's palm next to the crystal minstrel. Pressed into the clay were six letters, and the one that faced upwards was a *'J'*.
"J for Jessica and Jamie!" laughed Lepho.
"And Jonathan and Jane!" piped up Jamie.
"I shall show you how we play *Quintz* when we return, but meanwhile keep both tokens you hold in your hand. They will bring you good fortune!"
Jessica carefully placed the fool and the quint in her back pocket along with her charms.
"Do you ever long to explore the Upper World as a full size person?" asked Jessica as they walked along.
"I've often thought about what it would be like to climb straight over those great walls of stone up there and to pick up an acorn between my finger and thumb...but because I was born down here, I can only listen to

the tales of the Elders who can remember things like putting whole brambles in their mouths and riding on mammoth beasts called horses!"
It seemed incredible to Jessica and Jamie that Lepho had never known the full size Upper World as a full size person. But then again, *this* was *his* world and he seemed wonderfully happy. The Upper World was a different planet only to be visited when absolutely necessary!

The party walked on, sometimes everyone chatting at once, sometimes in silence, until Lepho suddenly stopped and pointed to a narrow passage leading off to the left.
"Time to change!" he announced with a flourish.
Everyone trooped into the passage and walked up to a line of hooks on the right hand wall. Dangling from each hook was a green smock made from beaten tree bark. All the Aqua Crystans quickly exchanged their heathery cloaks for the short smocks and Jonathan and Jane each slipped one over their clothes, suggesting that Jessica and Jamie do the same.
"The green keeps us well hidden from any passing Upper World eyes," explained Jonathan.
"Well *we* certainly didn't see anyone!" said Jamie.
"Mind you, we heard your horns once or twice!" added Jessica, remembering how the whole adventure had begun.
"That's our way of signalling to one another when we're too far apart to speak...different sets of notes mean different things. Otherwise we stay very, very quiet when we're up there!"

Back in the main passage, the way became gradually steeper and steeper, and darker and darker, as the rock changed into gritty sandstone, like in the forest cellar...completely without light giving crystals. But as the party rounded a bend, a glimmer of light gleamed in the distance in the shape of a small pyramid. As they approached, the glimmer became more and more brilliant, until Jessica and Jamie made it out to be a beautiful pile of fully glistening crystals. Again, the party was bathed in so much light it was like being back in *Aqua Crysta*.
The gleaming pyramid was a beacon marking a deep recess in the passage wall. Lepho stopped and pointed. This time, in neat rows along

the wall, shining brightly in the beacon's glow, were dozens of horns, all just like the one Jessica and Jamie had found at the *Charmstones*.
"You are now fully equipped for the rest of the journey!" said Lepho with a grin. "You have your light, your greenery and now your horn!"
The members of the party each took a horn and either attached them to their waist bands, or slung them over their shoulders with a plaited grass strap. When everyone was ready, the party once again began the upward plod towards the forest cellar, this time along a slightly less steep path. The glowing beacon faded behind them and the darkness returned. Soon, the travellers' luminous crystals began to reveal a narrower passage leading off to the left, even darker than the main passage. At last they had reached *Sigmund's Cave*, their first goal.

The deep, solid darkness set heartbeats racing as Lepho lead the way into the sharply dipping and steep cave, its floor strewn with rough rocks and rubble. In single file, occasionally tripping and slipping, the nervous explorers threaded their way carefully around boulders into the ever deepening darkness. There was no real path to speak of, nor steps nor hand rails. Jessica and Jamie began to think how difficult it was going to be to manhandle the Keys up into the main....
Suddenly, both of them nearly jumped out of their skins, as Lepho, just in front of them, stopped in his tracks and blew one long, warbling note on his horn. Everyone behind jostled to a halt and raised their eyes from the stony floor and gazed ahead in alarm!
Hanging in the darkness, pinned onto the blackness, were two green lights like emeralds. They vanished in a flash, then returned, closer, bigger and brighter.
"Hide everyone, hide!" called Lepho urgently in the dark. "Get to the sides of the cave, behind boulders, anywhere...*let it through*!!"
Heartbeats racing faster than ever, everyone scrambled for cover in any nook or cranny they could find, hiding their glowing crystals as best as they could. From their hiding places, nervous pairs of eyes gazed down into the black depths and watched as the two green jewels grew...and grew!

"Hide your crystals even more!" ordered Lepho. "Or it will have you!"
In the pitch blackness hearts pounded with fear as a loud, manic scuffling, scratching sound filled the dark. Then came the sound of heavy, rhythmic breathing...the wild panting of something alive!
Jessica and Jamie, wedged deep in a rocky crack, clutched one another tightly, panic stricken.
Their nightmare had begun!
The panting and scuffling was suddenly all around them, pressing them deeper and deeper into the crack.
Then, to their horror, they were suddenly trapped in their cold crevice by a wall of moving, warm softness...a wall of moving, smooth, silky fur!
They shut their eyes and held their breaths as the softness rushed by...and then, as quickly as it had appeared...it was gone!
The scuffling and panting faded, held breaths were released.
Whatever it was had gone...for now!
Jessica and Jamie gingerly stepped from their crack, as all about them, crystals slowly emerged from under smocks and inside pockets.
Worried faces appeared in the darkness and gazed back up the cave to the main passage. There was no sign of anything. The monster had gone, but in the gloom, it still held the travellers in the grip of fear.
"We must be alert for another!" warned Lepho, looking over his shoulder down into the cave. "At least their eyes give them away, so we must keep our crystals to the fore and *our eyes* peeled!"
"But, w..what was it?" stuttered Jamie.
"A *mouse,* young man, a mere mouse!" Lepho calmly replied, as though a Number 7 bus had just trundled by!
"A *mouse*!" chorused Jessica and Jamie in disbelief.
"You saw its eyes first, then its giant furry body! Definitely a mouse!" repeated Lepho. "Come on, there's no time to lose!"
For the first time, Jessica and Jamie, began to realise the dangers of being so small as they neared the Upper World. A mouse was not a mouse anymore. It was a rhinoceros! They shuddered to think what other perilous creatures may be scurrying about in the darkness. Shivers raced

up and down their spines,and they suddenly longed to be back in the cosy snugness of *Aqua Crysta*.
"Don't worry," Lepho tried to reassure them. "Such encounters are rare. The creatures of the Upper World keep themselves to themselves, and we hardly ever see them!"

But whatever anyone said, the experience of being within a whisker of that one, monstrous mouse had petrified them...but, believe me, it was *nothing* compared to what was to come!
Bravely, they tried their best to gather themselves and concentrate on the task at hand - the retrieval of the Keys. Lepho lead the way further into the cave, but now worries of simply keeping their footing had been replaced by a terrifying anxiety about what next could loom out of the blackness. The wonderful, fairytale dream had certainly turned into a heart-thumping, palm-sweating nightmare!

It was Lepho who suddenly jolted their minds and spirits back to what mattered - the tasks to grant the Queen her wishes. "We're here at last!" he announced, and pointed to a glimmer, not too far ahead, from a line of long, metallic shapes.
There they were...the giant *Seven Silver Keys of Sigmund*...all standing and leaning against the sandstone wall, balanced on their great, flat finger and thumb plates with their thick shafts pointing upwards. Each one sparkled as though it were brand new and unused, totally out of place in the rough, rocky cave.
They were huge, each one two or three times taller than Jamie, and they looked so heavy and unmovable. It was going to take a mammoth effort to move one, never mind all seven!
But, Lepho's plan was their match and soon the first metallic, ice-cold statue was hauled to the floor and then inched up the slope of

the cave. With much shoving and pushing, puffing and pulling, all seven were laid end to end, ready to be carried to the Harvest Passageway. The going was difficult, and with the thought of the mouse returning at the front of everyone's mind, the whole party was relieved when all *Seven Keys* were lying in the main passage, glittering in the crystal lights.

Everyone had a deserved rest, sitting legs asplay on the smooth floor, backs leaning on the gritty, sandstone walls. They were all exhausted, but knew that they hadn't far to go to the forest cellar. Soon the *Palace* would be alive with colour, movement and music as the Keys wound life into the metal toys. It was hard work but it would all be worth the sweat and toil!

Suddenly, Jessica stood up and listened in the silence.

"What was that?" she whispered, pointing up the dim passage.

"I'm sure I heard something from up there!"

Everyone froze.

Then everyone heard it!

A distant scuffling and scratching!

The mouse was back!!

Chapter 17

Far, far away...as far as straining eyes could make out in the gloom of the Harvest Passageway...something was moving! An uncertain shape, massive and bulky, jerkily filled the dim, distant tunnel. Lepho, without a trace of panic in his voice, ordered the travellers to get out of sight and cover their crystals, and, once more, every nook and cranny was filled, as the snuffling noises became louder and louder with the shape's every scurrying step.

Louder and louder, closer and closer.

Then it stopped.

Silence.

Just darkness.

Anxious eyes peeped from their hiding places and saw the two green jewels set in the blackness!

The travellers held their breaths. The mouse held its.

Then...it happened!!

From one of the hiding places, a dropped crystal clattered and rolled into the middle of the Harvest Passageway, illuminating all around. The Keys glinted...and there...almost close enough for Jessica and Jamie to touch, was an enormous, pink, quivering nose set in fine grey fur with long, silver whiskers frisking the air. Its great size took the children's breath away, as they flattened themselves even more against the rock in their cranny, trapped and in dread of the nose sensing they were there.

Its restless twitching and snuffling as it nudged the rogue crystal struck fear into them especially as the silvery whiskers brushed their legs.

Then, they saw one of the monster's great, black eyes, like a bulging, glassy cannonball with depths of emerald green...and then a huge, silky pink ear the size of a dustbin lid!
Suddenly, the mouse's attention moved to the first of the shining Keys. It pawed its fingerplate with both of its monstrous, pink feet, each claw like a small ivory tusk.
The Key moved and touched the next, the metallic clatter so alarming the mouse that in a sudden frantic scurry it suddenly darted over *all seven keys*!
The clatter of more metal on metal was like thunder in the cramped passage. The mouse panicked and fled down into the darkness of *Sigmund's Cave*, its huge grey body vanishing into the gloom followed by its great serpent of a tail behind it.
The snuffling and scuffling faded....and, then...silence...the mouse had gone.
One by one, anxious faces appeared and friendly crystal light filled the passage helping to drive away the fear. Lepho, his usual unruffled self, quickly gathered the party around him and explained that it would be wise to haul the Keys up to the *Palace* as soon as possible, although he wasn't expecting to see the mouse for quite a while after the shock it had had!
"You think the *mouse* had a shock!!" gasped Jessica. "I will never forget that mouse as long as I live! It'll be in my daydreams forever!"
"*Daymares* more like!" joked Jamie with a shiver. "And to think that I've always wanted a *pet* mouse! No-o-o, thankyou!"

The Aqua Crystans all laughed and began the task of lifting the first key and dragging it up the passage slope. The whole party heaved the heavy metal closer and closer to the *Palace* and it was just as they rested for the third time that Jamie noticed something ahead which made him call out with sheer joy!
"Look, there's the front door of the dolls' house...and there's a window on each side...and curtains!"
The travellers all laughed again. It was a sight they all knew well, but Jessica and Jamie just had to run ahead to have a closer look. A moment

later they were standing where the passage ended and opened out into the vast forest cellar - the *Palace of Dancing Horses* at last!

They ran and sat on the steps of the dolls' house and looked back along the Harvest Passageway to see the first, giant Key moving slowly towards them edged by countless sparkling crystals and the beaming faces of the Aqua Crystans. As their crystals came closer, more and more of the front of the dolls' house began to appear showing the fine, russet brickwork and the grand windows of the upper storeys. They could even see just beyond the house where the reds, greens, oranges, blues and yellows of the fairground toys awaited the Keys with as much excitement as the children and the rest of the party!

After the darkness of the Harvest Passageway, and, before that, the pinks and whites of *Aqua Crysta,* it seemed strange to see such a flood of colour...and even stranger still, to be sitting on the steps of what appeared to be an Upper World sized house!

They both would have loved to explore but they knew that they had to help with the Keys, and after that they would have to push on to the Upper World to retrieve the map. But at least they would be able to have a good look round as the party plodded through!

So with excitement bursting inside them, they joined in the carrying and dragging of the Keys into the *Palace*. Soon, all seven were propped up against the house walls waiting to do the work they hadn't done for many, many harvests.

"I suppose you two would like to investigate our beloved *Palace*?" suggested Lepho to Jessica and Jamie with a twinkle in his eye.

"You mean we've got time?" beamed Jessica, delighted by the invitation.

"We've made excellent progress despite the mouse!" said Lepho. "I think we can spare a few moments, but remember time is passing in the Upper World, so we will have to be on our way soon."

"Come on then!" burst Jamie, grabbing his sister's hand.

"We'll show you around!" chirped Jonathan, leaning on a windowsill, and very pleased to show off his nasty uncle's beautiful collection.

"Let's look around the house first!" called Jane, as she pushed open the maroon front door. "It's brilliant inside!"

"Before you go," Lepho reminded them, "remember we've still a long way to go to the map, so don't dilly-dally! The rest of us will meet you back here when you've seen all you wish... but don't take too long about it!"

The four *J's* jostled through the maroon front door into the flowery carpeted hall with its coat and umbrella stands. Before them was a wide flight of stairs and, to the left and right, dark wooden doors lead to several rooms.

The first room they entered was the lounge which Jessica and Jamie remembered seeing as giants from the other side of the house - the open side. It seemed so peculiar to be standing by the same dark, polished furniture and being able to sit on the velvetty, burgundy settee. Jamie picked up a violin which was lying on it and pretended to play an imaginary tune while Jessica accompanied him at the grand piano with crystal light shadows dancing on the ceiling. The children felt they were on a stage in a theatre, especially as the missing wall was filled with darkness.

Jonathan and Jane laughed at their companions' antics and then dashed through a doorway into the dining room with its twinkling chandelier dangling above a large, round table. It was set for a meal with white, gold rimmed crockery and silver cutlery circling an ornate candelabra. Richly wallpapered walls were decorated with gold-framed oil paintings of old country scenes and glass cabinets were bursting with china ornaments. A silver carriage clock sat on the carved marble mantel above the wide fireplace and a tall grandfather clock stood to attention by the doorway leading to the kitchen.

The kitchen was certainly the busiest room in the house. In the middle was another table set for a meal with a scrumptious, mouth watering pie surrounded with jars of pickles. Jamie, of course, just had to reach over and cut himself a slice, but was disappointed to find it as hard as rock, being made out of plaster! Jessica sat on one of the wooden chairs around the table and stared at all the pots and pans hanging from the walls, the great jet-black

fireplace with its oven doors and the tall dresser packed with more china plates. A white pot sink sat under the window and strung across a corner was the washing-line still sagging with pegged clothing.
"Race you to the school room!" shouted Jamie, as he suddenly turned from the pie and darted through the doorway, round the dining room table, through the lounge and into the hallway.
Galloping up the stairs, three at a time, they all poured into the classroom and collapsed onto the desk seats, puffing and panting. It was as though the bell had rung for the end of playtime and they were late for lessons!
"Who's been writing on the blackboard?" panted Jessica, recovering her breath and grinning at Jonathan and Jane. For, there, in neat joined up chalk handwriting were both of their names...the words that Jessica and Jamie hadn't quite been able to make out when they'd peered into the school-room as giants!
"Yes, it was us, the last time we were here!" admitted Jonathan. "We often play at school when we come up with a harvest party. It's great fun with all the others sat at desks chanting their five-times-table!"
"Come on, you lot!" urged Jane. "We ought to have a quick look around the fairground before we get back to Lepho!"
"O.K., race you to the front door!" challenged Jamie again, setting off for the front door at full pelt with the others trailing behind. They dashed down the stairs, across the hall and burst through the open front doorway, Jamie's crystal leading the way.
Outside was like daylight as all the crystals of Lepho's party greeted them. Lepho himself was standing at the foot of the steps.
"We've got to press on!" he announced, as the children tumbled towards him. "And as we've got to make our way through the fairground, as you call it, I am sure you will have ample chance to see the magic at close quarters!"

So, with crystals shining and lighting the way, the travellers marched past the house and then through all the motionless, metallic magic. Not toys now, but full size, life size Upper World marvels!
A little way beyond the house was the green and yellow striped helter-

skelter, now towering above them with its slide dizzily spiralling down the outside. At it's foot was a little door which Jessica and Jamie just couldn't resist!

"Lepho, can we have a go?" pleaded Jessica.

"Pleeease!" begged Jamie, almost on his knees. "Just one tiny little go?"
Lepho stopped, looked around, smiled and nodded.
In a trice, all four children, lead as usual by Jamie, were scrambling and clattering up the tin steps. Round and round, higher and higher until, gasping for breath, they reached the top. They emerged onto a little balcony which overlooked the whole fairground, its vivid and exciting colours gently lit by all the crystals below. Jamie pointed out the giant Ferris wheel which was even higher than the helter-skelter!
"It'll be brilliant when we wind up its clockwork!"
"It plays music as well, as it goes round," recalled Jonathan. "It was always our favourite after the carousel. That plays music too!"
"I can't wait to see them both packed with Aqua Crystans, all shouting and screaming as they whizz round! They'll have the time of their lives!" beamed Jane.
Jamie sat on the brink of the slide and looked down at the gleaming slope below his feet. "It's so shiny it looks as though it's been used every day!"
"It's because it doesn't have any clockwork parts," Jonathan explained, "so harvest parties use it every year. I think every Aqua Crystan has been down it at some time or another!"
"Well, here goes!" called Jamie. "Ger-oni-mo!!"
A moment later he'd vanished round the first corner and was quickly followed by the others, all whooping with delight as they sped down the spiral and crashed in a heap at the bottom with Lepho and the rest laughing yet again.

The travellers set off once more and wound their way through the fairground passing the beautiful carousel with its sparkling glass and dazzling white horses set frozen on their golden, barley-sugar pillars. How wonderful it would be when the horses really danced to the fairground music and had Aqua Crystans clinging on!

Next they passed the dodgems with a huddle of tiny, chunky, coloured cars all in one corner as though they were having a little get together. Then came some smaller roundabouts and side-shows before the party reached the end of the fair.

Beyond the fairground came all the rest of the toys. Before, Jamie had been able to pick up the green racing car with its dashing driver, but now he could look straight into the determined eyes of the helmeted racing driver with his stiff green scarf. He looked so keen to take on all the other racing cars, and Jamie could hardly wait to wind up his clockwork to see if he was as fast as he looked!

"I liked the motorcycles best!" said Jonathan, polishing a red and yellow motorbike and side-car with his shirt cuff. "I remember the one and only time our uncle let us play with them in the farmyard. He was in a good mood for a change! Coronation Day back in Nineteen-Fifty-Three...the day the Upper World's Queen Elizabeth was crowned, and a few days after Mount Everest had been climbed for the first time. This one was the fastest! Come and have a look at it!"

Jonathan introduced Jamie to the frozen riders, Bill and Bert, in their blue suits and gold helmets and he could see that the bike had definitely been Jonathan's favourite toy when he'd lived at *Old Soulsyke*.

"You can take Bert out of the side-car, but we've never been able to do that since we've been in *Aqua Crysta*. He's just too heavy for us now!"

As the flickering, twinkling line of crystals made its way slowly across the cellar floor, the roof could just be seen and the shadowy wall hollow with its row of rusty tankards and the tarnished ruby-studded dagger. Jessica and Jamie thought of the blue bicycle bell which they'd left on the shelf, but decided not to say anything to Jonathan and Jane.

Next came the life size railway with its line of beautifully detailed, green and cream, old-fashioned carriages set upon gleaming rails and headed by the maroon steam engine.

Jane climbed up into one of the carriages and waved from one of the open windows.

"I bet they're just the same as the ones that used to be at Sandsend - the *camping coaches* dad was telling us about," said Jessica.
"Did your father used to stay in the *camping coaches at Sandsend* ?" beamed Jonathan, suddenly amazed at Jessica mentioning them.
"That's a coincidence! So did we!"
Jessica and Jamie looked at one another, equally amazed!
"They were great!" enthused Jane. "Bunk beds and paraffin lamps! That week away from *Old Soulsyke* every year was the only time we were really happy. Even our nasty uncle relaxed and treated us like human beings! We played all day long with the local Sandsend children, rode donkeys, went fishing..."
"You didn't come across an...*Edward Dawson*, by any chance, did you?" asked Jessica.
"Come off it, sis!" laughed Jamie. "That *would* be a coincidence! Surely you don't think that Jonathan and Jane met dad?"
"Shut up, you!" retorted Jessica. "There's no harm in asking!"
But Jonathan and Jane looked at one another and shook their heads.
"No, I can't remember an Edward," said Jane, "but, mind you, it was a long, long time ago!"
"I can remember Jack...and Douglas...and William...and Ted, of course!" recalled Jonathan.
"...And the station-master, Mr Simpson," added Jane, "with his shiny buttons and whistle!"
"Then there was the tunnel we used to explore...!" remembered Jonathan.
"And stamping out the fires by the track!" suggested Jamie, thinking of his father's memories he'd related during their trip to Sandsend. It was amazing that the same sort of holiday seemed to have been shared by Jonathan and Jane *and* his father as a boy!
"How do you know about that?" asked a puzzled Jane.
"About what?" said Jamie.
"How do you know about the little fires caused by sparks from the railway engines and how we used to stamp them out?" repeated Jane.
"I told you, our dad stayed at Sandsend in the Nineteen-Fifties!" said Jamie. "He was telling us about it the other day. I suppose he used to do

the same things you did, and probably met the same local children!"
"But you must have stayed in the railway carriages during different weeks during the summer," Jessica concluded. "That would explain it all, but you must admit that its one heck of a coincidence!"

Suddenly, all thoughts of the past vanished as, in the gloomy distance, the shape of the great wooden door towered above them...the door that lead to the well...the well that had brought Jessica and Jamie into *Aqua Crysta* in the first place!

Lepho was the first to reach the massive wall of wood and there was such a wide gap beneath it, he was able to walk straight under!
The whole party filed under and were soon assembled on the wide rocky ledge where Jessica and Jamie had tightly crouched before pushing open the stiff door, what seemed a lifetime ago!
"Be careful of the edge!" warned Lepho, as they both gingerly walked towards the sheer drop of the well shaft.

In front of them, across the black emptiness, they could just see the huge stones of the opposite wall and an enormous iron rung. Jamie walked up to the very brink of the black hole and gazed down into the eerie void, just able to make out the next rung down in his crystal light, his hair blowing in the scented, warm breeze.
"But how are we going to get to the top?" asked Jessica looking back at Lepho. "Surely we can't climb the well's wall?"
"No, my friend!" replied Lepho. "We have a much easier way to the Upper World! You will see!"
Jessica and Jamie ran back towards the rest of the Aqua Crystans and found the whole party gathered around a mysterious new object glinting in the crystal beams. The huge, glassy disc was like a giant mirror doubling the crystal light, the reflections enchanting the curious Aqua Crystans.
"It's my torch!" called Jamie, as he ran over and tried to clamber onto the enormous, rubber battery barrel behind. With a shove from his sister he pulled himself onto the top and pushed the button with all his strength.
"It's...no...use, I can't press...it down!" he gasped.

"Pull me up!" called Jessica, on tip-toes, stretching her arms up the curved barrel. With Jamie pulling and Jonathan and Jane pushing, she managed to scramble up to her brother and then they both pressed as hard as they could onto the button. Suddenly it clicked down and instantly the ledge and the green, mossy wall were flooded with the brightest light the startled Aqua Crystans had ever seen! The whole party gazed around the rocky walls shielding their eyes from the sudden glare.
"It won't last long!" exclaimed Jamie from on top of the barrel. "The batteries were running out when we left the torch here on the way down!"
And indeed, as he spoke, the light from the magical mirror began to flicker and fade until there was just a faint glow from the bulb. Then, with a final splutter, the bulb vanished and the glass disc once more became a mirror for the crystal lights.

After Lepho had calmed his bemused, and slightly alarmed countrymen, and Jamie had tried to explain the power of his torch, the party moved towards a small cave entrance at the side of the ledge about halfway between the door and the well. Inside, the Harvest Passageway became gradually steeper and the surrounding rock was more crumbly and damp. The smells of soil and the forest floor's rotting leaves and wood were in the air. Smells that told Jessica and Jamie that they were nearly back in the Upper World!
"Not far to go, everyone!" encouraged Lepho, as the travellers trudged up the dark, dank and, sometimes slippery, tunnel.
Soon, the welcome, cool kisses of wafts of fresh night air played on the cheeks of the climbers, as they scrambled over the rough, gritty floor of the passage.

Suddenly, Lepho froze in his tracks and signalled frantically for everyone to flatten themselves against the right hand wall of the tunnel. Thoughts of the mouse immediately flashed through the minds of one and all, as crystals were quickly concealed...only to be brought out again as the first of half-a-dozen, heavily armoured woodlice trundled down the passage, antennae quivering and legs racing. Even though they were much, much smaller than the mouse, they certainly alarmed Jessica and Jamie, although everyone else seemed to take them in their stride! Each one was about as long as a tennis racket, and they looked like a herd of some kind of extinct prehistoric creatures! Thankfully, they seemed harmless enough as they just went about their gentle, nocturnal foraging, but it was definitely strange to see them this size! The last time they'd seen scurrying Upper World woodlice was when they'd lifted the well-head stone, and then they'd been no longer than a finger nail!

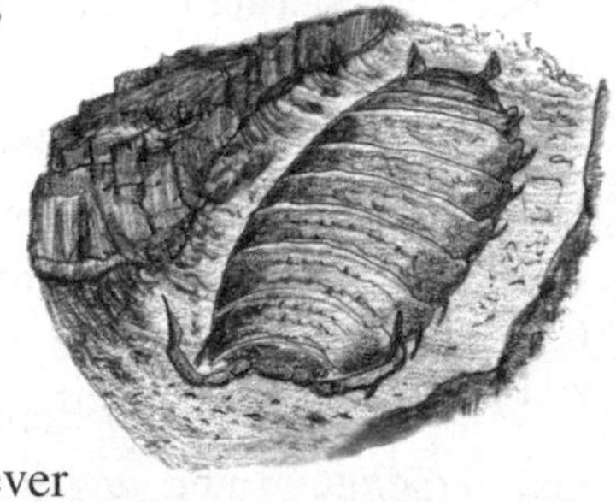

But the surprise of seeing woodlice was *nothing* compared to their next encounter with the Upper World!

"Worm ahead!!" called Lepho suddenly, pointing up the soily passage, and Jessica and Jamie nearly collapsed with fright! There, just in front of them was the greatest glistening, slimey, squirming snake they'd ever seen, emerging from a hole in the side of the tunnel. It was at least four or five times thicker than an anaconda, it's eyeless, tapered head weaving about menacingly from side to side like some man-eating, mythical monster!

"No need to worry!" reassured Jane, putting a friendly arm around Jamie, who was squinting through his fingers. "It'll be out of our way in no time. It's quite harmless!"

"Y..you're sh..sure about that?" asked Jamie a touch anxiously, suddenly imagining the creature coiling around him like a giant python and then swallowing him whole!

"Just think worm, think puppy!" laughed Jonathan. "We come across them every harvest and we've never had a problem yet!"

"Th..there's always a f..first time!" stuttered Jamie.

On and on, the huge creature squeezed out of its hole like never-ending, flesh coloured toothpaste and headed up the passage. Then, after its tapered back end finally emerged and followed the rest, its head seemed to be sucked into another hole. A moment later it had vanished, leaving just a sticky trail behind on the tunnel floor.

“That...was...*incredible*!” sighed Jessica at last, peeping from behind Lepho.
“It was! It was incredible!” agreed Jamie as calmly as he could, marching up the passage and suddenly finding his courage and his imaginary sword. “Worms! No problem at all! Next time, you just watch out, Mister Worm, the early Jamie will have *you*!”

Soon, small woody roots crossed the passage and formed obstacles to be climbed over...and then...all at once...they all felt the full force of the night breeze!
They had reached the end of the Harvest Passageway.
Beyond lay the Upper World.
Jessica and Jamie began to wonder what other little treats their own world would have in store for them. They looked at one another nervously, yet both were filled with excitement rather than fear. Somehow they felt safe with their new friends. After all, Lepho and the rest of the Aqua Crystans had been on countless harvest expeditions and returned safely. There was nothing to worry about! Was there?
‘*Stick together*!’ - their father’s words of advice - flashed through their minds, and they felt even safer. Jessica hugged her brother. Together, they could face anything!

The tunnel had ended in a vast, wooden cavern lit by an eerie, milky light.
“It’s moonlight!” called Jamie, as he darted out into the fresh air. “We’re there, we’re back on the surface!”
“Hello, *George*!” laughed Jessica dancing in the moonlight with her brother, but then they stopped and both began to realise that although they knew this *had* to be the forest, things were not quite the same as before.
In fact, things were *very different*!
Very different, indeed!!!
In an instant, their fears had returned!

Chapter 18

For a start, *George's* soft, bouncy floor of pine-needles was now an incredible tangle of slender, tapering woody stakes, each the size of a fence-post. Masses and masses of them, all overlapping and pointing in every direction, and quite sharp and lethal looking, although light enough to easily pick up. Scaly cones the height of the bedrooms back at *Deer Leap* were scattered about on top of the pine-needles, some half buried and some with their scales nibbled away by squirrels.
The occasional green grass shoot soared from the floor and swayed in the cool breeze above their heads, but the real shock was the woody cavern itself.

Its walls were the thick, flaky roots of a tree! The party had emerged from the Harvest Passageway at the foot of a colossal spruce tree. Jessica and Jamie stared upwards at the huge, dark, windowless skyscraper that towered higher...and higher... and higher into the night sky until sky and tree merged into one, amid a jumble of branches. It seemed to be a skyscraper the size of which the Upper World had yet to see. It was so gigantic in width and height it took their breaths away. It was absolutely awesome. Majestic, magnificent and menacing all rolled into one.
And, of course, it wasn't alone. Another monstrous colossus reached for the sky just beyond the distant ridge of pine-needles, its dark, fearsome shape almost overpowering Jessica and Jamie as their eyes followed its deadly straight walls up to its own tangled silhouette of branches and twigs. Both trees seemed quite capable of supporting the starry, black

sky which lay above them. Surely, no one in the history of the Upper World had ever seen anything as large...and it gradually dawned on them just how tiny, helpless and vulnerable they were!

Fearful, frightening thoughts flashed through their minds of deer crashing through the undergrowth, owls swooping down upon them, talons drawn, squirrels searching for fallen cones. It even occurred to them that a single, innocent, plummeting cone could wipe out the whole party in a split second!

Fear began to take a stranglehold on Jessica and Jamie. It had crept up on them and fingered their minds in a way that they had never known. Thoughts of dad and *Deer Leap* and even their snug memories of *Aqua Crysta,* and the homes of Jonathan and Jane and Queen Venetia couldn't fend off fear's tightening grip. Jessica was even beginning to feel tearful as she clutched her brother's hand. Jamie hugged her, knowing exactly how she was feeling. In a weak, jittery voice he asked Lepho how far it was to the well, so the business of the night could be seen to and they could return to the safety of the Crystal Water.

Lepho calmly reassured them that it was only about six trees away, as he put his arms around the shoulders of the clearly disturbed children.

"It's just up and down a few pine-needle drifts," he said. "Follow me and we'll soon be there and then we can complete our task!"

Jamie fingered his watch to ward off his nerves and suddenly noticed the seconds ticking away!

"Jessica, time has begun again!" he exclaimed. "It's now *four* minutes past two! It must have started again when we stepped back into the Upper World!"

"Indeed, you are correct," said Lepho. "Time marches on relentlessly up here. We must make haste so as not to lose too much!"

Fear began to lighten its grip on Jessica and Jamie as they thought about their promises to Queen Venetia concerning the rescue of the map and the bringing of life to the *Palace of Dancing Horses*. The awesome size of the trees and the dangers seemed to lessen as the party began to make its way over the giant pine-needles towards the crest of the first drift. Now, instead of solid rock beneath the travellers' feet, there was a scented springy softness, although the going was more of a scramble than an easy walk. They passed a huge, brownish, up-turned toadstool, its smooth dome etched with tooth nibble marks. And at the summit of the first drift was an untidy pile of cone scales, the tell-tale sign of a squirrel's picnic spot! Just beyond was the great gnawed stump of the cone the squirrel had stripped, a reminder that creatures the size of dinosaurs were at large in the dark!

Down dale and up hill they marched, passing two more towering trees as they went. At the foot of a third they rested, sitting with legs stretched out over the pine-needles and leaning against the cracked, flaky bark of the skyscraper. As Jamie stared upwards at the mighty wall, the crescent moon suddenly appeared from behind a mass of silver tinged cloud. The woodland floor was flooded with moonlight making everything almost as brightly, milky white as in *Aqua Crysta*. The giant trees cast giant shadows, the greeny brown needles became silvered and the deep, distant depths of *George* could be sensed. The children were certainly in the Upper World, but it was not the Upper World they had come to know. They felt as much like strangers here as they had been in *Aqua Crysta*!

Lepho rose to his feet and signalled everyone to follow.

"We must use the light!" he whispered, as though the wildlife of the forest was listening. "It will make our task all the easier, but, I have to say, all the more dangerous! Keep your eyes peeled!"

Soon, the wanderers were marching down a slope into yet another wide, smooth valley. Jessica, Jamie, Jonathan and Jane ran ahead and quickly climbed the opposite slope, hoping to see the flat, stone slabs of the well-head.

But instead, on reaching the summit, the four children fell flat onto the pine-needles and stared with disbelief at what was before them...or should I say...at *who* was before them!!

Chapter 19

Jessica turned and signalled to the rest of the party to take cover, keep quiet and conceal their crystals, as she and the others began to slither back down the slope so that just their heads protruded above the ridge of pine-needles, their eyes fixed on the monster ahead. For there, sat at the foot of the next tree was an enormous, Upper World man, clad from head to toe in white! White rubber boots, baggy white trousers, a chunky white top and a white beret perched above a black bearded and moustached face. Thankfully he was asleep, but one of his hands was grasping a long, thin tubular metal gadget...also white, with a great metal disc at its base resting on the pine-needles. It looked like some sort of vacuum cleaner!

"It's a metal detector!" whispered Jamie. "And I think he's a soldier judging by his beret!"

"But why is a soldier here, in the middle of a forest, in the middle of the night with a metal detector?" replied Jessica.

"And soldiers don't wear white, do they?" whispered Jane.

"They do in snowy places for camouflage," suggested Jamie, "but not normally in the middle of a forest at night! Unless, of course he *wants* to be seen!"

"But what's he doing here in the first place?" asked Jane. "And what's that metal detector for?"

The man remained motionless as the curious quartet looked on, gradually joined by Lepho and some of the bolder Aqua Crystans. Just his chest lifted and sank as he slowly breathed, in what seemed to be a peaceful sleep. He was a sleeping giant like the one Jack met at the top of the Beanstalk. Only this one was real and not in a fairytale! All of his hidden onlookers could have easily stood on his other hand, which lay by his side on the pine-needles, an enormous gold band glinting in the moonlight...his wedding ring!

"I can't understand why he's got a metal detector, either," puzzled Jessica.

"Perhaps he's looking for Roman coins!" suggested Jamie with a grin.

"Or perhaps he's just had a picnic and lost his knife and....!"

"Sssshh, listen!" Jonathan burst out. "I can hear something in the sky!"

A distant, whirring sound was silhouetted plainly against the silence of the forest. An incessant, throbbing sound. Like some kind of engine above the distant treetops. As the onlookers averted their gaze from the man and up into the darkness, the sound became louder...and louder...and louder!!

Suddenly, the white soldier giant awoke and his great bearded face looked around. The children and the Aqua Crystans flattened themselves against the pine-needles as a huge black shape in the sky moved over them, blocking out the moon.

The whirring engine sound became even louder, and then, all at once, a brilliant white light beam shot down from the shape to the forest floor. It swelled and brightened even more, the noise became deafening and then a breeze began to shake the distant mass of branches and twigs. The breeze turned into a wind that wrenched the treetops to and fro and rustled the undergrowth. Then the wind became a gale picking up the pine-needles and hurling them around the terrified party. The white giant got to his feet, his clothes billowing in the tempest. And then, in the confusion of wind, tossed pine-needles and the dazzling light, two more similarly white clad giants appeared from the depths of the forest and joined the first...all completety unaware of the chaos about their mammoth sized, rubber booted feet!

None of the travellers had experienced anything like it! The gale tugged relentlessly at their tunics and their hair as though it was trying to pick them up and toss them around with the needles. Petrified of being swept off the ground, they clung to one another and kept as flat as they could.

Through squinted eyes they could make out the equally terrifying moving white shapes of the soldier giants towering above them like a trio of animated, ghostly snowmen, realising that at any moment they could all be wiped out under the heel of a single boot!
The dazzling white beam had turned night into day, seemingly melting the branches and twigs in its glow. The noise was at its loudest, even louder than the raging gale, its throbbing beat shaking the forest floor!
"It's...a...*hel...i...cop...ter*!!" gasped Jamie, in as loud a voice as he could muster against the wind and knowing he would never be heard by the giants.
"It's a *helicopter*!" he called out again. "And look! There's a rope ladder being lowered through the light beam... it's coming down between the trees!"

Slowly, the twisting, jerking serpent wound down from the dazzling treetops, writhing in the buffeting wind, until its head was grasped by one of the giants. He steadied it while the other two began the upward climb towards the white brilliance that now seemed to fill the sky. Each soldier carried a metal detector and a huge, bulging, white plastic bag. As each monstrous soldier melted into the dazzling light, the third began his ascent, again armed with metal detector and bulky sack, and, as he, too, was swallowed by the light, the ladder again began to buck and twist as if suddenly stung. Then it began to shorten as it was wound in, until it vanished into the white.

The whirring engine roared, changed tone and lifted from the treetops. The white beam was extinguished as suddenly as it had appeared, and the gale below became a wind and then a breeze as hearts began to pound less loudly. The welcome moon peeped out from behind the shrinking shape and the nightmare was over, as peace returned to the forest. The whirring engine faded in the distance...and then was gone, hopefully never to return!

One by one, startled and shocked Aqua Crystans staggered to their feet and climbed to the summit of the ridge to join the

others who were standing on the crest bathed in moonlight. Lepho gathered them all together and spoke in his normal calm and quiet manner. Nothing, it seemed, could ruffle him!
"I can sense your shock, my fellows, and I, too, am shaken by these wonders of the Upper World, but our mission must be completed before we return. First, we must make our way to the map with the help of our friends, and then we must return to Queen Venetia."
He continued in an even quieter voice, and in even more serious tones.
"It has to be said that during many, many harvest visits to these parts, never before have I witnessed such sights! I sense that there is danger afoot. Our tranquil world is threatened, our Queen's realm is in peril, as foreseen by the candle flame, *Lumina*. Especially so if the men from the sky chanced upon the well-head and the map. We must make haste and discover the truth!"

And with that, Lepho began to sprint down the slope, followed by the rest of the expedition party, each and every member anxious to know what the giants had stumbled across. Had they found the well and the map? Was *Aqua Crysta* in danger?
They were soon to find out!

Lepho stopped sharply at the top of the next ridge. He raised his arm slowly and pointed ahead. What he had seen filled him with sorrow. The others, sensing his dismay, quickly gathered around their leader and gazed at what lay before them all. It was enough to fill their hearts with dread, and chill them to the core!

A tall, slender, red and white striped pole sprouted straight up from the forest floor, nowhere near as wide as a tree, but as tall as one of the soldier giants. It shone in the moonlight and at its top hung a gently fluttering yellow flag, reminding Jessica of the *Goldcrest's* sail. Next to the foot of the pole, where it seemed to explode from the pine-needles, was the great black opening which lay between the huge, flat slabs of stone which Jessica and Jamie had uncovered.
The well-head had been found!
And marked!

Suddenly, and quite unexpectedly, Lepho rushed wildly down the slope and flung himself desperately at the foot of the gigantic pole. Frantically, he pulled and tugged at it as though he was trying to uproot it. The rest were speechless as they looked on, totally bemused by this sudden change of character. What had happened to the calm, unflappable Lepho? It seemed that he had finally snapped!

"Don't just stand and stare!" he called angrily. "It's got to be removed as quickly as possible! Come and help me!"

Of course, the pole wouldn't budge a whisker, even with them all pushing and shoving at once. It had been well and truly planted in the ground by one of the soldier giants. No amount of effort would ever uproot it!

"We cannot allow such a threat to our Queen and her realm!" Lepho gasped, his strength beginning to ebb away. "But I feel so helpless!"

After one last effort he fell backwards from the stubborn pole and collapsed on the pine-needles.

"But *we* can help!" assured Jamie, kneeling by the distraught leader. "We will pull it up from the ground when we come up the well in our Upper World full size!"

"And we'll close the well-head and cover it!" added Jessica.

"But if some mishap should occur on your journey, you may not complete the task!" insisted Lepho. "We must remove the pole and conceal the well now!"

"But, Lepho, you know that is *impossible*!" said Jessica. "Surely we must return to *Aqua Crysta* and then begin our journey back here. It is your only hope!"

Lepho sadly looked up at the fearsome pole, his face as solemn as his fellow Aqua Crystans had ever seen it.

"You are right!" he admitted, with renewed hope. "After all, it is said that *you* are the *saviours* of our magical land and her people, so I will act on your advice. But first, before we return and leave this horror, will you see if the map is where you left it?"

Without a moment's delay, Jessica and Jamie, followed by Jonathan and Jane, were dashing over the pine-needles towards the two great, stone towers that arose from a tangle of thick, silvered ribbons of grass. Each massive, slightly leaning pillar was supported by a wall of enormous, chunky rocks full of mossy, dark caves and green vertical cliffs. Although merely gateposts they looked more like giant, prehistoric standing stones where ancient folk might have worshipped the sun. In the moonlight, the walls seemed like impenetratable barriers stretching away into the gloom of the forest, yet Jessica and Jamie remembered how easy it had been to climb over them...just a few minutes ago before the whole adventure had begun!!

As Jessica fought her way through the long grass and rounded the foot of one of the posts, she suddenly stopped and stared anxiously ahead. This was where she had left her backpack she was sure...by the post, propped up against its wall...but there was definitely no sign of it!

"I'm sure this is where I left it," she called, "but it all looks so different with everything so big!"

"What about by the other gatepost? Could you have left it there?" asked Jane.

Jessica shook her head.

"No, no, I'm sure I put it down next to this one," she said quietly, beginning to feel frustrated and annoyed.

"That means the soldiers must have taken it!" exclaimed Jonathan.

"But none of them had it when they climbed up into the helicopter!" burst Jessica, angrily.

"It must have been in one of those big, white sacks they hauled up!" suggested Jamie.

Jessica looked heartbroken.

"If we hadn't come here in the first place, none of this would have happened!" snapped Jessica, beginning to regret even finding *Old Soulsyke*. "The map would have still been behind the wallpaper at the farm and the well wouldn't have been discovered!"

"Nonsense!" said Jane. "If anyone's to blame, it's Jonathan and me for drawing the map and leaving it behind when we ran away! It was bound to be found sooner or later!"

"It's pointless arguing about who's to blame!" said Jamie, beckoning the others to follow him. "What we've got to do is get back to Lepho, break the news to him, and get back to *Aqua Crysta*!!"
"Perhaps we ought not to tell him," suggested Jessica. "He was upset enough seeing the pole. Imagine his reaction when we tell him the map's vanished too! It means that even with the pole uprooted, the soldiers will be able to find the well-head again!"
"No, I think we should keep him in the picture," insisted Jonathan. "He's put his trust in us. It would be unfair to deceive him. After all, he's just about the wisest person in *Aqua Crysta*. He'll know what to do!"

Jane and Jamie agreed, and so, with hearts thudding, the quartet returned rather sheepishly to the rest of the party. They didn't, of course, have to say a word to Lepho. He had guessed, and just stared at them with sad, distant eyes. Then he slowly averted his gaze to the open well-head that lead to his beloved, secret world.
Its beautiful, ancient, peaceful innocence open for all to find, plunder and destroy!
Although inwardly in turmoil, he remained calm and spoke quietly.
"We must not breathe a word of this to the Queen until you have fulfilled her wish to bring the *Palace of Dancing Horses* to life.
But we must act with all haste!"

Once more, he looked at the four children.
"Much will depend upon you when we return. First, you must make the hazardous journey up through the mists and into the well and on to the forest cellar. *Sigmund's Keys* are in place, ready for you to grant the Queen's wish. Then you must climb and destroy this wicked flagged pole and conceal the well-head...and, after that, you must discover the whereabouts of the map!"
He paused.
"Much rests upon your young shoulders! Are you equal to the deeds ahead?"
The children looked at one another and realised that they alone, all four of them, were the only ones who could save *Aqua Crysta*. They all knew

enough of the ways of the Upper World to know that if the enchanting realm beneath their feet were to be discovered, then its magic, tranquility and eventually its people, would be destroyed without doubt.
It was Jessica who plucked up the courage to reply.
"Each of us feels guilty for what has happened," she began, "but we will try our hardest to put things right. We won't rest until the well-head has been hidden..."
"And our map has been destroyed!" promised Jonathan.
"Then onward to *Aqua Crysta*!" Lepho suddenly exclaimed, in a tone of suddenly renewed determination and optimism. "Long live our secret world, and long live Queen Venetia!"
"Long live *Aqua Crysta*! Long live the Queen!" everyone echoed, as they all gathered around their leader, touched by his enthusiasm and strength. The tasks ahead *would* be completed, and any doubts *had* to be dismissed from their thoughts. Success had to be their goal...the only goal!

So, with a refreshed spring in their steps, the party followed Lepho back the way they had come. Back to the Harvest Passageway with its entrance nestled within the roots of the gigantic, moonlit tree. But, no sooner had they taken a dozen steps, that new determination suddenly vanished as one of the Aqua Crystans screamed a blood curdling scream, then the words they all secretly feared...
"Hide, hide, the monster from the sky is back!!"
Everyone froze and listened.
They all heard it.
The far away throbbing of an engine in the night.
The helicopter had returned!!!

Chapter 20

In next to no time the treetops were flooded with gleaming, white light, the silence of the forest was shattered and the still air was stirred once again into a fury. The travellers dived to the forest floor grasping either one another or bundles of pine-needles to avoid being picked up by the grasping wind which tore and tugged at their clothes and hair. Fear once again pounded in their hearts as the noise reached its loudest and night turned into day. But this time, fear turned into terror as a new, horrific sound filled their ears, much closer than the helicopter. A terrible crashing and breaking of branches, and a stirring and tossing of the undergrowth which numbed the party into a frozen, fearful despair.

The giant forest seemed to be falling down on them, as, through squinted eyes, they made out immense, fast moving, dark shapes...a tidal wave of slender legs, whirling hooves and massive bodies rushing through the trees. Flaring nostrils, staring, wild eyes and dashing sabre horns flashed by, only two or three pine-needle drifts away, accompanied by flying twiglets and tossed cones spinning from every direction.

A herd of deer, petrified and spooked by the noisy hovering invader had been sent rampaging through the forest as one, single great beast of the night!

In what seemed like a never ending dozen or so seconds this new monster had crashed by and vanished into the dark followed by the helicopter, its bright light fading and its throbbing engine melting into the welcome silence. Another nightmare was over and for a short while the travellers rested and soaked up the moonlit tranquility, hoping and praying that they would reach the Harvest Passageway with no more terrors to endure.

Thankfully they did. In fact the whole journey home was uneventful, not even the mouse making an appearance, and, as with all homeward journeys it seemed to take half as long as the outward one! Only stopping for a brief rest in the lounge of the dolls' house and to change back into Aqua Crystan clothing, the members of the expedition were soon returning their crystals to the chest near to the end of the passage. It was certainly a tired and exhausted party which was greeted in the Larder Caves with a celebratory feast fit for kings. Every table top was festooned with samples of food and drink from all over the realm. Jamie just stared with his eyes and mouth wide open.

"Now remember we've still got things to do, little brother!" warned Jessica. "You'll never get up the rope to the well if you eat too much!"

"For that I'll need energy!" replied Jamie, licking his lips. "And the fuel tank's getting a bit low!"

"Just don't overdo it, that's all!" said Jessica. "Nibble bits, don't gobble lots, as dad's always telling you!"

Moments later, every member of the expedition party was tucking into the delicacies. Apparently, Queen Venetia had ordered the feast as a thankyou to the brave travellers and to Jessica and Jamie in particular. And, as Lepho commented, the menu she had prepared was one of the best ever witnessed in *Aqua Crysta*!

MENU

Toadstool Roast with Fried Heather Tips
Acorn Slices with Fern Frond & Daisy Dip
Roast Chestnut Fingers with Dandelion Sauce
Seed Cake & Dried Buttercup Petal Flakes
Walnut & Sycamore Wing in Rowan Jelly
Hazelnut Chunks with Bramble
Meadow Sweet Loaf & Forget-me-not Dip
Royal Dried Wimberry with Bluebell Sauce

Every scrumptious mouthful was washed down with a variety of refreshing fruit juices, and, as you can imagine, Jessica and Jamie (especially Jamie!) enjoyed everything they tried! When they met the *Chief Cooks of the Realm by Royal Appointment* - Megan Magwitch of Torrent Lodge and Dill Stem of Middle Floss - they congratulated them on their tasty fayre and wished they could take a hamper back with them to the Upper World!

Not a word was uttered to anyone about the ordeals of the forest nor the missing map, and by the time the travellers were sailing down the Floss aboard the *Goldcrest*, all were so calm and relaxed it was as though the whole venture had never happened! *Aqua Crysta* was weaving its magic again and Jessica and Jamie almost felt as though they really *were* returning home...and home had strangely and magically become the enchanted kingdom itself. As they sped through the wonderful crystal cavern, towards the dangling rope to the Upper World, they both felt comfortable and safe. It was as though they'd lived there all their lives. They felt secure and amongst friends. Indeed, it was only the rope, which Jessica pointed out as the vessel began to slow down, that reminded them that *this* was *not* their real home!
Instead, their real home lay beyond the cavern's lofty mists and beyond the top of the well, in that nightmare of a forest! Although, as they both realised, the next time they would see *George,* at least they would be full sized Upper World people...or so they hoped!
Cones would be cones, trees would be trees and deer would be deer! Nevertheless, it was strange to feel so much at home in *Aqua Crysta* and to almost regard the Upper World as a distant planet...an *alien world*!!
In fact, the magic of the place had got such a hold on them, that if it hadn't been for the tasks they had to perform, and seeing their father and *Deer Leap* again, they would have been tempted to stay!
It was *that* thought that made them both feel uncomfortable and somehow guilty, as the *Goldcrest* came to a smooth halt on the pebbly shore of the Floss, at the very spot they had landed in the first place. And to their great surprise, standing on the shore, amid a cheering band of Aqua Crystans was Queen Venetia herself!

The Queen, dressed in green, her golden hair blowing slightly in the breeze, greeted Lepho and he smiled and bowed.
"The task is done, your Majesty," he began. "*Sigmund's Keys* are ready to set the horses dancing!"
The Queen smiled with a twinkle in her eyes, but then anxiously asked of the whereabouts of the map.
"And what of the map?" she asked.
Lepho spoke again, as calmly and reassuringly as he could.
"The map you speak of is safe and beyond the eyes of the Upper World. Have no fears, your Majesty!"
Lepho's words sent chills through the minds of the children and the rest of the party, but the Queen was convinced by the news and that was all that mattered for the time being. She then thanked the children for their endeavours so far and asked whether or not they were still determined to make the journey through the mists at the bottom of the well and risk the possible unknown dangers. Jessica answered for all four of them.
"We have talked about it many times during our visit to the Upper World, your Majesty, and we are all just as determined as ever!"
The others nodded and the Queen looked at each in turn with grateful and admiring eyes. "What is your plan?" she gently enquired.
Jamie answered, looking at the two dangling halves of rope that touched the shore.
"The middle of the rope is looped over the last rung of the well's ladder. If I secure myself to one half of the rope, and as many of your people as are needed pull on the other half, then I should rise into the mists! Then, as I grow back to full size, I should be able to pull myself up onto the ladder!"
Jessica carried on.
"Then he'll lower the raised half of the rope back to the shore for the next person to be pulled up! It's as simple as that! The only snag will be if he's eaten too much at your wonderful feast!"
Queen Venetia smiled, considered the plan and then spoke.
"Indeed, your plan sounds simple enough, but it will require great courage to enter the mists from below for the first time in our history. No one knows what will happen. Supposing you fail to return to your

Upper World dimensions and you and the rope are pulled through the last rung. You will fall back through the mists. The consequences are too horrifying to contemplate! If you die or shrink yet again for the sake of my wishes being fulfilled, I, and the whole of *Aqua Crysta* will grieve for many harvests to come. Is it all worth the risk?"

Knowing that not only the Queen's wishes were at stake but the very existence of *Aqua Crysta* itself, made Jamie, Jessica, Jonathan and Jane all insist that the risk *was* worth taking, but they were careful not to give their secret away.

All the travellers breathed sighs of relief as the Queen, at last, gave orders for the venture to begin.

Lepho took the hands of each of the children in turn and quietly thanked them for what they were about to do for the Queen and her people.

"We'll be back in the Upper World in next to no...!" burst Jamie, glancing at his watch and then staring at it in amazement. "Good heavens, how's that happened? It says *twenty two* minutes past two instead of *two* minutes past, and it's stopped again!"

"It started when we reached the end of the Harvest Passageway and entered the forest! Remember?" said Jonathan.

"You mean we were only up there for *twenty* minutes! It seemed like a lifetime!" laughed Jamie, picking up a piece of driftwood from the shore. "This'll make a good seat if I can knot it to one of the ropes!" he said, just beginning to feel the first twinges of fear in his stomach, as he looked up at the enormous distance the two ropes spanned between the shore and the swirling mists.

With the driftwood secured tightly to one of the ropes, he asked if a few of the party could pull on the other one to see whether or not they could move the seat upwards. Half a dozen took hold of the rope and heaved for all they were worth but the seat stayed exactly where it was. More members of the party joined in...but once again...the seat wouldn't budge in the slightest!

Jamie looked crestfallen.

"I told you that you should have nibbled not gobbled!" joked Jessica, to cheer him up.

Jamie looked at her grimly.
"The full sized rope around the last rung must be too heavy for us to shift!" he sighed. "I'm *never* going to get up there!"
Queen Venetia suddenly stepped forward.
"Try these!" she quietly urged. "Tie them to your wrists. Their magic will see you on your way!"
From a hidden pocket inside her velvetty, green gown, she produced a bundle of familiar, iridescent, jay feather strands, and handed three to each of the children.
Jamie busily knotted the bluey-green ribbons to one of his wrists and then braced himself for the next big effort of the tug-of-war band of Aqua Crystans. He grasped hold of the rope tightly with both hands.
"When I give the word," said Lepho, "just concentrate your mind on rising off the ground and I'm sure the good fortune entwined within the feathers will come to your assistance. Are you ready?"
Jamie shuffled more comfortably onto his makeshift seat and gripped the rope even tighter.
"Ready!" he called.
"Ready, men?" called Lepho. "After three!"
The team of Aqua Crystans strained on their half of the rope...and, wonderfully, the driftwood seat and Jamie began to slowly and jerkily rise above the pebble shore.
"Good luck!!" shouted Jessica and Jane together, holding back tears of excitement and worry mixed together.
"May good fortune be with you!" called the Queen, full of admiration for her noble explorer.
"We will meet again in the *Palace of Dancing Horses*!" called Lepho.
"See you in the well!" called Jonathan, waving wildly.

As more and more of the rope was pulled down by the Aqua Crystans, more and more joined the tug-of-war, making Jamie rise faster and faster. Up and up he floated. Occasionally he twirled round and marvelled at the magical view that no one in the whole of history had seen before him. When he dared to look down he could just make out the *Goldcrest,* but already all the people on the shore were merely dots. He would have liked to have waved but nothing would make him loosen his white knuckle grip on the rope! Instead he gently twirled round in the silence and gazed at the magnificent view unfolding around and below him.

It was like being in the basket of a hot-air balloon, but without the roar of gas-burners. It was so eerily quiet. Far, far below, the Floss had shrunk to a narrow, silver ribbon, its pebbly shore looking like sandy gravel. The cavern walls were steep and straight, soaring from the shore to the ever closer mists, their pinky white crystals glistening brighter and brighter. Huge stalactite points came into view, appearing out of the swirling clouds like fangs and sending shivers down Jamie's back. But on the whole, the journey was a wondrous experience. He was absolutely spellbound all the way, even grinning to himself every now and again. Being a hero wasn't too bad after all!

The first wisps of mist began to drift past him, his splendid view dissolving away only to re-appear again. He felt as if he was slowing down as the mist merged into cloud and wrapped itself thickly around him. He looked down and was slightly alarmed to see nothing but cloud beyond his feet. Somehow he began to feel that he'd completely lost contact with *Aqua Crysta* and he was between one world and another!

Then... he stopped.

He couldn't see a thing.

He gasped for breath and felt himself breathing in the strangely warm and dry mist. He began to feel light-headed and fear again began to wrap itself around him as well as the cloud. What if he was stuck there forever, what if he loosened his grip and fell, what if...? Suddenly...he could see darkness above his head. His heart bounded with delight and relief. He almost cheered in the strange, silent nothingness, as the mist cleared and he could see the round black hole that was the bottom of the well, and on one side his rope looped over the last rung! It was only an arm's length away as he grabbed the other half of the rope and pulled himself up.

He had made it!

The unknown journey was over and it slowly dawned on him that he was now a giant!
He had returned to the Upper World size without even noticing. This was *real* magic!!

He rested, his feet on the last rung, his hands grasping the third. Wedged up against the last rung was his faithful driftwood seat, vitally stopping its end of the rope from being disastrously pulled through and falling into *Aqua Crysta*. One slip now and the rest of the children would *never* be able to make the journey!
Carefully, he began to lower the raised half of the rope downwards and quickly his seat vanished from view into the milky distance. The mists had cleared and it seemed peculiar to look down toward the Floss yet see nothing but a narrow band of silver set in pale gravel with no sign of anyone at all. It all seemed just a jump away, like it had been when they'd first reached the bottom of the well...what seemed like days ago...but was actually only just over twenty minutes since! He glanced at his watch and yes, as he expected, time had started again.
'*Some twenty minutes*!' he thought to himself, hanging there between worlds, lowering the rope. Up above, the gloom of the well and the black night sky beyond seemed so cold and unwelcoming compared to the warmth and light of *Aqua Crysta* below! Strange thoughts once again flashed through his mind as he clung to the ladder, suspended between the world of *George* and *Deer Leap* and the world of *Pillo* and *Galdo*! Which one *was* his home?

Suddenly, both halves of the rope seemed to tighten, and then, a moment later, the rope, magically, by itself began to thread its way inch by inch over the rung between his feet. Jessica was on her way! The Aqua Crystans were tugging their end of the rope and the driftwood seat was rising towards the well.
Thoughts of his father back at the cottage, asleep in the middle of the night, merged with thoughts of the *Goldcrest* and the welcome party at *Pillo*. Then he pictured his bedroom and his computer, but these became mixed with images of the market place inside the island of *Galdo* and the beautiful crystal home of Queen Venetia. He struggled to think which lay in the real world, or had the whole adventure been a dream? Was he

really asleep...and if he was...was he in his bed at *Deer Leap?* Or was he in *Old Soulsyke* farmhouse? Or was he snuggled up beneath the trees of the forest near the well-head?

Suddenly, movement from below caught his eye and stopped his thoughts.

Mist swirled beneath his feet and then Jessica's hands, followed by bright, fluorescent green sleeves reached out towards him. He quickly climbed a couple of rungs to make way for his sister, who pulled herself up onto the last rung, and then rested, panting heavily.

"Welcome back to the *real* world, Jess!" laughed Jamie. "The time of arrival is twenty-seven minutes past two in the morning, local time, and the temperature is...!"

"Oh, stop sounding like an airline pilot, Jamie !" gasped Jessica. "What am I doing awake in the middle of the night clinging to a rope and perched on a piece of driftwood? What a strange dream I've had!"

"It's no dream, sis!" said Jamie. "Remember Toby, Quentin, Lepho...?"

"And Captain Frumo and Mayor Merrick," sighed Jessica dreamily, "and Queen Venetia!"

"And Jonathan!" laughed Jamie.

"And Jane!" gasped Jessica, a wide smile beginning to cross her face. "You've had the same dream as me *again*!"

"I tell you it's no dream!" insisted Jamie, pointing down into the milky light. "Thread that rope down and I'll prove it to you...*I think*!!"

Once again, the driftwood seat disappeared beyond the clearing mist towards the slender silver ribbon that seemed just a jump away. The rope dangled from the rung, its end invisible, like a crabline from a seaside quay.

"What's going to happen?" asked Jessica, not knowing what to expect.

"You'll see, just wait a sec!" said her brother from above, gazing down into the strange, milky paleness.

Then, as before, the two halves of the rope tightened... and then it magically began to thread itself over the last rung.

"Any minute now you'll meet someone from our dream!" announced Jamie.

Jessica looked up at him disbelievingly and then returned her gaze to beyond her feet.
The rope carried on slithering over the rung as though it had a life of its own. Then the mist began to swirl and two tightly clasped hands appeared with bluey-green feathery ribbons wrapped around them loosely. Next came Jane's beaming face with her plaits dangling over her flowery frock.
"See! Told you!" said Jamie. "Quick, let's move up a rung or two to make room for her. She's called Jane, remember? She was on the shore of the Floss a few moments ago, like we were!"
"Hello, you two!" panted Jane as she pulled herself up onto the last rung and delved into her frock pocket. "And look what I've got! You'll be needing this!"
And to Jessica and Jamies' surprise she produced a torch like a magician producing a rabbit from a top hat!
"Where did you find that?" exclaimed Jamie. "I haven't seen it since we dropped down from the well in the first place!"
"Lepho found it among the pebbles by the end of the rope," said Jane, passing it up to Jessica. "You must have lost it when you jumped down!"
Jamie reached for the torch and immediately switched it on, flooding the gloomy well with brilliance. Above them, the line of rungs, hammered into the walls by the ancient monks, marched towards the forest and the night. They thought of their last spine chilling visit, by way of the Harvest Passageway...the giant, skyscraper trees...the monstrous, throbbing helicopter...and the terrifying deer stampede! They truly hoped that this time things would be a little more peaceful... a little less eventful! But, as *you* probably know, things often don't *quite* turn out just how you hope they will!!

Chapter 21

"Here comes Jonathan!" called Jane, as she saw his familiar checked shirt sleeves and more jay feather strands emerging from the mist. He hauled himself into the well and rested a moment to catch his breath. "Queen Venetia and Lepho send their good wishes," he panted, "and the Queen has told me to tell you that, under no circumstances, have you to remove the feathers from your wrists!"

"No chance!" called Jamie, a dozen rungs above. "They've worked brilliantly so far! I only hope they give us good luck up here, too!"

"It's *magic* not *luck*!" gasped Jessica, thinking her brother was belittling the power of the jay feathers. "If we keep that in mind, then our mission will be completed. The magic's been with us all the way!"

"And it's been with *us* ever since we arrived in *Aqua Crysta*!" added Jane. "Magic is at the heart of her existence. That's why we've got to save her from the Upper World!"

"O.K., O.K., then!" called Jamie, feeling that he'd been put right by everybody. "What are we waiting for? Let's get on with it!"

The climb was uneventful, as they all hoped, although for Jonathan and Jane it seemed strange being back to full size after half a century in *Aqua Crysta*.

"It seems so weird taking such enormous steps from rung to rung!" said Jonathan, his voice echoing up and down the well.

"Wait until you see the toys in the forest cellar again!" said Jessica. "You'll feel like giants!"

Eventually, Jamie reached the ledge that lead to the small, arched wooden door.
"There's the torch!" he called, thinking of the last time he'd seen it and had to climb onto its barrel to switch it on. "I'll meet you three in the cellar. I'll go up and hide the pole and try and close the well-head. You take this working torch with you. It'll be pitch black in there and you need to start winding up the toys!"
"But you'll need it as well!" called Jessica.
"It's O.K., moonlight will do!"

Fortunately, the moon was shining in a cloudless, starry sky when Jamie pulled himself onto the silvered forest floor. It felt damp and cold as he clambered out of the well on his hands and knees. And how peculiar it was to be back in the forest with the trees back to normal, instead of never-ending gigantic pillars holding up the sky...and cones he could pick up...and pine-needles the length of his thumb nail!
And there...just by the well-head, the red and white striped pole with its yellow flag, now only a little thicker than a cricket stump and just a little taller than himself!
Without any hesitation, he yanked it clean out of the ground and then buried it under a heap of pine-needles. The dreaded marker had gone, but no doubt its position was in the memories of the soldiers. *Aqua Crysta* was still by no means safe, he thought to himself, as he anxiously looked around, half expecting a white clad soldier to suddenly appear or the helicopter to suddenly shatter the silence!

Next, he had to try and hide the well-head itself by covering the stone slab with moss, soil and pine-needles. He managed to lift it and let it fall back over the well-head, just leaving himself enough room to squeeze through onto the top rung. He stepped down onto the next rung and pulled as much soil and grass as he could over the slab, before stopping for a rest. He then tried to close the remaining gap but he just hadn't enough strength to do it completely, but at least it was smaller than before and probably much less noticeable from above. It would have to do for now, and anyway, he and his sister could hide it later.

So, with a shaft of moonlight guiding his way, Jamie descended the ladder and was soon scrambling along the cellar ledge. He could hardly wait to push open the door and, as it creaked open, he caught his first glimpse of the magic that Queen Venetia had wished for her people!

The *Palace of Dancing Horses* was already coming to life!

The other three *had* been busy! The clicketty-click of the tin, clockwork toys being wound up echoed around the cellar, like the croaking of toads round a tropical pond. Already, some of the toys were clattering away. Drums and cymbals were being beaten by musical, metallic monkeys, while clowns juggled with balls, dogs jumped through hoops and Jonathan was chasing his favourite motorcycle and side-car across the cellar floor!

Soldiers were saluting wildly, cats chased mice and the strongmen lifted their dumb-bells. Then Jane started the Ferris wheel, with its little passenger seats rumbling round and jerking in the torchlight.

It was a wonderful sight, and the best had yet to come! The railway, and, of course, the carousel with its glowing white horses on their golden, barley-sugar pillars!

"It's fantastic to do this again!" beamed Jonathan, picking up his motorcycle and giving the key another twist. "But it's all very strange and confusing! Only a few minutes ago I was polishing it and looking at Bert straight in the eyes! And look! Now I can take him out of his side-car...all ready for a Crystan to have a go!!"

"Everything go to plan upstairs?" asked Jane, winding up a red London bus.

"Yep, the pole's hidden and so is most of the well-head. I've just left a small gap for when we go up to find the map. Here, can I have one of the keys? I reckon I'll wind up this racing car!"

"It's amazing to think how enormous these keys were when we were dragging them up from *Sigmund's Cave*!" said Jonathan with a grin, as he handed one of them to Jamie.

As he pushed the key into the hole underneath the car, he suddenly stopped.

"What's that?" he whispered, straining to hear something among the clatter of toys. "I'm sure I can hear singing!"
"It's coming from the Harvest Passageway behind the dolls' house!" Jessica exclaimed. "The first of the Aqua Crystans must be almost here and they're singing the same chant they sang when the waterfall started flowing at Pillo!"
"Come on, then, let's get some more toys working for them!" urged Jane, as she wound up her favourite musical box in the shape of a treasure chest.

Soon, the shrill, tinkling notes of '*Greensleeves*' filled the cellar, mixed with the eerie, ever louder chanting from behind the dolls' house!
Ballerinas began to spin on pointed toes, crocodile jaws opened wide and snapped shut and more busby topped soldiers began to march on the spot. A London bus trundled towards the fairground followed by a fire engine with its bell merrily ringing. Jonathan wound up the dodgems and the chubby, multi-coloured cars sprung to life, darting and zigzagging all over the place, almost bubbling with the joy of being free at last!

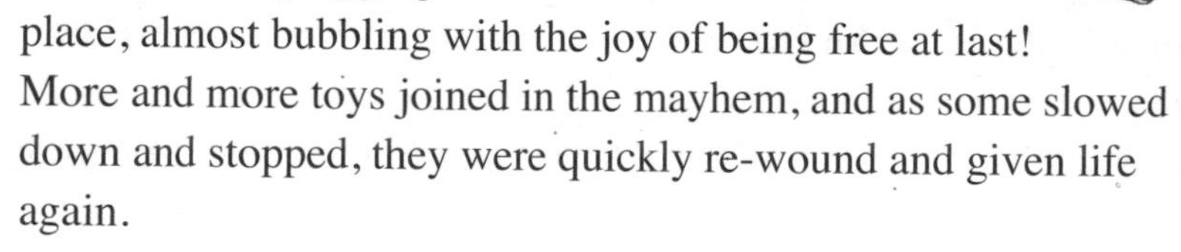

More and more toys joined in the mayhem, and as some slowed down and stopped, they were quickly re-wound and given life again.

Jessica switched off the torch and quietly squeezed behind the dolls' house. She knelt by the front windows awaiting the first Aqua Crystans at the end of their long, uphill journey, hoping they hadn't come across the terrifying mouse!
From the small hole at the foot of the cellar wall opposite the house's front door, she saw the flickering gleam of moving crystals...and, then, illuminated by one very bright crystal, she saw the first tiny figure appear! So, so tiny it was...and cloaked in purple! It was

unmistakably Lepho, with his fiery, ginger beard...and behind him, a winding line of his fellow countrymen, women and children all singing at the top of their voices, and waving their crystals!
So as not to alarm the travellers, she pointed the torch at the roof of the cellar and switched it back on. The light lit the dolls' house and the faces of Jane and the others, who had by now crept forward to see the Aqua Crystans arrive.
"Lepho!" she whispered. "It's us!"
Lepho and his followers all instantly looked up to see the illuminated faces of the four giants smiling down at them. For a second or two, the chanting wavered with the shock, but then quickly started up again, as the band of tiny people marched on into their magical *Palace*.

Just moments later, lit by torchbeam and crystals, it came alive with excitement and laughter, exactly how the Queen had wished. The fairground became awash with folk having the time of their lives. The dodgems were packed, a queue building up in no time. The helter-skelter had a never ending stream of cheering, screaming Aqua Crystans sliding down its spiral chute and, of course, the Ferris wheel was full of living passengers sitting on the knees of the tin ones!
But best of all was the *Dancing Horses* carousel itself, with each white horse galloping up and down, round and round, carrying two or three laughing, singing Aqua Crystans holding on for dear life! The railway platform bustled with rush-hour passengers anxious to scuttle round the shiny track in the green and cream carriages pulled by the smart locomotive, and Jamie was busy winding up a London bus for tours of the whole cellar. And Jonathan, of course, was giving one ride after another to his fellow countrymen in his motorcycle and side-car!
It was an incredible scene, with the children tip-toeing this way and that, keeping the magic going. Music filled the air as more and more travellers emerged from the Harvest Passageway, their eerie chanting mixed with tunes from musical boxes and the fairground toys.

When the Queen herself arrived she was delighted and could hardly wait for a ride on the train before making her way up to the small nursery at the top of the dolls' house. Once there, a fanfare of

horns amazingly brought silence to the cellar and she gracefully beckoned the children to come closer.
With all her people still and quiet, she spoke.
"I cannot thank you enough for the joy you have brought to my people," she began. "The risks you have braved in climbing through the mists and into the well will be talked of for many, many harvests to come.
The *Seven Keys of Sigmund,* which until now have brought only sad memories for me, will now remind me of this happy time, and your courage!"
Heartfelt applause and cheering broke out instantly from every corner of the cellar as the four children smiled and waved in the torchlight.
The Queen graciously raised her arms and the hubbub died down once again.
"And, on behalf of my people, I would regard it as a great honour if you, Jessica and Jamie, would come and visit us again in our secret kingdom!"
After another burst of wild applause and cheering, Jessica replied to the unexpected invitation.
"Such an honour is more than we ever expected, your Majesty! We have enjoyed our visit and our task, and we would love to come again.
Thankyou for the trust which you place in us. And thankyou for making us feel so welcome. There have been times when we haven't known which was our real home...*Aqua Crysta*, or the Upper World!"
With that, the Queen smiled and bade a final farewell, as did Toby and Quentin who had accompanied the Queen. It seemed ages and ages since Jessica and Jamie had first met them at the foot of the stairway to the Larder Cave, yet it was still only four o'clock in the morning according to Jamie's watch...less than two hours ago!
Lepho, too, bade his farewells and quietly wished the children good fortune for the tasks that still lay ahead...the quest for the map and for the reasons why the soldiers and the flying machine had been seen in the forest.
"I wish you well," he said, as the hubbub began below, "and I look forward to seeing you both again. Once the map is destroyed and the

well-head truly hidden I am sure the secret of *Aqua Crysta* will be safe! We are in your hands! *Lumina* can burn strongly and brightly!"
He smiled and waved and then followed the others down the stairs of the dolls' house, ready for the return journey to his beloved kingdom.

Jessica and Jamie felt sad as, one by one, their new friends disappeared, but at the same time they felt refreshed and determined to complete their task. The safety of *Aqua Crysta* was *definitely* in their hands. Of that, there was *no* doubt at all!!
But, if only they had known that the candle flame, *Lumina,* was beginning to weaken and flutter anxiously, deep below them, they would have realised that grave dangers lay ahead.
Very grave dangers indeed!

As the happy celebrations continued in the cellar, Jamie suggested that Jonathan and Jane might like to visit *Old Soulsyke* before they, too, made their way back to *Pillo*. They would be able to see their old home again, and the new forest, while they were still full size.
"We might find some clues about the soldiers and the helicopter, too!" he added.
"I've got too many sad memories of the place," said Jane. "I think I'll stay here and keep winding up the toys!"
"Why don't you two go and I'll stay here with Jane?" suggested Jessica, looking at the crowds of Aqua Crystans scurrying about the cellar floor. "I think she could do with another pair of hands, somehow!"

So it was decided. The girls would stay in the cellar keeping the toys fully wound up, while Jamie and Jonathan would climb up into the forest and visit *Old Soulsyke*. It seemed a simple plan, but if they'd only known what they'd find at the old, tumbledown farmhouse, they would have surely stayed with the girls in the snug, cosy cellar!! For, without doubt, they were both in for the shock of their lives!

Chapter 22

It was still dark as they emerged from the top of the well into the cool night, but the first streaks of dawn were just beginning to appear above the trees to the east.
Jonathan stared at the trees in amazement. He could put his arms completely around one with no trouble at all!
"These trees weren't even here when we left the Upper World! They were just the tiniest of saplings planted in rows across the heather moorland!"
He patted the nearby wall and was astonished to think that he could now jump over it in one leap compared to all the harvest visits when walls had to be climbed like mountains!
After they had hidden the well-head with twigs and pine-needles, but left it slightly open for their return, they began to follow the wall towards *Old Soulsyke*. More and more faint daylight marbled the sky and the first notes of birdsong began to usher in the dawn.

Soon they began to climb the purple crowned hill which held the ancient, broadleaf woodland aloft the rest of the forest with the farmhouse at its centre. Panting, they fell into the heather near the top and gazed through the gold tinged ferns.
What they saw made them gasp in bewilderment!
Neither of them could believe his eyes!

For instead of the farmhouse that Jonathan remembered from many harvests ago or the ruined one that Jamie had left just the day before, there lay before them a fortress of twisted barbed wire and red and white signs shouting at them:-

KEEP OUT!
by order of
The Ministry of Defence

It was an incredible sight, like something out of a war-zone, out here in the middle of nowhere, amid the peace and tranquility of the forest!

The low wall that surrounded the farm held an unceasing, knotted tangle of vicious wire three or four times higher than the wall itself, only broken at the gateposts next to an oak tree. Just inside the wall were three tall, metal towers each topped with a huge, unlit spotlight trained on the farm's ramshackle old buildings. A green, windowless metal shed stood by the gateposts with a long, slender aerial stretching beyond the treetops.

"It can only be something to do with the soldiers and the flying machine last night!" whispered Jonathan.

"But what on earth's going on?" wondered Jamie. "Come on, let's go up to the farm and see if we can find any clues!"

"Supposing there's still someone inside!" warned Jonathan, grabbing hold of Jamie's arm. "Supposing they've left someone on guard!"

"I can't believe they'd do that," said Jamie confidently. "There's no-one about for miles!"

"Then why surround it with all that wire and those '*Keep Out*' signs?" argued Jonathan.

"I don't know but we've got to find out for the sake of *Aqua Crysta*!" insisted Jamie. "We can dodge between the trees and keep low. Are you coming?"

Jonathan nodded, but just as they were about to dash for the first tree, he suddenly grabbed Jamie's arm again and pulled him back down into the heather.

"I just saw someone in white move in the window of the barn!" he gasped.

They both peered at the old, half-roofed barn, and then Jamie gently nudged Jonathan in the ribs with a smile, as a white cat majestically stepped through the doorway into the farmyard!
"It's only *Spook*!" he laughed. "We saw her yesterday. She gave us a fright *then* as well! Come on, let's go! One...two...*three*!"

From tree to tree they darted towards the gap in the wall of twisted barbed wire. There was still no sign of anyone as they crouched by the oak tree ready to enter the paved farmyard.
"Let's make for the farmhouse!" whispered Jamie, as though he was Robin Hood leading his merry men into Nottingham Castle!
Spook flashed back into the barn as they scampered across the paving stones and breathlessly crawled beneath the farmhouse window. Jamie cautiously climbed onto the water trough and peeped inside.
"It's O.K.!" he whispered over his shoulder. "There's no-one here!"
Jonathan's nerves had suddenly vanished as he had already stepped into the farmhouse and was full of wonder and memories as he gazed around his old home.
"I can hardly believe I'm here again after all these harvests!" he murmured, as he touched the pot sink and looked at the fireplace and then up at the hole into the hayloft.
"Where did your uncle keep all those toys?" asked Jamie.
"In a locked room between the barns but he hardly ever allowed us in!"
Jamie sensed Jonathan's sadness; the same sadness that had driven him and his sister to run away from the farm in the first place. He quickly suggested that they ought to have a look around for his backpack and then get back to the girls in the cellar.
"Before we go back, do you think I could just have a peep at the happiest place I can remember before we left the farm?"
"Where's that?" wondered Jamie.
"The old barn!" replied Jonathan with a gleam in his eye, thinking of the tricycle rides and the warm water baths he and Jane used to have in the trough beneath the barn's pump.

So, as the blackness of the night stealthily stole away, the two boys galloped through the forest, Jonathan unable to resist filling

his pockets with berries every now and again. It was so much easier picking them now that he had these full sized, Upper World hands!
When they arrived at the barn, Jonathan was sad to see that it had all but collapsed, so Jamie decided not to show him the squashed remains of his treasured tricycle.
"We saw a thin wisp of smoke here yesterday," said Jamie, as they both scrambled over the fallen chunks of rock. "It smelled sweet like the smell you have in *Aqua Crysta*."
"That's because we're directly above Pillo here," explained Jonathan, "and the smoke from nutshell fires drifts up through cracks in the rock!"

Jamie was amazed to think that beneath his feet, way below the ruined barn, lay that magical crystal cavern, the Floss and the beautiful village of Pillo. Memories flashed through his mind of arriving there aboard the *Goldcrest* with Captain Frumo and being met by Mayor Merrick. It all seemed so impossible, but if it was, thought Jamie, *who* was this with him now and *was* his sister *really* winding up dozens of tin toys in the forest cellar amid excited crowds of tiny Aqua Crystans?

But just then, before he could answer his own amazing questions, Jamie suddenly grabbed hold of Jonathan's arm and looked up into the treetops.
"Can you hear anything?" he asked.
Jonathan at first shook his head...but then, all at once, his face filled with a look of terror! The noise...*that noise*...was back!
It was last night all over again!
Both their hearts began pounding with fear!
The whirring, throbbing engine in the sky...*the flying machine was coming back*!!
Louder and louder, nearer and nearer...until there it was!

Not just a terrifying noise this time, but a huge, hovering blue and grey, metallic insect! It hovered above them like a giant dragonfly, slowly moving forward as though it was searching for prey. The boys crouched among the stones desperately hoping they wouldn't be seen. Again, like the night before, the treetops swayed and they could feel the whipped up air against their faces. Both of them covered their ears against the deafening din as it almost flattened them against the rocks.

"It's heading for *Old Soulsyke*!" shouted Jamie, as the monster glided beyond the treetops. "Come on, let's follow it and see what happens! We can hide in the heather!"

Under the cover of the trees, they soon reached the bottom of *Old Soulsyke's* hill. The helicopter was hovering above it like a giant bird about to settle on its nest. Panting and gasping, they clambered up the slope and plunged into the hill's heathery crown. Beyond them, chaos reigned in the calm heart of the forest. No wonder the deer had stampeded the night before! The upper branches of the trees had been stirred into a wild, manic dance accompanied by clouds of crazily tossed autumn leaves below. It was as though a whirlwind or a tornado had suddenly hit the hilltop!

There was no space for the machine to land, but as it gradually lowered and hovered above the fortress farm, the same madly writhing rope-ladder the boys had seen the night before wound downwards from a dark doorway in its side. Lower and lower it dived like a plunging sea snake until it reached right into the farmyard itself.

As Jamie and Jonathan watched from the deep purple, two white clad figures appeared in the helicopter's dark doorway, and one after the other, climbed down the ladder. When they were halfway down and level with the farmhouse roof, a third figure appeared at the top of the ladder. This one was not wearing white, but was dressed in blue jeans and a green anorak.

Jamie stared at Jonathan and then looked up again at the third figure.

"I can't believe it!" he exclaimed. "*It's my dad*!!!"

Chapter 23

The two white clad soldiers reached the ground and then steadied the rope ladder as Jamie's dad began rather gingerly to descend.
"What's he doing *here*, and why is he with the *soldiers*?" wondered Jamie, astounded at the sight of his father climbing out of the helicopter beneath its whirling rotor blades.
"I don't know, but I'm sure we're going to find out pretty soon!" shouted back Jonathan, equally amazed by the flying machine, the likes of which he'd never seen before.

When Mr Dawson was safely on the ground, his anorak and hair dancing as manically as the tree branches, one of the soldiers signalled to the pilot. The rope ladder was quickly hauled in, the huge machine rose into the sky and a moment later had vanished into the distance.
As the hilltop began to settle, silence returned and the other soldier began to speak.
"We'll have to get closer!" whispered Jamie. "I can't hear a word!"
Stealthily, they crawled through the heather and then darted from tree to tree keeping as low as possible.
"...so this area round the old farm will be the centre of the new complex." were the first words they heard clearly, as they strained their ears, crouching amid the roots of a giant beech tree.

"We intend to build command rooms here on the surface and underground too...and radar and tracking installations will spread about half a mile in each direction," the other soldier continued, although by now Jamie's father had begun to gaze wondrously at the ancient broadleaf copse.
"...and over there will be the main gates, with a road leading to the track where you have your cott..."
Mr Dawson suddenly turned and glared angrily at his two hosts.
"Just a minute!" he interrupted. "Do you mean to tell me that you're planning to *destroy* this beautiful patch of ancient woodland and put a road through to my cottage?"
"Yes, sir!" snapped the smaller soldier enthusiastically. "That's about it in a nutshell! And we intend to widen the country lane at the end of your track so it will carry military vehicles...!"
"And in addition," continued the taller soldier, "we'll be building barracks for over a hundred soldiers, not to mention houses for civilians!"
"You *have* to be *joking*!!" exploded Mr Dawson.
He wandered a few steps from the soldiers with his arms suddenly animated and pointing in every direction.
"Do you realise that I've seen finches, jays, nuthatches, treecreepers since that machine of yours flew off? And just look at the variety of trees! Birch, sycamore, ash, beech, sweet chestnut, oak...and look over there, there's even a *walnut tree*!! And you want to *destroy all this*? It would be *criminal*! It's glorious! Superb!"
"Look, Mr Dawson, we're not interested in all that!" barked back the smaller soldier.
"We've got our orders and today we start flattening the lot! We've been told to contact you as Forest Manager so that you can start the job of felling the forest for a distance of about half a mile in every direction from this farm with a wide corridor towards your cottage and the track!"
"Well, *I'm telling you*, Sergeant, that until I contact my superiors, I cannot agree to any of your plan, especially the felling of this part of the

forest! The sprucelands and the larchlands are one thing, but not this glorious, ancient broadleaf woodland!!"
The soldiers were certainly taken aback by the Forest Manager's outburst and they both stared at him as he again wandered away from them and touched the trunk of an oak tree as though it was a long lost friend.
"He loves trees!" whispered Jamie, admiringly watching his father as he sat down on one of the oak's gnarled old roots and gazed up into its twisted branches.

The two soldiers walked towards the farmhouse and one of them produced a mobile phone from an inside pocket, tapped some numbers and then seemed to have a heated conversation with someone. Then he slid the phone back, had a word with his companion and called over to Jamie's father in as pleasant a tone as he could muster.
"Do you want a lift back to your cottage?" he asked. "The chopper's on its way!"
"No, thankyou, I'll make my own way back!" came the short reply.
"Whatever you say, sir, and, oh by the way, there's a backpack belonging to a *Jamie Dawson* in our metal shed over there. We found it last night in the farmhouse and locked it away for safe keeping."
The smaller soldier walked over to the green hut by one of the spotlight towers and unlocked it.
"And we found another one belonging to a *Jessica Dawson* in the forest near a wellshaft. That's in there, too!"
"O.K.," replied Mr Dawson dreamily, his mind miles away among the trees and the birds. "They belong to my kids. They were camping out in the forest last night. You didn't see them did you?"
"No, sir, we didn't, but I'd get 'em home pretty quickly if I were you!"
"Why?"
"You'll see!"
As they talked, the familiar whirring, throbbing noise returned, gradually becoming louder and louder until the blue grey helicopter was above them like a giant dragonfly above a lilypad. The rope ladder wound down from its dark door and first one, and then the other soldier climbed towards the hovering aircraft.

When the sergeant was about halfway up he called back over his shoulder as loudly as he could against the din of the helicopter,
"Don't forget, Dawson, find those kids of yours pronto and get them out of here! The action starts today and there's going to be some pretty big machinery about!"
He spun round on the writhing ladder, and shouted again, "Our detectors last night gave some weird readings, especially round the wellshaft! The rocks below could be dangerously radio-active! We'll have to dig down and clear out the lot!!"

At the foot of the beech tree, Jonathan looked at Jamie with a look of horror on his face! This is exactly what he and his sister had warned the *Aqua Crystans* about when *they'd* ventured into their world all those harvests ago. Upper World men would one day come with great machines and destroy the whole forest, destroying the harvest lands...and now, even worse, there was the threat of digging down into the rock and discovering the magical kingdom itself!!
Something *had* to be done...and *fast!*

Silence returned to *Old Soulsyke* as the flying machine vanished, leaving Mr Dawson sat sadly at the foot of his splendid oak tree. A streak of white suddenly distracted him as a cat bounded across the farmyard. He smiled, but then nearly jumped out of his skin as Jamie charged towards him shouting,
"It's O.K., dad! She lives here! She's called *Spook*!"
Mr Dawson's head turned as if his neck was spring-loaded and stared open mouthed at the two boys rushing towards him. What, with the nerve-racking descent from the helicopter, discovering the secret woodland, the soldiers' news, the cat darting from nowhere... and now, Jamie and a mystery friend appearing from out of the blue...he was really beginning to feel the effects of shock!!
"And a very good name for her, too!" he mumbled, giving Jamie a hug and looking quizzically at Jonathan. "Your sister's idea no doubt! Talking of which...where is she?...and why did those

guys find your backpacks last night? And who's this?"
"Jessica's O.K. She's at our camp," replied Jamie a touch nervously, "and this is Jonathan! We met him and his sister yesterday. They're camping, too! They live..."
"Just the other side of the moors!" burst Jonathan, fearing Jamie was going to put his foot in it. He held out his hand and Mr Dawson shook it slowly, still rather puzzled by the appearance of his son's new friend.
"I'm *sure* I've met you before!" he said, as he carried on shaking Jonathan's hand. "I'm amazed by what you're wearing...corduroy short trousers, your sleeveless pullover and your grey socks up to your knees! You know? You remind me of me when I was a boy! It's crazy! Really peculiar!"
"No, sir, I don't believe we've met, but I'm very pleased to meet you, Mr Dawson!" Jonathan said calmly.
Jamie quickly changed the subject.
"We heard everything the soldiers said, dad! We've got to save the forest! But how?"
"It's going to be one heck of a battle with the authorities, but it'll be worth the fight to save all this!" said Mr Dawson, staring round at the woodland, but keeping a curious eye on Jonathan every now and again. There was definitely something familiar about this lad, but he couldn't quite put his finger on it!
"I'll have to move pretty quickly if we're going to stand any chance at all," he went on, "so I'm going to head back to *Deer Leap* and get started with a few telephone calls!"
He unfolded a map from his back pocket and worked out his route with Jamie's help, and just before he set off, he reminded him about the backpacks in the green, metal shed.
"How come you left 'em all over the place, by the way?" he asked.
Jamie was just about to come up with an explanation when his father started jogging on his way through the autumn leaves.
"Save it until later!" he called over his shoulder. "I'd better get going. You get back to your sister and make your way home, too! I'll see you back there! Bring your friends if you want!"

With a final wave he disappeared through the heather and down the hillside. Jamie and Jonathan looked at one another and sighed with relief

"That was all a bit tricky!" said Jamie, a bit embarrassed by his father going on about Jonathan. "Come on, let's look in the shed, and keep your fingers crossed that your old map's still in Jessie's backpack!!"

It was, and between them they managed to carefully unroll it. Jonathan inspected the thick, rough lines he'd drawn all those years before with that short, chubby pencil.

"Well, that's another task completed!" he said, as he cast his eyes around his old home, "I'll take it back to *Aqua Crysta* so it'll never fall into the wrong ha...!"

"*WHAT'S THAT* ?" Jamie suddenly shrieked at the top of his voice, jumping to his feet.

A new, deafening noise filled the air, shaking the metal shed, and forcing both of them to cover their ears.

Something was heading towards them and it certainly wasn't the helicopter. That had been loud enough, but this was ten times, no, a hundred times worse!

Then...like something out of your worst nightmare...they saw it or, rather...

they saw *them*!!!

Chapter 24

They were huge, gigantic mechanical monsters slowly appearing against the pale dawn sky above the trees. Three of them. Mammoth black and yellow machines each the size of a house, with enormous, out-sized, deep-treaded rubber tyred wheels each the height of a room. Great threatening shovels were slung in front of them ready to take the most fearsome bites out of whatever they could get their teeth into! And as if these monstrous machines weren't enough, above them were six even larger, greeny brown camouflaged helicopters...not like the small, single rotor helicopter that carried the soldiers but vast, double rotor machines! They hovered in pairs, each pair carrying beneath them one of the giant earthmovers in a cradle of chains!
The spectacular sight and sound of all this gruesome, hovering machinery just above the greenery of the forest was awesome and somehow spellbinding. The boys just stared, the sheer size of the machines and the thunderous, throbbing roar of the helicopters almost pressing and pushing them into the forest floor itself!
They watched, glued to the spot, as the monstrous black and yellow earthmovers swung in the air beneath their whirling puppet masters ready to bring havoc to the beautiful innocence below.

Slowly, and strangely gracefully, despite their brutal ugliness, the great machines were lowered between the churning branches of the dwarfed oaks and beeches. Ancient boughs snapped like matchsticks and fell among the tossed autumn leaves.

The destruction had begun without a single ignition key being turned!
Crash! Crash! Crash! One after another, the thick boughs hit the gentle hilltop's floor, as the earthmovers majestically floated to the ground...and then, with almost ballet-like precision, the terrifying trio crunched on top of them.

The boys imagined the damage that these monsters could cause if the mood took them. The sturdiest of trees and walls would just be crushed and swept away! As the soldiers had said, *everything* would be flattened! Nothing would survive. Nothing at all! They watched as the supporting chains were released all at once from the helicopters, plummeting and rattling and clattering around their loads and onto the forest floor.
Then in smooth formation, the six vast, thunderous helicopters rose into the sky and headed away, leaving everything to settle back into stillness.

Now, it was even quieter than before. The early birds had taken flight, driven off to the barren sprucelands where they would wait and watch. What was to come? Why had these sleeping, black and yellow monsters taken over their ancestral realm? The dozing dinosaurs lay in wait, ready to tear, and crush, and dig and smash! But for now, all was quiet. Very quiet, eerily quiet. Like a graveyard...the calm before the storm!

So, too, was the saddening mood down in *Aqua Crysta*! Quentin and Toby, the Guardians of *Lumina*, had returned to the terrace on the Larder Steps, and were sitting staring at their beloved candle flame. Before the children had climbed the well, she had been burning strongly and boldly, full of hope that the saviours would rescue

Aqua Crysta from doom and disaster. But now, she sensed tragedy and extinction were near. Her flame had withered to one that just about clung to the glowing wick. One so weak that a single puff of breeze could extinguish her. Quentin and Toby slowly cupped their hands around her and hoped, intently watching over their charge for any signs of recovery. For the moment they would say nothing to anyone, so as not to dampen the high spirits created by the wonderful happenings in the *Palace of Dancing Horses*. They clung on, like *Lumina,* to the hope that if the magic could revive the *Palace*, then it could work its wonders in the Upper World too! All they could do was watch and hope...only the passing of time would tell!

Jamie and Jonathan stepped from behind the metal shed, each of them carrying a backpack and Jonathan holding the precious, rolled up map. Tears began to well in his eyes as he thought about what all this meant for *Aqua Crysta,* the Queen and her people. He even began to think of the festivities being enjoyed in the *Palace of Dancing Horses* at that very moment as some kind of final get together before the whole dream was destroyed.
Jamie tried to reassure him, but he, too, knew that the future looked bleak. How could such a fragile kingdom survive not only the destruction of the harvest lands, but worse still, the quarrying of the rocks beneath the forest? Surely there was no escape! He just hoped that his father could do something about it, but secretly he had his doubts. After all, how could a mere Forest Manager take on the demands of the Military?
"We've somehow got to hold up their plans!" he said at last, as they began to jog back to the forest cellar. "That'll give m'dad a chance of getting through to 'em!"
"But what can *we* do to stop *this lot*?" sighed Jonathan as they scrambled by the mass of greasy, oily machinery and rusty chains.
They stopped and looked at the frightening tangle of powerful iron and steel, nervously half-expecting to be seen by a hidden eye somewhere amongst the mass of metal.

Strangely, for a moment, it felt like being back in the forest cellar as an Aqua Crystan, with the huge, towering rubber wheels and enormous shovels. The trio of deadly earthmovers looked like toys, rather than real machines with the power to destroy all before them! But the oil and grease, the caked mud and the smell of diesel soon put a stop to those thoughts! They were real enough! And so, too, was their dormant menace and evil!

The last of the long and winding, twinkling procession of joyful Aqua Crystans were just entering the forest cellar from the Harvest Passageway, as Jamie and Jonathan joined in the winding up of the toys and told their sisters of the happenings above. Both were heartbroken as they tried their best to keep the festivities going with the happy, laughing, tiny people running from ride to ride and from floor to floor in the dolls' house.

The four of them decided to say nothing about the earthmovers and the tragic plans of the Ministry of Defence, but to make sure the message reached Queen Venetia that the well-head had been sealed and the map retrieved. Returning Aqua Crystans would do that.

"But what are we going to do?" sighed Jane. "There *must* be something!"

"We've *somehow* got to hold them up, stop the earthmovers from starting!" said Jamie, as he wound up the clockwork railway engine. "But we've got to think of something *fast*! The sergeant said the *action* would be starting *right away*!"

Flocks of Aqua Crystans piled on board the train, totally unaware of the anxious conversation going on above their heads. When the carriages were full to bursting, the engine set off around its circular track with beaming passengers waving from every single carriage window! As the train clicketty-clicked along its silver track, the passengers began singing the same joyful chant they had sung when the Pillo Falls had begun to flow. In next to no time, *every* Aqua Crystan in the cellar had joined in. The sound was at once both gloriously celebratory and anciently eerie, like an echoey cathedral full of chanting monks from centuries ago!

As the amazing sound reached its crescendo, Jessica's eyes mysteriously moved first to the ribbons of jay feather still tied to her wrist and then to

the railway carriages packed full of chanting Aqua Crystans. Somehow, the magic of their homeland was working again.
Somehow, by some unknown means, she had the answer!
And down below, *Lumina* swelled and whispered her news into the minds of her two Guardians. Quentin and Toby looked at one another and smiled, the growing candle flame reflected in their eyes. Hope had returned!

Jessica's plan was magnificent...but would it work?
The first problem was letting the Aqua Crystans know that they were going to be part of a top secret mission to save their world! Once told, they might panic and rush down the Harvest Passageway and spread chaos from one end of the Floss to the other!!
The second problem was just a minor one! *Taking about one hundred and fifty Aqua Crystans to Old Soulsyke in the six railway carriages and a London bus*!!

Fortunately, Jane was popular with everyone, and as all the toys began to unwind and stop and the music faded away, she calmly asked all the Aqua Crystans in the cellar to make their way to the dolls' house. Then, when the hushed assembly were all seated comfortably on the lush carpets and sofas and chairs of the downstairs rooms, Jessica slowly knelt in front of them.
You could have heard a pin drop as the scores of tiny faces looked up at her enormous face. She smiled and whispered her plan, holding her audience spellbound. After she had spoken there was much excited mumbling as the tiny people filed out of the house and headed towards the railway station platform where the six carriages and the bus were waiting.
Straight away, twenty Aqua Crystans filled each carriage and another thirty clambered onto the double-decker bus. Those left over, although disappointed, began to make their way back to *Aqua Crysta* to pass on the good news about the well-head and the map, but not to mention anything about the new venture into the Upper World.

Soon, the children were making their way up the well, clutching their precious cargo. One by one, they carefully rested the green and cream carriages and the bus on the forest floor. They looked quite peculiar sitting there in the early morning sunshine, up to the tops of their wheels in pine-needles and with tall, gold-tinged fern fronds swaying above them. And even more so with two or three tiny Aqua Crystans poking their heads out of every window, all chattering away as though the whole business was one great big adventurous day out!!

After concealing the well, the children headed towards *Old Soulsyke*, Jane this time amazed by all the trees which she remembered as small saplings, fifty Upper World years ago. But her biggest shock was when they approached the farm with its barbed wire, '*Keep Out*!' signs, towers and, most of all, the giant, sleeping earthmovers! Jessica could hardly believe her eyes, too, as they crept past the monsters.

And as for the chattering Aqua Crystans...they were suddenly dumb-struck, staring around with terrified, astonished eyes! Their mouths dropped open in awe! Could anything be *that* enormous?

Jamie checked his watch. It was just after seven o'clock.

"It won't be long before the men come to get these things moving!" he called to the others.

The four children held the six carriages and the bus together.

"Are you all ready?" whispered Jane to her fellow countryfolk.

"Yes, Miss Jane!" chorused the tiny passengers.

"Good luck, everybody!" wished Jessica. "Let's make a start!"

The children began to climb up into the lower branches of the ancient trees that surrounded the gigantic machines. It was a bit of a struggle with the carriages and the bus to carry, but when they were far enough off the ground, they let the eager passengers clamber out onto the thick boughs.

Seconds later they were all hidden amongst the woody nooks and crannies and the foliage.

Not one could be seen!

"Just in time!" called Jamie from his tree. "I can hear a helicopter! Quick, climb down and hide!"

Swiftly, they shinned down the trees, pelted through the gap in the barbed wire, across the farmyard and into Spook's barn. Above, the sound of the helicopter became louder and louder as they peeped through the old window.

The tops of the trees began to sway and thoughts of the tiny Aqua Crystans clinging onto branch bark and leaf stems flashed through their minds. Would the plan end in disaster there and then, with the tiny folk being scared witless and blown out of the trees?

Jessica gripped the jay feather strands around her wrists and wished as hard as she could.

The magic just *had* to stay with them!

The helicopter hovered above the farmyard as the familiar, snaking rope-ladder wound downwards. Then a whole troop of men wearing green and brown camouflaged clothes climbed down...ten, eleven, twelve of them. As each soldier jumped to the ground he darted off to one or other of the earthmovers or to the green metal shed.

When all twelve were down, the ladder was wound up and the helicopter throbbed into the distance, its noise replaced by the soldiers barking orders at one another!

The children in Spook's barn peeped through the window and watched every move.

So did the Aqua Crystans up in the trees.

And below ground, the eternal candle flame was still burning strongly.

Two or three soldiers climbed onto each earthmover and fiddled with bolts and levers and removed the heavy, clanking chains, while others dragged equipment from the metal shed. As they beavered away, they shouted at one another less often, until the woodland became quiet again except for the clinking of metal on metal.

It was then that it happened...just as Jessica had planned!

Gentle, haunting musical notes began to float through the air from one of the old oak trees. It was magical and mystic, once again like the chanting of ancient, ghostly monks in a distant, echoey abbey. It was so eerie that it sent shivers down the spines of the children as they watched and waited.

The men hadn't noticed, they were so busy gathering up the rusty chains and tinkering with the mammoth engines and shovels...but, then, one of them stopped and listened.
"Dave, can you 'ear owt?" he shouted, staring up into the trees with a puzzled look on his face.
Dave leaned out of one of the earthmover shovels, grasping the biggest spanner you've ever seen, and he, too, listened intently.
Then all of them stopped what they were doing, stood straight and gawped all around...up and down...side to side...and then speechlessly at one another, scratching their heads.
The haunting chant from the oak tree became louder.
The men gazed at one another, frozen to the spot, with their mouths wide open and their eyes beginning to pop out like organ stops!
Their foreheads began to glisten with beads of sweat...and tools, one by one, dropped from their hands.
And then suddenly, as if commanded by a hidden choirmaster, the chanting swelled as the other trees joined in...an ash, a beech and another oak!
The sound was terrific! Beautiful...but very, very scary...as if it was coming from nowhere!
The men were directly beneath, as the hidden choir became even louder and louder...and their frozen panic was a joy to behold!
They didn't know whether to cover their ears and run for it...or get down on their knees and pray! After all, they were *soldiers* not mice!
They just couldn't run away from nothing!
Louder and louder the trees wailed!
The men remained motionless, dumb-struck...until suddenly, the nerve of one of them broke!
In a mad scurry of arms and legs he slid down from one of the giant earthmover cabs, crashed to the ground and ran for all he was worth towards the heather at the edge of the hilltop.

Then, as though on cue, there was a terrifying, echoey blood-curdling screech from inside the metal shed! Spook the cat flew out with her back arched, her fur on end and her tail sticking up as straight as a poker! Then, like a creature possessed, she pelted through the mass of tangled metal, in and out of the massive wheels and between the legs of the quivering soldiers, screeching and hissing all the way!

At the same time, the chanting of the trees reached its electrifying, spine-tingling crescendo, charging the air with even more panic and fear!

It was the last straw!

The men couldn't stand it a second longer!

In a mad, manic rush of boots and camouflaged suits, the petrified soldiers deserted their machines and bolted across the woodland towards the heather, as though they were being pursued by a battalion of bees!!

Back at the barn, the watching children just collapsed in a heap, roaring their heads off!

"That was *brilliant*!" laughed Jessica, wiping tears from her eyes.

"Did you see their faces?" chuckled Jonathan. "They were absolutely horror struck!"

"And wasn't Spook fantastic? Right on cue!" giggled Jane.

"But will they be back?" said Jamie cautiously. "Surely, trained soldiers can't be driven off by ghostly trees and a phantom cat!"

Outside, the chanting began to fade until, once more, the hilltop woodland was completely quiet.

"We've got to be ready for them!" whispered Jamie, swishing his imaginary sword.

"I don't think that even *real* swords will be much good against those monstrous machines once they get started!" replied Jessica. "We've held them up, it's true, but I don't see how we're going to stop them for good!"

"If only we could make them *disappear...vanish*!" said Jonathan, with a twinkle in his eye.

"Don't be daft, Jonny!" giggled his sister. "How do you make machines as big as houses *disappear into thin air*?"

"You just hold your horses, sis!" continued Jonathan slowly, with a cunning smile on his face.

"I *think* I've got an idea!"

Chapter 25

From the barn window, the children scanned the hilltop for any signs of activity. The soldiers seem to have been driven away, but they knew that with their camouflage and training they could be anywhere! As for the wonderful Aqua Crystans, they were still up in the trees, knowing perhaps that their job wasn't quite over. One thing was for certain, though...they had definitely enjoyed themselves! They'd never sung in the Upper World before for fear of being heard. But this had been different and the normal rules just had to be bent. So they sat and relaxed in the morning sunshine and chatted about their musical heroics and a possible encore!

Suddenly, everyones' nerves were on edge again as a familiar, distant whirring sound broke the silence - the faint throbbing of a helicopter returning to the farm. Closer and closer it came until it was visible above the dancing treetops, forcing the tiny Aqua Crystans to dash for cover in the hollows of the ancient branches. The children peeped from the barn. Was it a rescue mission to save the petrified, spooked soldiers? Or perhaps reinforcements to take on the ghosts?

The helicopter hovered noisily above the hilltop and the rope-ladder once again wound down between the trees. This time, however, just one, solitary, most important looking soldier climbed down. He, too, was dressed in camouflaged clothing but he seemed a lot older than the other soldiers, with a distinguished white moustache which curled up at the ends over his rosy cheeks.

He jumped to the ground and annoyingly waved the helicopter away as though he was swatting at a wasp. Instantly, the ladder was wound up and the flying machine roared into the distance. As its engines faded the soldier stood and gazed around, a look of anger mixed with determination etched on his craggy, ruddy face.
"*Where are you? You cowardly worms*!" he suddenly bellowed, shattering the peace.
The children ducked out of sight almost thinking he meant them!
"*Come out, you half-wits*!" he bellowed again.
Shapes began to appear sheepishly from the heather as the twelve soldiers, heads bowed, began to walk towards him.
"*I can't believe* it!" he barked at his flock. "*You mean to say you've got me out here because...let me get this right...because the trees started SINGING*!"
He was like a headmaster bawling on the playground at a bunch of pupils who had just kicked a ball through his study window!
"*Do you think I was born yesterday? Singin' trees m' foot! It'll be flute tootin' forget-me-nots next! You worthless pack of worms! Call yourselves soldiers*?"
" 'onest, sir!" bleated one of the soldiers at last. "If we 'adn't all 'eard it, we'd never 'ave believed it ourselves!"
"*What were they singin' then? 'Tie a Yellow Ribbon Round the Old Oak Tree', I s'p'ose*!!"
Suddenly, he stopped in his tracks as all the soldiers cupped their hands to their ears and stared into the trees around the earthmovers.
In the barn, the children gasped as notes drifted on the air once more.
"Th..they've st..started again!" stuttered one of the soldiers.
The senior soldier started tweaking his moustache anxiously as his eyes began to bulge in amazement and disbelief. He stood there, his mouth wide open, but with nothing coming out for a change! A gold tooth glinted in the sunshine.
Louder and louder...even louder than the first time...the encore of eerie chanting filled the woodland.

Spookier and spookier!
Louder and louder!
The sounds of a haunted monastery at dawn drifted on the breeze as ghostly monks chanted their wordless songs among the ancient pillars of an ancient abbey. Sweat once again broke out in torrents on the soldiers' foreheads...even the one above the quivering, white moustache.
No one said a word. They just gazed, entranced, up into the trees where the sound seemed to be coming from...from everywhere, but nowhere!
At last, they could stand it no longer!

One after the other, the white moustache in the lead, they made for the heather and dived headlong into its purple depths hoping to smother the sound ringing in their ears.
The children, again, collapsed in a heap of laughter! The plan had worked for a second time! The earthmovers still hadn't budged an inch...and what's more...a few minutes later, the helicopter returned, lowered its rope-ladder and the whole bunch of soldiers, including the barking white moustache, scrambled up from the woodland floor, extremely glad and relieved to be departing the haunted hilltop!

But, best of all, now that the coast was clear, Jonathan's idea could be put into operation! It was another long shot, but if it worked it would hold up the military plans even further!
First, though, the children couldn't wait to congratulate the Aqua Crystans on their splendid efforts. They ventured from the old barn and walked towards the phantom trees, the pillars of the ancient abbey!
"You were all fantastic!" called Jane, as the tiny folk began to scurry up and down the boughs, waving and chattering.
"*Terrific*!" called Jessica, clapping her hands above her head.
"Tree-mendous!!" exclaimed Jamie. "And, Spook, if you're listening, you were *purr-fect*, too!!"

Down below, *Lumina* shone even brighter, and the smiles on the faces of her Guardians grew wider. But they knew that only a battle had been won...not the war! Their beloved realm was *still* in danger!

After Jane had reassured the Aqua Crystans that they would be safe in the branches until they returned, Jonathan lead the way to the collapsed barn, first opening the green metal shed and grabbing a couple of buckets for each of them to carry. Soon, they arrived at the tumble-down barn and Jonathan instantly lead them to the water pump and its stone trough. It was dry and overgrown with moss and fern, but, even after all the years since Jonathan and Jane had pumped warm water for their winter baths, the long, curved, wooden handle still worked. Jonathan and Jamie pulled and pushed on the handle, yanking it up and down...but not a single drop of water dripped from the spout.
"I suppose it was just too much to hope for!" sighed Jonathan, his plan in ruins.
"Come on, Jonny, one last go!" urged Jamie.
Once more, they pulled and pushed on the handle, but again, not one drop dripped from the rusted spout.
"Let me and Jane have a go!" suggested Jessica, flexing her muscles. "We'll show you couple of weaklings a thing or two!"
"What? *You two*!" laughed Jamie. "You couldn't knock the skin off a rice pudding! If *we* can't do it, you two don't stand a chance!"
The two girls pumped the handle as hard as they could, but the spout yielded nothing.
"I think we'd better get back to *Old Sousyke*," said Jamie glumly, as he gathered his couple of buckets. "It was a good idea, Jonny, but..."
There was a sudden gurgle from the spout, followed by another and another.
The children gathered round as another volley of gurgily splutters came from the old pipe.
"What was that about *rice puddings*?" smiled Jessica. "Come on, Jane, one more go should do it!"
The two girls heaved the handle up and down once more, and low and behold, a splutter of water gushed and splashed into the trough, followed by another splutter and then a torrent!
"We must have loosened it up for you!" insisted Jamie with a grin, as he shoved one of his buckets under the flow. "Now you two keep pumping while Jonny and I fill the buckets!"

"And it's *warm*!" shouted Jonathan. "Just like it was when we used to come from the farm all those harvests ago! And now we know it comes from directly under the Pillo Falls!"
Jessica and Jamie remembered the thick, crystal encrusted pillar on the waterfall they'd seen from the balcony outside Jonathan and Janes' house in Pillo. It seemed incredible that the pump spout lead straight to the magical kingdom they were trying to save!

One bucket after another was filled to brimming by the boys as the girls madly pulled and pushed up and down on the handle, and soon all eight were standing in a row ready to be carried back to the farm.
As the water slowed to a dribble and then to a last drip or two, thoughts flashed through the minds of each of the children about what lay ahead. How *could* Jonathan's idea possibly work? Surely it was beyond the power of even the strongest and most powerful magic! Still, the magic had been with them so far...but would it work yet again?

Back at the farm, Jonathan arranged all eight of the buckets of water under one of the mammoth black and yellow earthmovers. They looked tiny under the great monster, but when they were all in place, he stood back and checked to see that they were all in the best positions.
"I think we need *three* buckets under that huge shovel, instead of two," he suggested, rubbing his chin. Jamie quickly moved one from underneath the engine and placed it beneath the shovel.
"Right, keep your fingers crossed!" said Jonathan, rolling up one of his checked shirt sleeves, "It's now or never!"
He bent down and crawled under the enormous machine. Then he squatted next to the bucket behind one of the gigantic rubber tyres, took a deep breath and plunged his hand into the warm water. Instantly, he began to swish the water as fast as he could...and...in seconds...the water began to bubble, and froth overflowed the bucket's rim and glided slowly down its side like lava from a

volcano...the same pale green colour as the rafts of froth on the Floss! And, at the same time, clusters of bubbly froth floated upwards and clung onto the greasy, metal underbelly of the sleeping mechanical monster.
"So far, so good!" Jonathan exclaimed, his face beaming. "Now, you lot, swish as many buckets as you can!"
In next to no time, froth was pouring from every bucket, and sticking to the underside of the earthmover, its shovel and wheels.
"Right, wipe all the froth from your arms and hands and stand back!" called Jonathan. "The fireworks are about to begin...I hope!"
From behind a beech tree, the children stared intently at the earthmover, as too, did the hordes of patient Aqua Crystans still up in the branches.

Froth kept on churning and churning out of the buckets and soon there was almost a solid bed of the stuff beneath the vast machine. The children and the Aqua Crystans watched and watched, and waited and waited...but, *nothing* happened!
Even Jessica was beginning to have doubts that anything *would* happen.
"But how can the magic work here anyway?" she asked. "Perhaps the water's only magical below ground in the Floss Cavern!"
"Well, according to legend," explained Jonathan, still convinced that *something* would happen, "the bubbles hold a magical mist which comes from the rocks way, way beneath the Cavern and the higher the mist travels, the greater is its magical power!!"
"So that's why all the mist gathers near the roof of the Cavern...the highest part of *Aqua Crysta*!" suggested Jamie. "And that's why people shrink when they jump through it!"
"But we're even higher here and there's still no sign of any mist!" said Jane.
"I vote we go and have another swish!" whispered Jamie. "Perhaps even more bubbles are needed...to make the *mist*...to make the *magic*!"

Jonathan agreed and lead the quartet back towards the sleeping machines, watched curiously by the Aqua Crystans, who had gathered in small groups along the branches. As they crunched over the autumn leaves, keeping their eyes fixed on the bed of froth and trying to spot the almost buried buckets, they all suddenly stopped in their tracks.

The froth had started...*climbing*! Climbing, *all by itself*, as though it had a mind of its own... around every nook and cranny of its monstrous, mechanical host!
Streams of the green coloured froth wound themselves around the huge shovel, the wheels, the engine and the cab like a writhing mass of serpents. The froth had become a living creature, wrapping around the great machine like the arms of a huge octopus!
And then, when it had its prey well and truly held in its grip...the most amazing thing happened! The frothy arms dissolved into a white mist, completely hiding the earthmover from view as though it was in a thick, white cloud! The mist swirled and lapped around the giant shape of the machine, touching and caressing its every inch, wrapping itself around every single nut and bolt!
But then...the unthinkable happened...striking fear and horror into the children and the tiny Aqua Crystans alike...the monstrous machine was beginning to get bigger...and *bigger*...and *BIGGER*!!

Chapter 26

The horrified children stared at the vast cloud of swirling mist as a corner of the earthmover's shovel began to emerge from the white shroud, slowly growing as it edged towards them. Then the yellow roof of the cab appeared above the cloud, swelling by the second. It was as though the whole machine was made of rubber and was being slowly inflated! Next, the upper rim of one of its huge, black tyres thrust itself through the mist, growing all the time. It was an incredible and terrifying sight!

Jonathan could suddenly stand it no longer!

He ran wildly towards the machine!

"*Stop it*! *Stop it*!" he screamed, as the top of the swelling monster crept nearer and nearer towards the branches holding the tiny Aqua Crystans. Then, just as he had almost reached the gigantic, bulging tyre, he tripped on a fallen branch and plunged head first into a crunchy drift of autumn leaves. He spluttered bits of leaf from his mouth and gazed up at the tyre. It was beginning to deflate...become smaller...shrinking back into the mist!

The same was happening to the shovel and the cab!

The whole, fearsome monster was shrinking before his very eyes!

The cloud began to shrink around it too, as the earthmover began to wilt and sink in the ever decreasing, swirling mists, like a punctured blown-up toy! Soon, all its bulky height and menace had sunk into the

exhausted, churning mist which was hungrily consuming the beast as though it hadn't been fed for months!
There was no struggle. The earthmover had just shrivelled to nothing...helpless to resist!

The other stunned children rushed forward and helped Jonathan to his feet. Before them, the remaining small cloud of mist began to clear. The froth had all disappeared, and where once stood the great earthmover, now stood a ring of eight empty buckets, each drained of every drop of water...and sat in the middle of them, like a lonely chick in a nest of fallen branches and twigs was...a tiny, black and yellow toy...a mere model of the earthmover and no higher than a matchbox!!

Jonathan stepped cautiously forward and slowly picked up the tiny, shrunken machine and sat it on his hand, almost feeling sorry for it! The others gathered round and closely examined it, somewhat nervously, as though they half expected it to suddenly spring to life and bite them with its shovel!
Jonathan lifted it to show the watching Aqua Crystans just as if he was lifting the F.A. Cup at the end of a soccer cup-final!
His tiny countrymen, as one, burst into a torrent of wild, excited cheering to match!
It had been an incredible few minutes!
How could swished water and bubbles have done this? How could the froth and mist have shrunk something so huge and solid into something so small and delicate?
Shivers ran down the children's spines. They were standing within a magical mystery beyond their understanding, but one thing was for sure. The magic had worked again!
The question was, would it work on the remaining two monsters that towered above them? They knew that there was only *one way* to find out!

The air of wonder lingered with the children as they busily gathered the buckets and returned through the forest to the pump. Again, the girls worked the handle up and down as the boys collected the precious water, all four of them lost in thoughts about the magical happenings they had witnessed. Soon they were carrying the heavy buckets back to the farm trying not to spill a single drop and anxiously listening for the return of the dreaded helicopter. Surely, *someone* would come back to the fortress farm to investigate the strange events! The Ministry of Defence and the Army couldn't be scared off *that* easily!

Jonathan, beginning to feel like some kind of wizard's assistant, arranged the buckets as he had done before...this time underneath Monster Number Two. When all was ready, the swishing began. Instantly, the warm water began to produce its bubbly froth, which began to dribble smoothly down the sides of the buckets.
"Right everyone, back to the beech tree!" ordered Jonathan. "Let's see what happens *this time*!"

The children crunched back to the tree and sat amongst its stout roots, watching all the time for any signs of action. The froth, like last time, carried on pouring from the buckets making a thick bed under the earthmover. Patiently, they waited to see if it would again begin to climb over the vast machine.
They waited and watched along with all the Aqua Crystans. Would it all happen for a second time? Or was the magic exhausted? It wasn't long before they had their answer!
All at once, the first stirrings of the froth began, as several arms started to emerge from the thick bubbly bed and creep over the enormous, black and yellow body that towered above the woodland floor.
"Will it grow bigger before it shrinks, like last time?" whispered Jane, as she watched the arms slither over the machine like a mass of serpents.
"I think that's because the mist makes things bigger as well as smaller," whispered her brother. "Remember how *we* grew when we came *up* through the mist into the well?"
But this time the magic didn't dither in the slightest! Its mind was made up! Once the froth had melted into the mist that shrouded the whole menacing but helpless earthmover, its amazing power to shrink the vast machine sprung into action!
Even faster than last time, the second great monster dissolved and withered away and when the mists cleared all that remained was a

second harmless toy in the middle of a circle of empty buckets, gleaming in the strengthening sun!
Another threatening menace had bitten the dust!

The trees cheered wildly as Jamie picked up the toy and carefully placed it with the first at the foot of the beech tree, snuggled between two of its chunky roots. Although the tiny earthmovers were metallic, cold and heartless, the children almost treated them as fallen fledglings from a wind tossed nest! They somehow needed caring for, looking after, their wide open shovels begging for food!
And, strangely, they even felt sorry for the remaining machine, standing there alone, awaiting its fate. But, thoughts of the damage that even it, by itself, could inflict on both the ancient, innocent woodland and the secret kingdom below, quickly encouraged the children to refill the buckets for a third time!

The last earthmover was the largest and most fearsome, its shovel twice as big as the others put together! This time, as the mystic water was swished into its full power, the children hoped and prayed that the magic would work just *once more*!

As they retreated to the beech tree and watched the spell's every move unfold before their eyes, the froth and mist again set about their mysterious deeds. This time, the white swirling cloud was bigger than ever as it enveloped the sleeping tyrant! When its every towering inch was finally covered, the wonderful magical climax once again astonished all its onlookers. The cloud began to shrink and with it the last of the great mechanical monsters!
The mist cleared and in the midst of the eight empty buckets was the third baby earthmover, all alone, as though just hatched from a prehistoric egg!
Jane placed it carefully in the nest at the foot of the tree, and together, with their shovels wide open, the hungry trio looked as though they were awaiting a fat, juicy worm from their mother!
Jonathan gently covered them with autumn leaves.

Deep, deep below, the candle flame swelled and reached new heights. Quentin and Toby looked at one another and their faces beamed wide grins. They shook hands. They felt sure that the threats to *Aqua Crysta* had gone!

The magic was over, and so, too, was the danger from the vast machines. The children, still astonished by what they had seen, wandered into the tangle of fallen, broken branches which was all that remained to tell of the earthmovers' arrival and presence.

Jessica picked up a strand of chain that had borne the whole weight of one of them as it had been lowered from the sky. The chain had shrunk along with its cargo, and now was no more than a short necklace with tiny, rusty links. Carefully, she felt in her back pocket for the charms she and Jamie had found.

One by one she threaded them onto the chain...first the tankard, then the horn, and the silver baskets...all of their finds except for the dagger which she placed back in her pocket. Then she tied a knot in the delicate chain and slipped the glittering charm bracelet over her wrist next to the ribbons of jay feather.

Meanwhile, the others had put the buckets back in the green, metal shed and fetched the railway carriages and London bus from *Old Soulsyke's* barn.

As the excited Aqua Crystans crowded into them for the return journey to the forest cellar, Jonathan and Jane said their farewells to the old farm. It had been wonderful seeing the old place again as full sized Upper World folk, but they could hardly wait to return to their little house in Pillo, even though the future of *Aqua Crysta* was still uncertain. The soldiers and machines had gone for the time being, but would more soldiers and new machines be flown in? Or would Mr Dawson's protests be heard and taken notice of? Everything had worked out so far...but the magic and good fortune had to run out *sometime*...surely?

The *Palace of Dancing Horses* was silent and dark when they arrived but it wasn't long before the cellar was alive with laughter and singing after Jamie switched on the torch. Jane quickly

calmed her countryfolk and thanked them all for their splendid efforts and pleaded that they say nothing of their ventures once they reached Galdo and Pillo.
When all of them were well on their way down the Harvest Passageway and their joyous singing had faded away into the distant depths, the time had come for the pairs of children to part.

Even though they'd known one another for only a few hours, somehow it had seemed like a lifetime, with hazardous and magical adventures packing every single minute! In their hearts they knew that they would all meet again...someday...but they were all sad as Jonathan and Jane perched on the ledge outside the cellar ready to climb back down into their magical world.
"I'll keep shining the torch on you as you climb down!" said Jamie, training his beam on the mossy walls of the well. "Then I'll follow you down and pull up the rope!"
"Are you going to use the rope or jump when you get to the last rung?" asked Jessica, trying to hold back tears.
"Definitely jump!" replied Jonathan in a flash. "I think we'd better do everything the same as we did the first time! Just to be on the safe side!" He stepped over to the rungs and climbed down a couple to make room for his sister.
"See you sometime!" called Jane in a trembly voice. "Hope your dad manages to do *his* bit!"
"Bye!" called Jonathan, as he began his descent. "Looking forward to meeting again!"
"Bye!!" chorused Jessica and Jamie sadly. "Good luck!"
"Good *Magic*, you mean!" Jonathan reminded them from down the well.
"Sorry! *Good Magic*!!" chorused Jessica and Jamie, feeling their jay feathers.

They watched as the dark shapes of their friends gradually melted into the blackness beyond the torchbeam. Jessica called a final, echoey '*Goodbye*!' into the gloom and a tiny distant call from Jane returned. It was as though they had shrunk already.

Then they heard no more.
They sat on the edge of the ledge in silence.
Had Jonathan and Jane jumped through the mists? Had they landed safe and sound?

Jamie began his descent to retrieve the rope which was still dangling from the last rung into *Aqua Crysta*. Jessica shone the torch for him as he, too, disappeared into the darkness. The milky glow from below lit his way beyond the torchbeam and soon he was clinging on to the last but one rung, his feet firmly planted on the next.
Not a sound could be heard.
The swirling mists lapped the last stones of the well...and then, as he watched...they began to clear.
He squinted as he stared down into the glowing cavern.
The scene was just as he remembered from two minutes past two that same morning.
Just a thin, glistening ribbon of milky water winding between craggy, glowing rocks.
It was all just the smallest of jumps away, yet he now knew that it was the leap of a life-time. One slip now and he'd be back in the magical kingdom. Its sweet smell drifted in the air and its warmth touched his cheeks as he gripped the rope and slowly began to pull.

Unknown to him, far, far below, Jonathan and Jane were sitting by the Floss gazing up into the cavern's heights, as the rope began to wind its way up and up and out of sight. Chilling memories flooded back of the rope-ladder from the flying machine writhing and twisting above *Old Soulsyke*!
They looked around their beautiful homeland and hoped that the terrible threats from the Upper World would somehow come to nothing.

Above them, Jamie was thinking exactly the same thoughts as he wound the rope around his shoulder and began the climb back to Jessica. He pictured the *Goldcrest* sailing down the Floss, her yellow sail billowing in the breeze. He imagined her slowing down and gliding to the shore with her banks of oars...Jonathan and Jane climbing aboard, being greeted by Captain Frumo and then whisked off homewards to Pillo or perhaps to visit Queen Venetia at Galdo... depending, of course, on which way the current was flowing!

What a wonderful world they lived in! If he was honest with himself he envied them, and could almost feel *Aqua Crysta's* attraction pulling him back down the well...but he carried on climbing until the magical, milky glow was left behind and the torchbeam drew him back to reality...well, almost reality!

First, he and his sister just *had* to have one last look in the cellar!

They pushed open the arched, wooden door, crept into the amazing room and shone the torchbeam over all its wonderful treasures. The fairground with its glassy carousel of prancing, white horses, the railway with its green and cream carriages smartly back on their silver line, as though they'd never been away...and, of course, the magnificent dolls' house with its splendid rooms decorated in such fine detail.

Jamie wanted to take back a memento of their visit, but Jessica persuaded him that it was best to leave everything just as they'd found it. Nevertheless, he couldn't resist reaching up to the stone shelf and slipping the blue tricycle bell into his pocket to remind him of Jonathan and Jane.

There was no doubt about it. They were both missing their new friends already, and deep beneath their feet, their friends were missing them just as much! As they stood at the bow of the *Goldcrest* as it plunged along the Floss towards Galdo, they couldn't help thinking about Jessica and Jamie making their way back to *Deer Leap* and their father in the bittersweet Upper World. But they had no doubts about where *their* home was!

It was definitely *Pillo*! The Upper World held no temptations for them now! Not one!

With the well-head hidden for the last time and their backpacks slung over their shoulders, Jessica and Jamie walked briskly back towards *Old Soulsyke*.

By now, the sun was over the treetops and shining brightly. Birdsong was even creeping back into the forest, and the busy buzzing of insects filled the air. Everything seemed as normal as it had been the day before. The children just hoped that they would find the old farm as peaceful as when they'd left it and that their father by now had managed to pull a few strings!

What they saw when they reached the farm was certainly *peaceful*...but not *quite* in the way they had imagined!

Chapter 27

An ants' nest couldn't have been busier! Dozens of soldiers were working everywhere, but hardly a single sound could be heard! Silently and hastily, the barbed wire fencing was being rolled up, towers dismantled, the green metal shed taken apart!
Jessica and Jamie crouched in the heather and watched.
"They must have arrived while we were in the cellar!" whispered Jamie. "Look over there... it's the guy with the white moustache!"

Stood by himself in the middle of the farmyard, looking dazed and bewildered, was the soldier who had lead the final retreat from the haunted woodland. Mumbling to himself and gazing up into the trees, he seemed totally confused and somewhat anxious, as if he expected the woodland to begin its eerie chanting once again!
Jessica and Jamie couldn't help smiling...but then, to their surprise, a figure not wearing military uniform suddenly appeared at the farmhouse door.
"*Dad*!!" they yelled as they rushed from their cover towards the farmyard.
The soldiers all stopped working, glanced at the children, and then carried on. They were obviously under orders to finish the job quickly and seemed, sort of, in a rush to get back to base for some reason!
Mr Dawson hugged Jessica and Jamie as the quivering white moustache came uncertainly over to the delighted, happy huddle.
"I just can't believe it!" he grumbled. "I just *can not* believe it! A couple

of hours ago there were three of the *biggest* and *most powerful* machines the world has ever seen, standing right there, ready for action!"
He walked towards the gateposts, slowly shaking his head from side to side and nervously stroking his white moustache.
"And now...they've *gone...vanished into thin air*! No trees knocked down! No tracks! Nothing!"
He wandered into the tangle of fallen branches where the machines had once stood waving his arms about as though he was suddenly expecting to touch one.
"How *could* they have disappeared like that?"
"Woodland fairies, perhaps!" joked Mr Dawson with a smile across his face and a twinkle in his eye.
Jessica and Jamie beamed at one another broadly, enjoying their wonderful secret, while the white moustache rambled on.
"And what about the racket we heard in the trees? The singing? Scared the pants off us good and proper, it did! And, I don't mind admitting it! No amount of training can prepare you for that kind of thing! I know our detectors picked up some pretty weird readings up here last night, but that can't explain the trees singin' and the diggers vanishin'. I just *can not* make head nor tail of it!"
"I'm sorry I can't help you, Major!" said Mr Dawson, trying his best to be serious. "It sounds like some mysterious, inexplicable forces are trying to drive you away, besides *me*!"
"Or the *woodland fairies*!" risked Jamie, with an equally serious look on his face.
The soldier glared at him and tweaked his moustache.
"Well, you've certainly got what you wanted!" he grumbled again.
"What do you mean?" asked Jessica.
The Major went on.
"Orders have just arrived from H.Q. for us to abandon the *Soulsyke* site pronto! The whole blinkin' project's going hundreds of miles away! Too much hassle here!"
Jessica and Jamie couldn't help but let out a cheer and their dad punched the air as though he'd just won a million pounds!

"That's wonderful, wonderful news, Major!" Mr Dawson exclaimed. "It's amazing what a phone call can do!!"
"Don't forget the *fairies*, too!" laughed Jamie, nudging his sister who was trying her best to keep her face straight!
"But what *I* want to know," continued Major Moustache, "is what about my *diggers*? Nobody's goin' to believe I lost 'em!"
Jessica and Jamie glanced at the foot of the beech tree and then at one another. 'If only he knew!' they thought. 'If only he knew what lay under that drift of leaves among its roots!'

As the soldiers carried on dismantling *Old Soulsyke's* ugly metal mask, the chilling, and all too familiar, throbbing noise of distant helicopters shattered the peace. But at least, the children reckoned with relief, it would be for the last time!
Never again would they return to the beautiful hilltop woodland nor to the harvestlands of *Aqua Crysta*. Soon, they would be gone forever!

And indeed, when every piece of equipment every single nut and bolt, had been packed into the several large, wooden crates that floated down on chains from the vast, hovering flying machines, Jessica and Jamie began to realise that the magic had finally worked. They felt the ribbons of jay feathers still wound round their wrists and Jessica touched her new charm bracelet.
Strangely enough, at the very same time, deep below the forest floor, Jonathan and Jane were just untying *their* ribbons and handing them back to Queen Venetia on the quayside at Galdo! She accepted them and gratefully thanked them for their endeavours. Lepho shook their hands.
At the small terrace half way up the Larder Steps, Quentin and Toby were enjoying a tankard of wimberry wine each as they gazed at the boldly burning *Lumina*. Next to her was a ragged edged, rolled piece of paper. Quentin picked it up and offered it to the candle flame. Just moments later, the old map from *Old Soulsyke's* hayloft wall had burnt away into black ash. It had gone forever!

Meanwhile, the soldiers, lead by the white moustache, quickly climbed the dangling rope-ladders, and then, with a final roar, the helicopters buzzed away from *Old Soulsyke,* never ever to return! As the throbbing faded, the woodland began its celebrations with birdsong. Birds returned to their ancient realm from every direction. Chaffinches, robins, thrushes, nuthatches, the lot! Even a couple of jays settled on a lower branch of one of the oak trees.

"What *was* that guy *talking* about?" asked Mr Dawson, at last, sitting on the half buried wall by the gate-posts. "How *do* three giant earthmovers just *disappear into thin air*!"

Jamie could resist no longer!

Jessica gasped in disbelief as her brother beckoned his dad to follow him to the beech tree! Before she could say a word to stop him, Jamie swept away the autumn leaves around its roots and revealed, to his astonishment...*absolutely nothing*!!!

They'd gone! Vanished! Completely disappeared!

Jessica and Jamie were absolutely flabbergasted!

"Bu..but they were *here*!" Jamie stuttered. "*Three earthmovers*! Great shovels! Huge wheels...*right here*!"

"What *are* you talking about, Jamie?" laughed his father. "Don't *you* start talking about *vanishing diggers*, too! You're beginning to sound like that barmy Major!"

"But they *were* there, dad, I promise!" pleaded Jessica, clearing more leaves away with her brother.

"Oh no! Not *you,* as well!" their father exclaimed, raising his eyes to the sky and shaking his head.

"Mind you," he went on, sounding puzzled, "I *do* think there's something pretty spooky going on round here!"

"What do you mean, dad?" asked Jessica.

"It was when I came here earlier this morning! Your friend...Jonathan, I think you called him! I was *sure* I'd seen him before *somewhere*!"

"But you can't have, dad!" insisted Jamie. "*We* only met him and his sister *last night*!"

"Yes, but I reckon...and this is going to sound *ridiculous*! I reckon I knew him *fifty years ago, when I was a lad*!!"

Jessica and Jamie looked at one another, shocked by what their father had said.
"But, dad," said Jessica at last, "what are *you* talking about now? How *could* you have possibly met Jonathan all those years ago when he's only about *my* age?"
Mr Dawson reached into the back pocket of his blue jeans and produced a small, dog-eared, black and white photograph.
"Have a look at this then!"
He straightened the corners and passed it to Jessica and Jamie.
It showed an old railway carriage with three children sitting in front of an open door on a couple of steps leading onto what looked like a station platform.
There were two boys and a girl with pigtails.
"That's me in the middle. I was about ten or eleven years old...!"
Jessica and Jamie stared at the photo in amazement!
There was no doubt about it! They knew exactly who the other two children were, but didn't say a word.
"It's our holiday camping-coach at Sandsend Station, and those were m' best mates, Jonny and Jane! They used to stay in the next door carriage every summer during the same week as me and your gran and grandad stayed in this one! They called me Ted in those days, not Edward, and I reckon that lad you were with this morning is the spitting image of Jonny!"
"But, dad, it *can't* be!" laughed Jamie, slightly uncomfortably.
"He'd be the same age as you are *now*!"
"Well, *I* certainly can't explain it!" said Mr Dawson. "Even his *clothes* were the same! Just look at his pullover and his corduroy shorts!"
Of course, Mr Dawson, was absolutely correct! The children in the photo *were* Jonathan and Jane! Was this the last amazing twist in the tale?
The two children who had hosted the party in Pillo, helped bring the *Palace of Dancing Horses* to life, churned the Floss water into its magical mist...had also been the summertime friends of *their own father all those years ago*? It was unbelievable!

But, it was true! And at that very same moment, deep, deep, in the secret world, way beneath the forest floor, the very same children were sipping fizzy bramble wine and nibbling toasted chestnut slices in the crystal home of Queen Venetia!
It *was absolutely* incredible!!

The bright sunshine glinted off Jessica's precious charm bracelet as she sat on a drift of golden leaves by one of the farm's half buried walls. As she stared dreamily into the depths of the forest she was sure that she caught a glimpse of two flashes of white! Possibly a phantom cat named *Spook* and an albino deer named *Chandar*?
She couldn't tell!
But somehow she knew the magic was *still* with her!
She reached into her backpocket and produced a small cube of clay with a '*J*' on one of its faces and a delicately carved crystal minstrel with a three cornered hat. 
'Lepho's!' she thought to herself. She'd forgotten to give them back to him.
'I'll just *have* to return them someday! After all, he can't play *Sanctum* with a missing *fool*, or *Quintz* with a missing *quint*!'

She rested her head on one of the moss covered stones, closed her eyes and felt herself drifting into sleep...

...as she heard...

...the haunting sound...

..of a single...

...silver...

...horn...

The History of
Aqua Crysta

IN THE BEGINNING, long before Aqua Crysta was discovered by folk from the Upper World, a ***Crystal of Eternity,*** from the far depths of the Universe, fell to Earth. It came to rest deep in a great, dark and desolate forest which spread over the hills of what became the North of England. The crystal's magical powers, unknown to anyone, seeped into the rocks around this place, and awaited their discovery.

Unaware of the Crystal, a splendid ***Abbey*** was built on a windswept clifftop where the great forest met the Northern Sea. Beneath the Abbey's perch a village grew within the shelter of a cliffy inlet. It became known as ***Whitby*** and grew into a ship building, fishing and whaling harbour.

In the Upper World's 16th.Century, the Tudor King HenryVIII fell out with the Church and destroyed many of England's Abbeys including the one perched on the Whitby clifftop. As the Abbey burned, the monks fled taking with them many of the ancient building's treasures.

THE DISCOVERY OF AQUA CRYSTA

Murgwyn, the monk in charge of the Abbey's Refectory, was entrusted with hiding the riches of the ruined Abbey. He discovered an ancient well near Old Soulsyke House in the great forest, not far inland from Whitby. He and his followers hid the silver and gold treasures in a secret room down the well, and in the Upper World year 1550, the venturesome monks climbed further down the well and discovered the magical realm which came to be known as *Aqua Crysta*.

The following history uses Upper World years, which equate to the Aqua Crystan "Harvests"

1552 MURGWYN crowned as the First King of Aqua Crysta. Carves the Throne of Elmwood and Crystal

1561 PILLO township named after Murgwn's brother PILLONIUS, who built its first streets, houses and the market place

1580 GALDO island hollowed out & inhabited by half of Pillo's population

1581 first "*Goldcrest*" launched to sail between Pillo & Galdo along the two-way River Floss

1585 Murgwyn moves into a new Palace at Galdo. PERSEUS becomes the first Mayor of Pillo

1590 Beginning of much felling of the Great Forest in the Upper World, for fuel, house and ship building by Upper World inhabitants

1641 "Meeting Hall" opened and "Torrent Lodge" hollowed by the Magwitch family

1642 Pathway completed along the whole length of the *Cave of Torrents*

1645 Upper World "Civil War" - many new arrivals into Aqua Crysta

1652 KING MURGWYN drowns in the Great Flood of Lake Serentina. His son, ARGWALD becomes Second King

1660 ARGWALD orders first expedition into unknown territory beyond the end of the Cave of Torrents. Fearsome sounds reported and further exploration banned. Instead Argwald produces the first map of the whole of Aqua Crysta

1666 Great Fire of London and The Plague - more arrivals from the Upper World

1669 Everlasting Toadstool Forest at Galdo begins to grow from spores brought back on harvesters' feet

1671 Arrival of MERRICK Building of walls on the moorlands which have replaced the Great Forest in the Upper World

1691 New Crystal Quarry opened near Pillo and Heights of Merrick village built by Merrick

1700 PENWORT becomes Second Mayor of Pillo on the death of Perseus

1720 First Regatta Festival held with competitions between teams from Pillo and Galdo

1741 MiddleFloss village inhabited
1742 First musical instrument made by Cleff of Galdo - a flute. More instuments follow and eventually an orchestra debuts in the Meeting Hall
1752 Discovery of the Great Galdo Crystal Vein
1759 Roofed towers added on summit of Galdo
1789 Great Crystal Quarry Rock Fall - 21 killed
1799 New "*Goldcrest*" launched
1801 Death of Argwald. His eldest son, SIGMUND, crowned Third King.
1802 River Floss at unusually low levels for three Harvests
1804 The game of SANCTUM invented
1815 Upper World "Napoleonic Wars" - many new arrivals, plus many more due to changes in farming in the Upper World and growth of cities and industry The game QUINTZ invented
1840 birth of LEPHO, future adventurer & Royal advisor
1851 MERRICK becomes Third Mayor of Pillo on death of Penwort
1862 After the Great Goldcrest Disaster (27 killed when the ship sank in the Narrows) the third "*Goldcrest*" launched under the command of CAPTAIN FRUMO
1905 100th Sanctum Championship
1906 First Pillo Regatta
1915 Upper World "First World War"- more arrivals
1920 Larder Caves extended to cope with extra Harvest collections
1922 The Great Jay Disappearance - for fifteen Harvests no jay feathers are collected in the Harvestlands
1930 The Great Harvest Disaster. 78 Aqua Crystans killed in storms in the Upper World mainly by two falling beech trees
1932 Bridge to Far Pillo opened
1939 Upper World's "Second World War" More arrivals
1941 Ogwood's Flying Machine fails to reach the roof of the Floss Cavern, resulting in the inventor's death when his machine plunges into the Floss
1955 The Great Planting of the Pine Trees begins in the Upper World LUMINA senses doom & disaster Arrival of Jonathan and Jane from the abandoned Old Soulsyke Farm - the last new arrivals into Aqua Crysta Naming of the *Palace of Dancing Horses*
1961 Death of Sigmund, crushed by the *Seven Silver Keys of Sigmund* Crowning of his wife, VENETIA, as the First Queen of Aqua Crysta
1965 Pillo Theatre opens and first play performed, "*The Crystal Tale*" written by Penlop of Middle Floss
1978 Regular musical concerts begin in the Meeting Hall amphitheatre, and musical compositions encouraged by Queen Venetia
1991 Aerial network of rope bridges built inside Galdo. New pier built at Pillo
1995 First pine cone seeds harvested and used to make implements. Megan Magwitch introduces pine-needle tea at Torrent Lodge
1999 New Larder Cave extensions begin Pixwith Stem develops the new pastime of painting using pigments from the Upper World
2001 Roof collapse in Harvest Passageway, but everyone rescued. Mouse excavations blamed
2002 New freshwater stream discovered when Crystal Quarry extended into a new vein
2003 Willip, a descendant of Murgwyn, writes her "*History of Aqua Crysta and her Folk*"
2004 LUMINA senses doom & disaster

Kings & Queens of AQUA CRYSTA

Murgwyn	1552 -1652
Argwald	1652 - 1801
Sigmund	1801 - 1961
Venetia	1961 -

Mayors of PILLO

Perseus	1585 - 1700
Penwort	1700 - 1851
Merrick	1851 -

a letter from Jessica

Hello!

I'm sitting in our little wild backgarden at the moment. Jamie's up in his bedroom on his computer and dad's out checking a newly planted larch nursery on the other side of George!

We've settled in now at Deer Leap after our move from Scotland and we're really enjoying living in the middle of the Yorkshire Moors. What's it like where you live?

It's a lovely day so I'm letting Harry have a bit of exercise in a wooden run I built with Jamie. Harry, incidentally, is a hedgehog dad brought home. He found him by the side of the road near Goathland. He's been hit by a car but luckily he's not too badly injured. He likes mince meat chopped up in warm milk. We should be able to let him go soon, before he becomes too tame! We haven't got any pets yet. Have you any? At school we're doing Elizabethan England. I would loved to have been a lady at the court of Queen Elizabeth or perhaps married to Sir Francis Drake or William Shakespeare! I would have liked to have acted in one of William's plays...but I think all the women's roles like Lady Macbeth and Cleopatra were played by men! No women acted in those days according to my teacher, Miss Penny. What do you like best at school?

I still can hardly believe that I've met some one who was born just half a century after Queen Elizabeth died! Merrick, who was born just before the 1666 Great Fire of London! He's a great old man! But I liked Lepho best!
One day soon, I'll return his minstrel Sanctum piece and his quint! I've got them safely in my bedside drawer, along with my charm bracelet made from a chain which carried those terrible machines! I shudder when I think of them!!

Anyway I must go as I'm supposed to be making tea with Jamie...always a nightmare, as he eats it as we go!

Bye for now,

love Jessica

a letter from Jamie

Hi,

I've got to say that I'm no great shakes at writing letters! Give me the phone anyday, or text, or e-mail. But I'll have a go!

At the mo I'm in my bedroom sorting out my models. Dad's put up some shelves to display them and they look great. I like old railway engines best! Not far away is the North Yorkshire Steam Railway, so I can see the real thing! They're great, the ancient steam engines, hissing away and belching out all that steam! Ace!

I also like small Matchbox toys from the 1950s - dad's always on about them...when he's not listening to his 1960s music. Mind you, I like that too, especially the Beatles! What do you like? Do you collect anything?

I like playing on my computer. Do you? I like car race games best, but I'm going to try and get one with motorbikes and sidecars, like the one in the forest cellar - the one Jonny liked! It was really great meeting him and his sister! Can't wait to see them again, and try that super grub down there in AC!

I liked the toasted chestnuts and the dips best! And then there was the bramble juice! Deeelicious!! What are your favourite foods and drinks up here in the Upper World? Watched Leeds United on the telly yesterday! Dad's a real fan. He used to live there as a boy and go and see them play! Do you support a team?

Before dad went out to work today he made a super toad-in-the-hole for dinner. I like grub as you've probably guessed, and luckily I like healthy stuff! What do you like? Well, I've run out of space - writing a letter wasn't too bad after all!

See you, Jamie

a letter from Jonathan and Jane

Dear All,

Glad this letter has found you in the Upper World. As we write it we're perched on the edge of our balcony overlooking Pillo. It's a wonderful view of the Floss . As you know, we live in a house carved into the pink rock just above the town.

After we awoke we spent some time working in the grass plaiting workshop making sandal straps and cloak belts. Everyone in Aqua Crysta has a few small jobs. Before we sleep again we'll be crystal polishing next door helping our neighbour Elfrin. He's really ancient - about 250 harvests ,we think! He's an expert maker of crystal Sanctum sets. He and his wife Tilly have invited us round for tea. I bet Jamie wishes he was coming! He loves our food here! I hope to see him and Jessica soon. We miss them! What's life like where you live in the Upper World? Do you have jobs to do? What's school like? Would you like to visit Aqua Crysta? Do you play any of the games we played up there before we came to Aqua Crysta, like chess and draughts,ludo, cards and snakes & ladders?

Television had just started when we came here , but our uncle didn't have a set. What's it like? Are there any good shows? Do you like sport? Jane played netball and I liked cricket!

love from J and J

AQUA CRYSTA

Part 2

If you've been drawn into the
magic of *Aqua Crysta* and would
like to visit the mystical realm again,
watch out for:

'DEEPER THAN YESTERDAY'

It begins with Jessica and Jamie at home, at *Deer Leap,*
a few months later, on a very snowy Christmas Eve.
Beneath the forest, Aqua Crysta is in danger again, this
time from a peril that lurks in mysterious caverns deep
below the River Floss and the townships of Pillo
and Galdo. Meet the evil, plotting Tregarth and the
fearsome creatures which inhabit the rocky depths.
Travel back in time along the Whitby coast with
the four 'J's and Lepho as they attempt to save
The Land of the Crystal Water.

Aqua Crysta Part 3 **Forever Crystal**
Aqua Crysta Part 4 **StoneSpell**